OLD FACES

Yet More Tales from Tipperary

Edward Forde Hickey

Grosvenor House
Publishing Limited

This book is published by
Grosvenor House Publishing Ltd
Link House
140 The Broadway, Tolworth, Surrey, KT6 7HT.
www.grosvenorhousepublishing.co.uk

A CIP record for this book
is available from the British Library

ISBN 978-1-83975-664-1

CONTENTS

FOREWORD

Edward Hickey writes with a clear, crisp command of English which helps to transport the reader back to the sometimes-forgotten era in which his material is set. In this, his latest publication, he relies on his beautiful way with words to convey the stories and tales from yesteryear and to bring them to life so convincingly with a language which is inspiring and insightful.

Edward is a prolific writer who has endeavoured to fill a void in what has become a real niche in the literary world. However, his speed of productivity has not in any way diminished the quality of his work which remains original and quite brilliant.

Old Faces is sure to strike a note with readers, not just with a sense of nostalgia and of looking in the rear-view mirror with rose tinted glasses, but also with a sense of recognition. The stories told and the characters featured are from all of our childhoods and from every era - a sure sign that despite how far we have come as a global community, people are still people, humanity is still humanity, and life is still life.

This book will certainly rekindle memories for many a reader.

Noel Dundon
Deputy Editor of The Tipperary Star newspaper, and author.

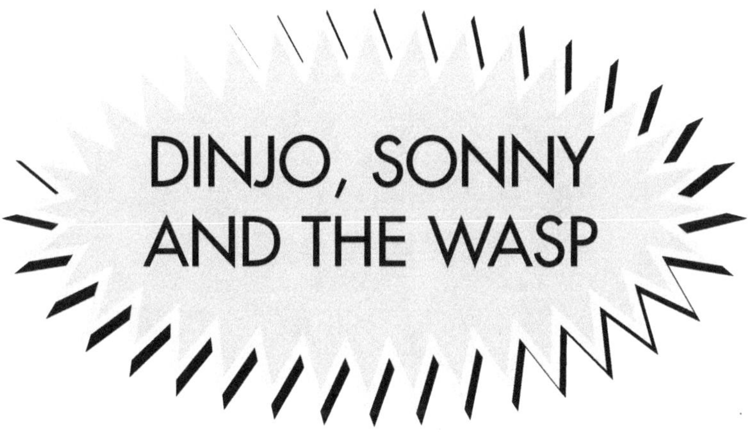
DINJO, SONNY
AND THE WASP

1

Some years back, just before it was her time to give birth, Molly-rattle-the-tea-and-sugar-bag had felt the stabbing pains of an imminent childbirth at the damnedest of times. She had been on the road to the pig-killing at Red Scissors' house and was barely able to crawl back home.

At the time of the birth, it was our two good neighbours from Sheep's Cross, Freckles and Cheerful Nan, who came to the fore as usual. By the time Cheerful Nan had rushed up to help Molly give birth, Freckles had already stepped in the half-door with a fine big currant-cake to cheer things along and was down on her knees tending to Molly's skirts inside in the bedroom. Cheerful Nan had to laugh out loud for she had brought another fine currant-cake along with her.

After the birth of little Dinjo, and while she was still wiping the sweat from her jaw, Molly was more than surprised when (six minutes later) his brother Sonny popped out his head. There had been no twins in the history of her family. Indeed, these little boys were the first twins anyone had ever heard tell of in our part of the world, and Cheerful Nan and Freckles couldn't believe what they were looking at and slapped each other on the back for a job well done.

And as they grew to manhood, Dinjo was seen to have a forest of crisp red hair and a jaw as smooth as a little piggy. Sonny had the most beautiful jet-black hair imaginable but was otherwise ill-kempt with a blue unshaven jaw on him. Their days were uneventful for most of the time where they lived with their parents – out by the gravel pit in a quiet lane, overgrown with ancient nettles. It lay to the east of Clashing River and west of the Lisnagorna Woods and a mile from the

Little Bald Plain. Their father (the old gossips called him Cantankerous Nick) was as cross as a briar and went by the name of the Wasp. In addition to the Wasp's bad temper, there was always a gloomy sort of air about him anyway – even before he opened his mouth to speak. It was as though he had eaten something bilious which then affected his liver. His own father had been much the same sort of fellow, and our forefathers had given him the charming nickname of the Malignant Eye.

The Wasp's nervous and half-crazed wife was the daughter of the shepherd, Grim-and-Gripe. At her birth, she had been given the name of Molly-the-second-one, the previous child having also been called Molly but dying at birth, poor thing. However, Molly-the-second-one was soon attributed with the much longer name of Molly-rattle-the-tea-and-sugar-bag for in those days of scarcity, she was forever tottering down the road and rattling her empty tea or sugar bag and looking to borrow a grain of tea or sugar. She once asked her friend (Dowager) for the loan of a match to light her fire and Dowager's eldest lad, My-Son-Jack (wasn't he the wag?), asked her on what day she'd be returning the precious match to him. As a result of her general antics, the neighbours were forever hiding under the table like little mice as soon as they heard her boots stomping down the road.

A short way up the creamery road lived Moll-the-Man and her husband (By-Jiggery). Their children loved the sight of Molly's ass-and-car tearing down the road – herself and her peculiar antiquated headgear (the green tam and it full of holes) and her shawl sailing back behind her in the breeze. She was the fastest ass-driver they had ever seen on our creamery road, and they would stop playing their jackstones on the flagstones as soon as they saw her flying by. She'd be standing high on the lat-board of her blue cart and whaling her ash-plant like fair hell onto the backbone of her poor old ass (Lock-Jaw).

There'd be a lather of pink sweat on her cheeks as she cursed the poor innocent creature because he simply wasn't breaking the record for ass-and-car speed. It was usually five o'clock in the afternoon when they caught sight of her, and she'd be in a dreadful hurry in case she was going to be late for the shops in town.

'Jiggery! Jiggery! Will I be late for town?' she'd roar at By-Jiggery (it became a saying among us) as she came sailing past the flagstones.

'No,' was By-Jiggery's whimsical reply, 'it'll still be there in the same spot where ye left it last time.' He knew, of course, the reason for her speed with the ass at this hour of the day. The lazy article was never able to get herself out of bed in time for anything and was always finding herself late, be it for Sunday Mass or her messages in town. Indeed (thought By-Jiggery), she'd be late when the day came for her own funeral.

The twins had a sister (Hanoria) who was two years older. She had left the gravel pit at the tender age of 20 to go and settle in Galloping Will's slate house (he had long given up on the thatch) to start a new life with him to the north of Chieftain Hill, 3 miles away. Not long after she left, we heard that she'd acquired a number of new skills, having, for one thing, become the best baker of apple-and-rhubarb tarts imaginable as well as learning the art of sheep-dipping and cleaning maggots from the sheep's wool during the hot summer. She'd even been seen delivering new lambs from the ewes in the middle of the harsh winter. It was amazing what an upstanding young husband like Galloping Will could get out of a damsel these days, said By-Jiggery with a smile.

2

Molly's husband (the Wasp) wasn't the fastest ass-driver in the world. But he was a first-class craftsman when it came to the use of the trowel and mortar. Hadn't he won fame for himself by building half the houses in Copperstone Hollow? And a decade later he was to prove himself the man-of-the-hour all over again. It was the year everyone would remember as the Year of the Deluge. For on a certain night that nobody would ever forget, a savage storm decided to make its way through the length and breadth of Tipperary. Folks could hear the wind whistling like an out-of-tune orchestra as a veil of heavy black clouds came sweeping down on them from Bog Boundless and rolled over Shy Dennis's shack.

'The Devil is out this evening and riding his black horses,' said Dowager as she listened to the howling blasts roaring down her chimney.

Next day, the grey dawn came frowning in through the windows and farmers were trapped indoors, listening to the trees dripping wet as the fierce rain went on hammering upon lanes and fields. What a sight met their eyes when they struggled out of bed! Never in living memory had so vast an avalanche of water hurtled down on them from the hills above. It uprooted the smaller trees and snapped them into matchwood before floating them on into Bog Wood and choking the turbulent waters in the river.

Men, women and children raced down the slope, only to see that the river had completely overflowed its banks. Its waters went on pitching and tossing in a ferocious temper for the rest of that day till they eventually covered the fields up as far as John's Gate, threatening to drown all the small farms and animals. Indeed, one or two bewildered calves were seen swimming alongside the submerged tree-trunks and the cows running around in circles and bawling deliriously after them.

It took a fortnight before the waters went down sufficiently for all to see the proper state of their sad river. By that time the old wooden bridge had entirely vanished and its stone arches and copingstones, having tumbled into the water, had been swept away along with it. Folks were cut off from town and couldn't get themselves in as far as the shops. They sent for the men above in Lisnagorna Woods, who cut down two huge poplar trees and brought them down the road in the hope of throwing them across the water from bank to bank.

Then one or two ambitious young clerks came out from town to inspect the flood-damage and see what they could do to help matters. It was at that precise moment that the Wasp came into the picture since he was the nearest thing the small community had to an educated engineer. He went cap in hand to Lady Elegance's back door (more in hope than expectation) and asked her to help him install a new bridge. Much to his surprise, not only did the good woman dig deep into her personal piggy-bank, but she took proceedings a lot further than the Wasp or anyone else could ever have imagined and asked him to draw her a pencil-sketch for a new bridge.

The result was that very soon folk found themselves the proud owners of a shining new metal bridge. With the help of Father Honesty and his bucket of holy water, they gave it a royal christening and named it the Lady Elegance Bridge, though to the children it would be known hereafter as Echo Bridge because of the ringing echoes of their voices when they played underneath it. Everyone sang the Wasp's praises as never before for being smart enough to cause Lady Elegance to donate this new bridge. As you can imagine, there was no excuse needed for a bout of royal feasting, dancing and carousing on the floors of Din-Din-Dinny's long-house.

3

Shortly after the deluge, the Wasp and his engineering skills made the news yet again when the yellow floodwaters had finally subsided and the last of the wooden bridge's debris was just about to sail from view. Every man jack headed down to the river with their ass-and-cars and worked like Trojans to carry off the floating timber for their firing. Before the night had settled in, the river was as clean as a whistle.

The Wasp took his paper and pencil and went down to inspect the state of the riverbed. By now the torrent had eased, and he was able to get a good look at the damage to the paving stones that lay on the riverbed. He couldn't believe his eyes for the river was now in a sad and sorry state. Not only had it swam some animals and timber away out of sight, but the long-established paving stones were utterly destroyed and floating somewhere far-off in the Shannon River and heading out for the great ocean.

Each evening the wise man tapped his pencil on his lips and got his engineering mind to work. If you peered in his window, you would see him and his ruler, his goggles perched on the tip of his nose, designing a grand mosaic for the riverbed, a cornerstone here and a keystone there. After all, it was his grandfather (the Gawk) who had laid out the last riverbed at the time of the famine with the help of 20 men, once they'd finished making the ditches that marked out the present fields. At that time his riverbed paving-stones had been greatly admired. God bless the Gawk was the prayer on everybody's lips, a prayer that was short and sweet each night.

The Wasp took his horse-and-cart over to the Yellowstone Quarry next to the schoolhouse and brought back enough slabs to fill the entire river. They were all sorts of colours, oyster-grey and pigeon-blue and irregular in their shape and size – to give them that bit of variety (he said). Smart man that he was, however, he couldn't have selected a worse band of rascals to lay the riverbed's pavement than the three prime byze from Abbey Cross, a few yards further down from the river itself. They were Peter-the-Hare (ganger-man-in-chief) and his assistant (Clever Jack) and his assistant's assistant (Tom Tatters, the son of Split-the-Wind). These three were the most imaginative fellows and could see the end of the week quickly creeping up on them and all the fine drinking they'd be doing in Curl 'n' Stripes drinking-shop when the work was finally finished. They spat on their fists and with a right good will at first, set out to repair the floor of the river.

From his stately perch on the bank, the Wasp saw that the work was going along nice and handy and for a while, his well-known phlegmatic crotchetiness had no need to raise its head. Then came the most critical moment for the workmen's endeavours – the time for laying the last few detailed paving-stones. To the amusement of the three rascals, the Wasp began to get more than a little frustrated and to show the three of them the depths of his testy nature. In the end, he turned himself into a raging tornado, twisting his body this way and that, the spit flying out of his mouth as he waved his arms frantically at them. He was like a sergeant-major from the Daffy-Duck Circus as he tried to show them where the last few bits of his jigsaw should be placed. Couldn't the thundering eejits see where these last few stones were to be placed? Had the simpletons never been inside a schoolhouse?

Regrettably, he made a singular mistake, a fatal one, when he cursed their harmless mothers for having given birth to them and rearing them to their present state of stupidity. Anyone could have told him that he'd gone a step too far, that a harsh word against their saintly mothers was far too painful a thing to bear for the likes of Peter-the-Hare, Clever Jack and Tom Tatters. Like everybody else, they had always loved their mothers most dearly, more than life itself. And another thing – they were not in the best of humour this same morning, for the danglers between their thighs (said Tom Tatters) were frozen to death on them from the icy coldness of the river. Their toes were absolutely icebergs from the constant water soaking the insides of their wellingtons. With thoughts of the Wasp's insult to their mothers continuing to boil in them, the wily devils knew what they were going to do with him and his snotty-nosed orders. It was he himself, they whispered, and not his overburdened minions that was going to be the bleddy simpleton a minute from now.

And then those timeless and inspired fairies, *the Trickeries*, who forever haunt the riverbanks, made their appearance to the three rascals and stepped out to help them in their wicked scheme, offering them the gifts of a fox's cunning and craftiness. They made a bet with each other to see which of them would be first to make the Wasp jump into the river and rinse his good trousers and give the insides of his wellingtons a right royal christening.

Peter-the-Hare had started the day in the merriest of moods, having loaded himself with a few glasses of his father's raw-gut potheen before hopping up on his bike. Already it had started to give his scholarly imagination a bit of a lift, and he now showed himself to be the clumsiest clown in Christendom as his poor befuddled head made a number of vain efforts to fathom out where he should lay the last few paving-stones. His assistants were quick to join in the fun and made puzzled sheep's eyes up at the Wasp, all the time squinting and winking at one another behind his back.

And then the Devil came out from his hidey-hole and whispered a little sin into Peter-the-Hare's ears, who lifted the biggest slab in his hands and, looking like some timeless statue, gazed at it for a minute-and-a-half as though it were a long-lost friend. In imitation of the Wasp, he started twisting this way and that, wondering where he was supposed to place this gem. The other two devils scratched their heads as though they were trying to work out a mighty big sum from previous schooldays. Finally, Peter-the-Hare looked up pleadingly at the Wasp and begged him to give him the fruits of his inspiration.

'For the love of sweet Jesus will ye come and help mee poor aching brain? Can't ye see how misfortunate I am? Can't ye see how I'm stuck here in this cursed river, not knowing which way to turn?'

Now, apart from the insult offered to their mothers, there was something else that bothered them. They were as jealous as hell of the Wasp and his credentials – an important engineer with a hundred wonderful thoughts stacked inside in his scholarly head. It was the Wasp, they thought, and not themselves that was in charge of these important operations, wasn't it? Which of them could cross their hearts and say they owned a pencil or a ruler? Not one of them. Which of them had ever owned an engineer's goggles? Not one of them. Which of them had ever been asked to design a bridge and a riverbed? Not one of them.

Matters now moved along fast. Seeing that his fine mosaic was never going to get completed at this rate, the Wasp forgot his important status and in pure desperation took a running jump straight into the middle of the river. Furiously he snatched one of the last paving-stones from Peter's hands and placed it in the exact spot meant for it. Then he did the very same thing with the next stone.

Tom Tatters now approached the great man from behind and stood awkwardly on the Wasp's left wellington, peering over his shoulder to see where the two stones had so cleverly been laid. Clever Jack kept his own wellington firmly on the Wasp's other wellington with a grip a badger would be proud of. The freezing water came in over the top of the poor man's wellingtons, soaking him to the skin. And now, the shadows of Tom Tatters, Clever Jack and Peter-the-Hare seemed to be all around him, each of them feigning their utter perplexity as to where the wise man was going to place the final slab. When he laid it to within an inch of perfection, the rascals rolled their eyes round in absolute amazement and clapped him on the back at this unheard-of stroke of an engineer's pure genius.

'Aren't ye the bleddy marvellous man!' they hooted and laughed to see the puffed-up smile on the Wasp's face as he beheld the completion of his perfect riverbed mosaic. He made them a little bow and forgave them wholeheartedly for their lack of a proper brain.

But then there came a change in the weather as Peter-the-Hare showed his appreciation for the Wasp's burst of magnanimity by holding onto the back of his startled collar. Clever Jack held onto the buttons of his jacket. Tom Tatters turned his attention to his britches, which were not yet slightly wet. The river sport then got going in earnest, and it wasn't long before the poor Wasp regretted getting out of bed in the morning. What happened next was an absolute scandal, leading him (*'ye feckin whoors, may ye rot in hell!'*) to scream out the foulest of curses – curses unfit for the ears of any riverside fairies that happened to be nearby.

Still sorely wounded from the insult that the Wasp had bestowed on their beloved mothers, the threesome began pitching their engineering friend across the river from one set of hands to another. It was like a game of handball as they tossed him over and back, over and back. In the end, their arms grew stiff from all the sport and, just before the Wasp lost his balance entirely, as well as the remains of his lordly composure, they gave him a kick up the arse and left him flat on his back in the river.

Oh, mercy-me, such unseemly conduct. Was this the way to treat a fine scholar like the Wasp? Was this the way yeer mothers reared the three of ye? And they hopped out over the railings and went off to enjoy the finest few pints of stout they'd ever been privileged to wrap their lips around. The news of the laying of the riverbed mosaic went speeding round the hills and laughter like no other laughter echoed round the creamery road. What with the unprintable curses of the Wasp in his rage and his drenching among the paving-stones, no-one got a blessed day's work done for the next week-and-a-half.

Everyone's joy, however, was soon to be followed by a bout of genuine sadness for the Wasp when they heard that he hadn't long to live and that the gates of Saint Peter were beckoning him to the Beyond. The soaking in the river hadn't done him a drop of good and had brought the wretched pneumonia into both his lungs. At 70 he was old enough anyway and was ready (so he told himself) to meet up with the angels even without the wetting he had gotten from the river.

DAYS OF TEARS AND LAUGHTER

1

It was said that if Molly-rattle-the-tea-and-sugar-bag, like many a good widow-woman before her, didn't quickly nurse herself out of her grief, she would soon be going to join her husband in the Beyond. For like one of Lord Elegance's swans when losing its mate, she was seen daily pining away for the loss of her sound man. But, frail and lonely as she was after the Wasp's death, it wasn't her time to die for yet a while. In the days following his death she began to feel stranded, not knowing what to do with herself. The Wasp had always stood by her side and supported her, and she was soon starting to grow sick and tired of keeping up the fresh appearance of her house and little farm.

And another thing – Dinjo was inside in the Limerick Hospital, and she didn't know when, or if ever, he was going to be brought back to her. A month before this, he had lost his arm in the mineworks, catching it between the sidewall and the cage. A terrible thing, for all could picture him as once he was, him and his rosy face and his blue shirt and his stylish Sunday boots and his new brown suit and his Woodbine fag dangling from the corner of his mouth. Would he ever again be able to strike a match to light a fag for himself?

On the other hand, his brother, Sonny (that lazy good-for-nothing-son-of-hers), was spending every day lying in bed till noon. When he did rise up, he would snatch the last few grains of tea from the canister and roll them inside in a bit of brown paper to make a handy fag for himself and smoke it to his heart's content. What earthly use (said Molly) was this lazy article to her? What use was he to anyone else for that matter? And she made up her mind she'd no longer carry on breaking her backbone for him. Instead, she'd get up on her ass-and-car and go and join her daughter, Hanoria, and Galloping Will at the back of the hill.

But before she went off on her long journey, there was the good fortune of seeing her raise her spirits for a last time. She was coming home from town late one evening worn to a thread from traipsing around the town and her arm aching like hell from all the handshakes of sympathy given to her for the loss of the Wasp. By the time she got home, both herself and her ass were wet to the skin from a sudden downpour of rain. It was almost dark when she reached the lane, and the crows had long gone to roost.

She entered the yard and knocked on the door. There was no answer. She pressed her screwed-up nose against the windowpane and peered in on her tippy-tiptoes. There sat Sonny, her impudent son, sound asleep in front of the fire with the whiskey-bottle resting half-empty in his fist. The cat (good Lord-in-heaven!) was halfway up the dresser and eating the last of the delicious sausages hanging down on a string from a nail under the hob.

'Let me in! Let me in, blasht ye!' whined his mother. 'For the love of sweet Jesus on the cross, let me in!'

Her good-for-nothing son blinked one eye open and fired his sizzling spit onto the hob. He slowly dragged his tottering feet over to the window where he stood grinning bleary-eyed out at her. Once again, he had made himself a dainty fag from the grains of tea. He puffed the smoke at the window-glass and with a few choice scurrilities pointed his tea-fag leeringly at her but refused to open the door and let her in. Instead, he went back and threw a few more furze-bushes onto the fire to heat up the skillet-pot of leftovers and get himself a hearty feed of sausages and grease before finishing off the last of the whiskey.

Suddenly, Molly heard the thieving cat, its mouth full of the stolen sausages, giving the wildest of screeches. For when Sonny had seen that the sausages were nearly all down the cat's belly, he developed a terrible rage and chased the hissing animal round the room before catching it by the tail and throwing it into the fire. Whereupon, seething like the Devil's housemate, the misfortunate creature jumped as high as the rafters and made its escape up the chimney where it hid in the smoke rather than ever venture down again.

Sonny was having a fine old time of it, warming his toes in front of the roasting fire and his father no longer alive to chastise his arse with a belt of the ash-plant. From that day forth, he went on leaving his poor mother locked out whenever he felt like it. There was nothing she could do but cry her eyes out and sit there in the lonely yard. With no Wasp or Dinjo to give her a bit of a lift, she spent night after night in the pig house with the angry sow where she cried herself bitterly to sleep.

2

A fine morning arrived and somehow or other Molly welcomed in its rosy light. She heard a noise and looked across the yard and in over the ditch. Sonny the villain had recovered from another feed of greasy meat and whiskey and was out in the nettle field, himself and the frisky ass (Lock-Jaw). After several vain attempts, he finally managed to get up on the creature's back. In and out amongst the nettles, he gaily rode this jaunty animal, and no lark could have been as cheerful as our bold gamecock this blessed day.

But Lock-Jaw (fair play to him) was a unique individual with his own inborn way of thinking things out, and he carried Sonny to the corner of the field where the nettles grew as high as a house. From a safe distance, Molly was able for once in her life to get a little glimpse into the future. She got down on her bended knees and joined her hands in prayer. She begged her Saviour to show pity on her for the state of her miserable life. Would He please grant her this one last sweet wish? Would He deliver a strong dose of medicine to this noble son of hers?

As though it were indeed the Last Judgment, her humble prayers were answered on the spot. The early morning horse-bees had been assiduously working round the ass's gable-end for the last hour or so. Suddenly Lock-Jaw felt one or two sharp stings beneath his shitty tail where the little buzzers continued to swarm so as to get at the sweet ammonia smells pouring out from that quarter. He lowered his head and made a fierce jump into the air, sailing his back legs out from under him. With tail amok, he ran round and around through the nettles before executing a very dainty turnabout worthy of the town's show fair and pelted Sonny into the depths of the nettles after first leaving him half-dead from the fierce kicking he gave him. This wonderful creature then jumped out over the gate and disappeared from view. He wasn't caught and captured till a week later. By this time, he was half-ways to Tipperary Town (said the smirking drinkers below in Curl 'n' Stripes' shop).

His mother, with feelings of righteous revenge, ran across the lane and leaned in over the gate.

'Sonny! Dearest Sonny,' she snarled, 'tell me this – and tell me no more – how do ye like yeer new nettle-bed?' Her harsh words only added to the poor fellow's pain from the stings of a thousand nettles for he knew that his mother, having witnessed this little comedy, was sure to report it to the rest of the creamery road. He'd be a figure of fun for the rest of the year, and men would never tire of asking him the same old questions. How did he like the dance-steps of his lovely ass, Lock-Jaw? Were the nettles as high as they were reported to have been? He heard his mother's boots retreating across the lane, her sides bursting from an unstoppable fit of laughter. She felt she could hear the Wasp laughing out loud from his bed beyond the clouds. Enough said.

No-one knew when (or even if) Dinjo would be coming home from hospital. Molly couldn't wait any longer to get some news of him, all the time fighting these wretched battles with Sonny. The morning after the rascal's quarrel with Lock-Jaw and the nettles, she was ready to depart. She took down her brown suitcase, the same one that she'd stuffed long ago for a trip to Baltimore in the Land of the Silver Dollar before she met up with the Wasp. So, without a word of goodbye to her bold son, she started out on her journey to Hanoria and the sheep-farm.

In the following days, Sonny continued to doctor his face and arms with the dock-leaves to get rid of his nettle-stings. Realizing that his mother's ass-and-car had gone out the lane and that she'd never be returning as a result of the way he'd treated her, he became overcome with grief. There may even have been a small trace of guilt in him. Of course, what the lazy lump was going to miss most of all was his mother getting him out of his comfortable bed before noon and giving his heartless belly a feed of greasy sausages along with his two boiled eggs (the rascal).

Not long after all these ructions and rows, however, news arrived that Dinjo was on his way home. There was great excitement. Folk left off whatever they were doing and lined the creamery road and waited for his arrival. The younger children were more than anxious to see a man with only one good arm. The older ones wondered if they'd ever see this old friend of theirs sitting with them in the blue-button field. They remembered a few years back when they were looking at the antics of Dowager's son (Stylish) after he'd returned from Dublin where he was learning the bar-room trade of wines and spirits. They told the younger children how Dinjo would lie down with them in the thistles, watching the dexterity of Stylish and his hurley-stick and shammy ball, how Dowager's grumpy old ass (the Lightning Whoor) would look out greedily at them from the haggart, envying them their spot amongst the thistles (for he loved nothing better than eating thistles) and how Dinjo would pick the flowers off of the clover (another favourite dainty of the Lightning Whoor) and fill out his lips with a flowery display to make them all laugh. Oh, how the awestruck little ones sighed when they heard these tales about Dinjo! His likes were far and few between, and they couldn't wait to get a good look at him as soon as he arrived.

The grown-ups wanted to know if Dinjo would be the same as he always was or would he be a changed character with his heart bristling angrily inside his shirt and his spirit as sad as the town's railway yard for the great wrong he imagined the minework had done him. Would he keep everyone at a distance? Would he be riding his bike one-handed? Would he be able to carry his fishing-rod out to Growl River? How would he get into town to see his beloved hurlers at the next hurling match? These were some of the questions that old and young alike kept asking themselves whilst waiting for him to arrive. He had always been the politer one of the twins.

With his disfiguring stump of an arm, the sad youth came into view. Black Bess, the nurse, handed him down gently from her truck and into the arms of a tearful Sonny, who for once in his life was full of genuine concern at the sight of his twin brother *('mee other self')* and his misfortunate lack of an arm. Dinjo's white shirtsleeve was flapping across his chest in the afternoon breeze and pinned back at an angle with a few gigantic safety-pins. His coat was thrown across his other good arm. He looked different, like a man coming home after fighting a mighty battle. He was strange, almost fierce. There was no longer a merry gleam in him or a smile out of him, and his eyes seemed to have reddened since his accident, giving him the appearance of a wild gander about to spring forth and attack the rest of the neighbours.

The following day, a chosen group of children went shyly up to the gravel pit to comfort the poor man and his stump of an arm. They brought him piles of sweets from the shop, enough to rot his fine teeth. Men sent him up several packages of the best fags – his favourite ones, the Gold Flake, the Craven 'A' and the Sweet Afton. What with the several other gifts that every household felt obliged to give him, it was as if a hundred Christmas Days had been rolled into one for the poor lad.

3

Though his mother was now very far away, she continued to ask God what had she ever done that He should bestow on her this wretched gift of Sonny and all the sufferings that came parcelled up with him. Unlike Dinjo, this second child had very large feet on him, turned out awkwardly at a severe angle like those of his great-grandfather (Gunpowder). When he came stepping down the creamery road, he had such an ungainly way of walking, as if he was treading on broken glass.

'He's the very same as a string-halted ass,' said Dowager and in spite of themselves, both herself and My-Son-Jack had to laugh. Even the skin under his black whiskers was that bit pasty and puffy like his mother's dough and with none of Dinjo's pink rosiness. And another thing – Dinjo hadn't an ounce of bitterness in him and wouldn't hurt the fleas on an ass's back, and he always kept himself as clean as a whistle – even after he had lost his wretched arm.

By the time of Dinjo's cruel accident, the twins were a shade over thirty. In the last few years, Sonny had been in a dreadful hurry to show that he was no longer a youth but had become a real and proper man. Unfortunately, by this time he had developed a few unsavoury habits. Whereas other men cleaned out their nostrils with a twisted bit of rag, this uncouth fellow became an expert at placing his finger alongside his nose, letting loose a fine spray of juicy snot onto the flagstones whilst bidding the world good-day before wiping his oily hands on the leg of his trousers. Furthermore, he rarely if ever put a razor to his jaw. His toenails, as men witnessed when they stripped off annually in Growl River for the full washing with the carbolic soap, were as twisted as corkscrews.

'That's the reason,' said My-Son-Jack, 'why the little devil walks so awkwardly as though his britches were full of shite.' Nor did he use the penknife like the rest of us to pare his fingernails.

However, there is always a second side to a brass copper, and Sonny had the most beautiful head of hair, like a Spaniard's, and as thick and curly as a sheep's wool and as black and shiny as a jackdaw's wings. He was forever combing it back with soapy water so that it had a higher wave in it than anybody else's. He also had a great set of teeth on him – or at least he did have until Sally-from-the-Valley's left fist came in contact with them at the house-dance at Shy Dennis's above in the Valley of the Pig.

It was the first dance of the evening. 'Who can dance the polka?' said Sonny. He led the comely Sally out onto the stone floor. He could see the way the other men were watching the tidy style of his dance-steps, and he was growing in confidence as the dance and music went on. During the round-the-house-and-mind-the-dresser spin, he made the fatal mistake of removing his hand from this fine young damsel's waist. He placed it firmly on her ample arse and gave it a little squeeze. Whereupon (and before he could even blink an eye) Sally gave the brazen heathen the finest clatter up into his jaw and sent him hopping off of the wall and landing in the fire. For the rest of that evening, he didn't enjoy a single bit of the fun and carousing. Nor did he drink a drop of the raw-gut potheen or eat a slice of the currant-cake.

As mid-January came around the weather was getting colder. What would life be like on these cold days for Dinjo and Sonny with their mother gone out across the hill? That's when Sonny found himself a new role – that of mother housemaid. He kept the black burner on the hob full of the oily grease grown from generations of fat bacon piled high and never cleaned out. The ashes from his alarmingly huge fires of furze-bushes were never taken out to the ash-pit but left halfway up the hob, spreading out across the floor.

Sometimes he played host and invited a few friends home from the drinking-shop after a feast of stout. They were royally entertained at the sight of Sonny attempting to light a blaze with furze-bushes, stretching them from the fireplace to the centre of the welcoming room. With the wobbly frying-pan poked out in front of him over the ever-increasing blaze, he would try to fry up a few tasty bits of mutton and one or two sausages that the cat had only half-eaten, wiping them on his trousers. It was a miracle the entire place didn't burn to the ground. The bemused cat peered down from his hidey-hole to see what was going on but (no fool was he) dreaded to put in a personal appearance and remained safely hidden in the depths of the chimney rather than join in the fun and get pelted into the flames a second time.

And whilst all this liveliness was going on, what of poor Dinjo and his one arm? He was lying in his bed behind the hob and pining for his beloved mother. Now that she was gone, he had time on his hands to do nothing but think things out for himself. He guessed that whilst he was on the broad of his back in the hospital, Sonny must have shown their mother cruelty beyond belief, seeing that she had been unable to stay a minute longer to look after himself and his one good arm, especially since he and his mother had always been as close as two sides of a dinner-plate. But then one or two of the nightly visitors let slip the unsavoury news to him – how Sonny had spent his days making homemade fags and smoking all the grains of tea in the canister, how he had left their mother standing in the rain abroad in the yard (a pure disgrace) and how she had to go and sleep with the angry sow in the pig house.

Sonny, however, wasn't completely without a heart. Although he had quickly seized the few warm blankets that Molly had left behind, he thoughtfully brought in several armfuls of hay and surrounded Dinjo with it in a made-up crib in the corner of the room behind the warm hob. The hay in Dinjo's new bed would keep him nice and snug (said Sonny to himself). Indeed (said he as he looked back at his brother from the bedroom door), anyone would think that his twin brother was the very same as Jesus lying in the manger, so comfortable and contented did he look.

Dinjo (fair play to him!) didn't take too kindly to this well-intended treatment of him with the hay and began to plan some sort of revenge on Sonny *('I'll put the frighteners on that lad. I'll teach the little fecker a thing or two')* – a revenge that he'd remember for the rest of his life, for he could clearly see that his twin brother was growing worse and worse as the days went by.

As soon as the clock struck 10, the heathen was out the door like a shot from a gun and seldom seen for the next few hours. There was no entertainment for him at home, no more fun from abusing his mother by smoking away the last grains of her precious tea, no more locking her out of the house and seeing her crying in the middle of the yard. He couldn't stay looking at Dinjo and his godforsaken arm for the rest of the day, could he? It was enough to make any man run for the nearest glass of stout. And so, as soon as he had milked the cows and had filled the creamery tanks (or had spilt the milk halfway round the yard as a result of the previous day's fine feed of booze), he took his pounding boots down to Curl 'n' Stripes' drinking-shop. Once inside the door, he took on the serious job of improving his drinking-skills and wiping the froth from his whiskery lips.

4

Unknown to himself or to anyone else, Dinjo's mood swings were growing darker by the day. His shaky nerves, after the rawness left by the operation on his arm, were causing him to lose all sense of direction in his distraught wits. By the time the winter came on, the poor fellow had descended into a state of relative deliriousness, and at times he removed himself from his bed to go parading round the countryside.

And then the genial spring season began to grow lush and time was seen dashing along like a merry little steam engine. One afternoon, three of By-Jiggery and Moll-the-Man's children (it was Young Jim, Leppity and Battlin' Sal) were coming home from school when who should come streaking down from an overhanging tree but a wild creature with no shoes on his feet. Was this strange apparition a vision from Paradise? Might it be Saint Patrick? Was it the Devil? He was wearing a blue, raggity shirt, a brown pair of britches with a rope tied round it and a woman's pair of calico knickers outside the britches. The children's carefree homeward stroll had suddenly been turned into a living nightmare, and they were soon pissing themselves.

'Keep back from me, little children, keep back, I say!' roared the wild man, convulsive screams pouring from his spitty lips.

Oh, no! It was Dinjo. Yes, Dinjo and no other. Having seen him before his accident, they had loved him as the gentlest of souls, but now he was anything but sound in his mind. Not only had the live nerve-endings on his armless shoulder vanished but the nerves inside in his handsome head had also disappeared; that's what their mother said when they staggered home later and gave her the news.

For a minute they were left frozen like statues, not knowing which way to turn, only staring at the empty shirtsleeve pinned into the centre of Dinjo's chest, giving him the look of a character from a storybook, perhaps a pirate from some foreign shores in the Indies. They suddenly got back their breath, and with terrified screams that would match a Cork orchestra *('run, let ye! run like the wind!')* they ran towards the opposite ditch. This seemed to alarm Dinjo, and he rushed after them like a mad bull, chasing them here, there and everywhere round the road. Matters got worse as he started cursing them and their race, threatening to take them off to some imaginary grotto amid the tombstones in the graveyard. They couldn't stay there bawling like a pack of sick donkeys, and they ran like hell as far as Ducks-and-Drakes' hayshed, leaving behind them the bewildered Dinjo running around in little circles as though he was trapped in a sally hole whirlpool.

Next day, they were too afraid to walk up High Straits to school. They couldn't get Dinjo out of their heads and kept wondering what was he planning to do with them once he captured them and took them away to his grotto. The best way to avoid meeting this monster was to take a roundabout way to school through the ferns in Red Buckles' field even though the dew would soak them to the skin.

Young Jim took off his coat and held it out like a shield in front of the other two so that they could follow in a line behind him like young ducks and avoid getting a drop of water on themselves. It was no use. Leppity and Battlin' Sal were much too frightened to continue their journey, and they sat down and began to bawl. Things were desperate. They made up their minds to go home and miss school for the first time in living memory. It was better to face the wrath of their mother than face the frightening spectacle of their new ogre, and the three of them retraced their steps to Echo Bridge.

Young Jim (wise child that he was) decided to run Leppity and Battlin' Sal into the river like cattle. He ordered them to stand side by side and face what was called the Kerry direction where the wind and rain always came from. Then he pelted the water up generously onto their coats and legs so that it looked as though the rain had suddenly come on while they were traveling along High Straits. Their mother knew it could be raining like hell up near the school and yet not a drop seen below on the creamery road.

Soon, Young Jim had soaked his young brother and sister fairly well, careful enough so as not to drench them entirely to the skin. They in their turn pelted the water up at him, making sure to do a believably good job of it. For a finish, the three of them looked the same as they did on those other rainy days when the master (Dang-the-skin-of-it) saw them entering the schoolhouse like wet rats and put sheaves of papers down their miserable backs to soak up the water from them.

As soon as they were satisfied with their appearance, they started out for home. Finally, they came in across the flagstones, their faces sad and downcast (the little play-actors). Moll-the-Man and her shocked face was coming down the pig house gap with an armful of sticks to throw on the fire and was just in time to greet them. She stopped in her track and stared at the three little faces in front of her. She put on her thinking cap. She was puzzled and perplexed. Then she gave a little smile and stood her children in a row. She ordered them to turn around. It was just as she had suspected: their coats were as dry as a board. She almost laughed out loud for her little scallywags hadn't thought of soaking their backs, had they?

Something had to be done. She marched across the yard and brought back the yard-brush. She belted them like blazes round the yard and out across the stream, cursing them as never before.

'To think this is why I brought ye into the world!' To miss a day's schooling was a crime in her book second only to missing Mass. However, she didn't know the half of the misery her children were feeling on this wretched day for their hearts had almost jumped out of their bodies at the dastardly appearance of Dinjo and his monstrous antics and the way it had been able to bring a halt to their usual cheerfulness. It had been the first time in their young lives that they'd begun to understand the meaning of true fear. They were no fools and remembered their schoolbook tales and the fireside stories of ghostly ogres. They began to wonder if there could be some truth in these great mysteries. Were there such things as other monsters in addition to the ghosts of their ancestors, who appeared in the dead of night to one or two men, especially when they were coming home drunk? And then (young though they were) they had another little thought: was Dinjo really the one and the same Dinjo as before? Maybe some devilish spirit had now taken over his body, removing the real Dinjo from them forever? Questions, questions and still more questions. It was the first time they'd stopped to think about such deep matters and reflect on the strangeness that lay at the back of life itself. One thing was sure: they'd be on the lookout for Dinjo, their horror-of-horrors, from this day forward.

5

With the spring season well underway and Dinjo no longer confined to his bed behind the hob, he began to enjoy more and more his bouts of new freedom. After frightening the school-children, he was more or less in his element. He had acquired for himself three little pigs which Shy Dennis had given him as pets so as to draw him out of his newfound misery. He gave names to each of them, and they followed him everywhere, out across the fields, down the road and on towards the river.

'My little curly tails,' he would sigh when he saw them standing behind him at the well where he was gamely trying to bring back a bucket of water with his one good arm. If the day happened to be too wet, he would turn on them angrily and order them to stay at home in the hayshed in case they caught a cough.

If he was traveling to the shop, he had the choice of making his trip home either across the fields or by way of the road. When his pets grew tired of waiting too long for him in the hayshed, they discovered that they had a new power previously hidden from them inside their bodies. They realized instinctively which route Dinjo would be taking home. To his complete amazement, they always pre-judged which way he'd be coming, and they'd meet him half-ways either across the fields or else half-ways up the road, depending which route he'd decided on. This left him scratching his head as to how the little devils had managed this smart new trick. Weren't they the clever little piggies! What need had they of schooling?

People began to take notice of this new version of Dinjo. He appeared to be far less shy than anyone would have have imagined for a man with one arm and, as the days moved on, his deranged mind began to get him talked about by young and old alike. He not only frightened the children out of their wits but scared the hell out of the young ladies one starry night when they were cycling home from the Platform Dance-in-the-Fields. The loneliness and anger had increased in him from day to day to such an extent that, though he was unable to go off and enjoy a night's dancing himself, he was at least able to take to the stage and put on a bit of a performance in front of this new audience, the dancing girls. He dressed up in a white bedsheet stolen from Cheerful Nan's bushes and placed himself inside the graveyard. In his hand, he held his brother's flash-lamp.

As soon as he heard the dancers' peels of joyful laughter, he wrapped the sheet round his body, covering his head, and lit the folds of it with his flash-lamp, thereby highlighting his manic appearance. Swelling with rage, he emerged as a savage ghoul from behind a tombstone and stood there motionless as though he were a heron ready to strike a fish. Then he ran dementedly round among the tombstones, scampering in and out of the ancient abbey ruins. Never in all their days had the dancers seen such a sight as this. Dinjo's latest antics put a sudden end to their cheerful memories of the evening's dance-steps and those shy bits of fumbling and kissing that they'd exchanged with their young fellows behind the dark haystacks. The creamery road became filled with their wild screams, and old men rose up in their beds and wondered where they had placed their shotgun. How would these young ladies ever forget the wailing groans or the wolf-like howls that this new ogre started making at them?

For Dinjo, these nights were the greatest moments so far in his life – appearing before his audience on his theatrical stage and delivering a truly tremendous bit of jack-acting (there'd be more performances to come). Some of the more religious dancers thought that the graveyard's dead bodies were about to come back to life, that this might well be the Day of

Judgment. Others thought that it was one of their own family ancestors now coming back to drag them off to the graveyard and down into the gloomy tomb alongside them.

For a few more weeks, Dinjo continued to take to the stage and frighten even the bravest of men until a night came when Tom Tatters' cousin, Mick-the-Ass and his two younger brothers, after arming themselves in the drinking-shop with a boozy skinful of stout, proved men enough to step into the graveyard at midnight and face up to what others by now believed was the Devil incarnate. Seeing the ghostly-sheeted shape once more doing its bit of a war-dance round the tombstones, they gave chase until they finally outran it and caught a hold of the sheet and tore it off the ghostly spectre.

Ah no! It was Dinjo! And though he and his lost arm was a terribly sorry sight to behold, they gave his skinny ribs a few handy belts of their axe-handles so that he'd have a few purple bruises on him for days to come. The bruises would do nicely in keeping his dead arm company (they told everyone).

Following his escapades amongst the tombstones, Dinjo took up a new hobby and stole into the churchyard when dusk was coming on. Men returning from the minework saw him genuflecting in front of each statue. They saw no harm in this carry-on. Next morning, however, they found that Dinjo had taken on a new tack when their backs were turned and that one or two statues and tombstones had miraculously (Dinjo having but one arm) changed places during the night. The news of such outlandish behaviour spread like the wind and was pounced on by the gossipy old women, who said such a terrible act as Dinjo's had never been heard tell of in all the annals of Tipperary and that it called for a vengeance from God.

A week later, Dinjo took to religion in earnest and was seen kneeling down and saying his prayers in front of Curl 'n' Stripes' drinking-shop window. To cap it all (with his one good arm again) he hoisted the ten-foot wooden crucifix from the churchyard in town and staggered away with it before being caught by Tom Tatters. A day later the self-same Tom (he was always a humorous wag) said he saw Dinjo holding a polite conversation with a few dewdrops inside Free 'n' Easy's stile and that he had seen him saluting a little field-mouse as it ran out past him in the grass.

What was to be done with poor ill-starred Dinjo and his broken nerves? People were at a loss for words. It was time (said some) for him to be removed to a more permanent place of peace and quiet – time for him to be taken away and locked up in the House for Nervous Disorders. But the ever-patient Guards, though mindful of his recent fights with statues and tombstones, were happy to let matters rest for a while and they did nothing. Mindful too of the huge crucifix that he and his one arm had carried away from the churchyard, the patient Father Honesty did nothing either. There was still a great deal of sympathy for a man with only one arm, and folk were left asking themselves a simple question: what would be the state of their own nerves and what would they be doing to pass the time of day or night if they had only one arm like poor Dinjo.

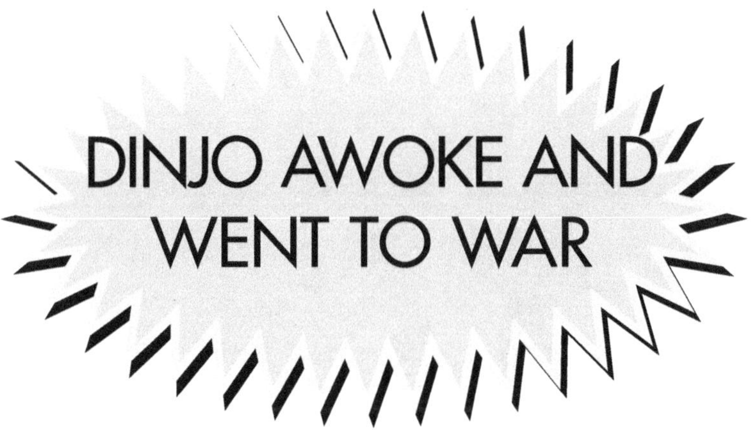
DINJO AWOKE AND
WENT TO WAR

1

As time slipped onwards, the poor wretch grew weaker and weaker, spending most of the day asleep in his bed. He continued to miss his mother and was more lonesome than ever for the loss of her. He had nothing to do for half the day but listen to the cattle coughing in the nettle field and the rattling chains of a solitary horse-and-cart *('who's that passing by, I wonder?')* and wait for hours on end with his ear cocked for the sound of Sonny's jingly bike-bell coming back up the road from the drinking-shop. Apart from the ache in his chest, he had an unearthly hunger in his belly and was raving more and more and talking to imaginary spooks and fairies round the bedroom.

In the dead of night when Sonny was sleeping off his fine feed of booze, Dinjo started to walk out along the roads. At three in the morning, he'd be chatting with the hobgoblins inside the ditch and shaking his fist at the peppered stars in the moonlight above him. He began to bathe in the cold waters of the river, his pile of clothes lying on the bank.

The seasons changed, and the grass was ready for cutting and all would soon be busy mowing and turning the hay, but Sonny seemed unaware of the need for action in the meadow. He was still away for most of the morning, doing the fine carousing with his gable-end resting on the beer-casks inside in the drinking-shop and his six good pints of the black stuff wobbling around in his belly. It was the same routine every day. At 10 o'clock he'd leave home after surrounding Dinjo with his own quilt and as much hay and straw as he could fist into the bed to keep his brother's body warm and snug (he said). Dinjo could daydream about faraway field-flowers and mauve hills beyond in Clare and Killarney (he said).

'I'll be back in a tick with the pound of sausages, and then we'll have the finest of feeds from the burner.' The rascal couldn't wait to hop up on his bike and race the dust off of the road before whaling into his boozy medicine. Anyone could see that he was rapidly racing his way through the Wasp's horde of carefully-saved money. Once out the door, the scamp lost all sense of time and forgot the promise he had made to his twin brother.

As the days rolled on (and to the merriment of the other early drinkers), he was fast becoming the finest of scholars, parading round the drinking-shop and entertaining one farmer or another as they nipped in for a livener on their way back from the creamery. By the time he was into his third pint of stout, he was foaming at the mouth, and his eyes were turning somersaults in his head.

The drinkers were now in for a bit of a mid-morning show. They knew what was coming as Sonny started throwing out his hatred against the British above in what he called the Black North. The nudges, smirks and jokey laughter of one or two young rascals only added to Sonny's rage. They couldn't get enough of his hobnail boots dancing and stamping in temper across the floor. They could see him marching his way up to the Black North. Yes, they could. They could see him marching twice as quickly back home with his britches pissed. Oh yes, they could!

As they goaded him further, Sonny worked himself up into an even grander head of steam, drilling his military goose-steps and making sharp-wheeled turns with an imaginary rifle on his brave shoulder – up to the door and back to the counter.

'Pon-mee-oath,' he cried, 'which of ye little whipping-boys is man enough to come with me and put up a bit of a fight in the Black North?' The young men left down their pints of stout and slapped him on the back.

'We're behind ye, Sonny – every man-jack of us!' Then there followed another bout of laughter. 'More power to yeer elbow, Sonny!' and they filled his glass for him once again. But

Sonny told himself they were nothing but a pack of rotten whoors and merely laughing at him – that it was simply a way of passing the time of day for them.

'By-jakish, if none of ye feckers will go with me, I'll go meeself and set fire to the British basthards.' And again, the shop resounded with delighted laughter at the picture of Sonny putting up a bit of a fight for the freedom of the Black North. By noon the promise of a feed of sausages for poor bedraggled Dinjo had turned into a load of hot air, and the proposed feast lay forlornly in the depths of Sonny's shopping bag on the handlebars of his bike outside the shop door. Dinjo's belly would have to ache with hunger for another hour or two at least.

2

With Dinjo pondering, pondering, pondering and with nothing else for him to do but grow angrier, angrier, angrier as a result of his life's drudgery, it was high time for the battle between himself and Sonny to reach gale force. A fine spring morning came on – a merry little day and not a day for serious quarrelling. Dinjo was awake early and had promptly hopped out of his straw nest. He got down on his bended knees and, like his mother had done on the day of the ass (Lock-Jaw) and the stinging nettles, began to pray to his heavenly Saviour, asking Him to grant him one sweet wish – that a suitable and just punishment might rain down on Sonny's head for spending half the day in the drinking-shop and not bringing back the sausages for his breakfast. The good God-in-heaven listened to his prayers and sent him down what seemed like an inspired masterplan. Sonny, purple-nosed and bleary-eyed as usual, brought his turned-out toes teetering into the yard. It was past noon by this time, and he laid his bike with the bag of sausages against the wall.

Dinjo, with an eye that looked as if it could spot a trout in brown water, was shielding his eyes from the sun and gazing up at a bit of thatch to the right of the chimney. Sonny stood watching him and trying to fathom out what this new mystery was.

'I own-to-God, Sonny,' said Dinjo coyly, 'for the past hour I've been watching a crowd of dirty jackdaws at their work. Do ye know what the basthards are doing? They're tearing our precious thatch to bits over behind the chimney. The little feckers are building a nest with our good straw.'

There was a soft side (not often seen) to Sonny, and it was likely to come to the fore on these occasions when he was back home after his feed of strong drink. He didn't need to be asked twice what he should do but went to the turf-shed and brought back the tall ladder and placed it against the side of the chimney. He mounted to the top to try and find the jackdaws and see where their nest was hidden. He was determined to teach these bleddy jackdaws a lesson they wouldn't forget. He straddled himself on the roof near the chimney and clambered his way gingerly along the ridge, all the time looking for the nest that the jackdaws were building.

'Over this way, Sonny! Over this way! A little bit more to yeer left,' directed Dinjo, ensuring that his brother was as far away as possible from the top of the ladder. He now felt his stomach-muscles clench and his heart turn into a block of ice. Oh, the bile that had grown inside in him! Oh, the rage! Sonny was firmly in his sights for the damage that was about to come his way. With a hefty heave of his boot, Dinjo sent the ladder toppling towards the pig house door. Then he reached behind the bushes where he had prepared a huge heap of rocks.

For the next half-hour, the misfortunate Sonny found himself in a cloud of pain as Dinjo hammered rock after rock off of his head. You could hear the screams and shrieks of him all over the Little Bald Plain as his face turned into a picture of bloody crimson. What amazing strength and determination Dinjo had – for a man who had only one arm to his name.

'Aren't ye the little bantam-cock, Sonny! This is the day I'll make ye tremble,' he roared. 'This is the day when I'll teach ye the Irish language on the back of yeer poll.' He was the very same as a demented ass. 'I'll chastise ye – mark mee word – for drinking away the last of our dead father's few shillings on us!' And at each pelt-of-a-stone Dinjo kept reminding Sonny of how lonesome he had been feeling all these sunny mornings, left alone for hours on end without a bite to stave off his hunger-pains.

Sonny was an absolute disfigurement (even redder than Rambling Jack's recently killed pig), and it was only the arrival of his cousin (Red Scissors) that stopped him from being fully dispatched from the earth. With a sick stomach, the big man climbed up the ladder and brought down the dismantled remains of Sonny. He was scarcely breathing. Everyone ran up (the children galloping ahead) to see what was happening. Opposite their astonished eyes, Red Scissors carried the poor fellow into the welcoming room, and the services of Doctor Glasses were quickly sent for, to come and repair Sonny's wretched limbs. He was speedily carried into the Limerick Hospital, where he spent the next week in a coma between life and death. Father Honesty drove his car in to see him. Fearing that he was about to die, he gave him the Last Rites of Holy Mother Church.

When the rest of the creamery road got to hear of Dinjo's bitter work, they were shocked out of their wits for a day or two. But when they gave themselves a bit of time to think seriously, they remembered the terrible way in which Sonny had blackguarded his misfortunate brother – staying in the drinking-shop with his fist wrapped round a glass of stout for half the day and not having the consideration to come home with Dinjo's breakfast, starving him to death more and more as the days went on.

'Ye wouldn't treat an ould sow like that,' was the view expressed by the men standing at the creamery gates.

'It was good enough for the rascal, and a broken arm or leg was what the whelp richly deserved,' said the women at the well-hole.

3

When Dinjo realized how close to death Sonny had come, he was full of remorse and sadness. All he had wanted was to chastise his brother and break a few bones in his body, not leave him at death's door. And from that day onwards his disturbed mind brought him further down the hill. But still, neither the Guards nor Father Honesty had a wish to interfere in this domestic war between the twins. They prayed that the storm would pass and that all would be well again. Indeed, a month after the outrageous attack from Dinjo and his heap of rocks, the nurses said that Sonny would soon be returning home with his wounds almost healed. From that day forth he'd have the good sense (they said) to fear his brother and keep the new promises he'd made to them in his hospital bed – to return from the shop in good time each morning and bring Dinjo back a supply of sausages huge enough to feed a house in a famine.

It was finally the time for the harvest. With Sonny laid low for another day or two in his hospital bed and not yet fit for work, Dinjo decided to save his hay. Up until now (and till he knew that we had all forgiven him) he had remained too shy and ashamed to come out into the open air except in the dark of the night when his confidence showed itself in its own strange ways, such as his swimming at night in the freezing river or his tidy dance-steps with the tombstones inside in the graveyard. Hammer-the-Smith came down and mowed his hay for him and for the next few days, the hay lay drying in rows in the fields on the other side of Fort Dangerous.

Then a very strange thing happened as the children were returning from school. They couldn't believe what they were witnessing when they looked in over the ditch and saw the undaunted Dinjo and his one arm, the handle of his hayfork wedged under the stump of his dead arm. It brought a tear to their eyes – the sight of him as he tossed the hay in the air and turned the dried-out hay-rows with just his one good arm. With Sonny still recovering in the hospital, Dinjo's heart had become as stout as a terrier's in his need to support his injured brother. A man with two good arms ('twas said) couldn't have done a better job with the hay. With the turning of the hay with his hayfork, it was felt by all that Dinjo had made a lasting retribution and had carried out his Christian duty fair and square.

Sonny would soon be coming home. The nurses sent word that he wasn't dead (only half-dead), and his face was still the colours of a rainbow. He'd be far too weak to do much about bringing in the hay. The one-armed bandit (as Dowager began to call Dinjo) would soon be getting his great big breakfast shovelled into him each morning by Sonny as never before. By-Jiggery and My-Son-Jack felt obliged to rally round and come to the rescue and in the next week, filled the haycart time after time and brought the last trams of Dinjo's hay home safely into his hayshed. This year, when the twins' hay was eventually sold, the price of it would stay firmly in the pockets of the one-armed farmer whereas previously most of the money from the sale of the hay had found its way into Sonny's pocket and from there had found its way nice and neatly into the cash-box of Curl 'n' Stripes in his drinking-shop.

4

The turning of the hay with his one good arm, however, was to be the last noble deed seen from Dinjo. He was tired after his harvesting, and he went back to his bed once more. He still had plenty of time to think. It wasn't only the pelting of rocks at Sonny that started to put shame and sorrow into him. He was beginning to regret his previous wild and savage deeds: the time he had frightened the women and children, the time he had interfered with the statues and tombstones in the graveyard, the time he had taken away the crucifix from the churchyard.

Following those past outbursts of what he felt was his unheard-of wickedness, Dinjo wondered what he should do for a penance so as to get himself absolved from his sins and get a chance to see Heaven in the afterlife. The first anniversary of his accident came around, and he walked the 5 miles to town. He had the price of more than one pound of sausages in his pocket. He had never been a man for drinking more than a single glass of stout and, with the numerous tablets that Doctor Glasses had given him to kill his pains, to be sipping the black stuff all day long wasn't the best thing he could have done. He spent a few hours drinking pint after remorseful pint in one drinking-shop after another, and the evening was upon him before he knew it. It would be a long and weary walk back to the hills now that he was accompanied by the several pints of stout rattling around inside his shirt.

It was a dark and starless evening, and he came home the way he was used to traveling on his midnight rambles – along by the quarry-hole known as the Deep Green Pool. In his sorry state from the drink, the poor befuddled soul misguided his steps at the bend of the road. A grey wind led him on towards a gap, and he went in through a broken fence and staggered on across the fields towards the edge of the deep pool. He looked down into the murky waters 60 feet below him, and a miserable ache rose up in him. No-one knew for sure what happened next, although those narrow-minded old gossips assured everyone that the wicked spirits of the pool (the same spirits that must have haunted Dinjo's dreams since the day he lost his arm and his nerves) caught hold of his jacket and dragged him down under the waters before he could stop them. Of course, the neighbours were well-used to the damned lies of these old dramatists, and they scorned them out of hand these days. Everyone knew the truth – that poor Dinjo's feed of drink (he not being used to it) had led him in off of the road and into the misty darkness where, like many another lost soul abroad in the bog, he had tumbled in and got drowned.

Next morning, everyone ran down the creamery road to see could they find their dear friend, Dinjo – even the younger children like Leppity (the fastest of all the children) and Battlin' Sal, who also ran there faster than the rest of the crowd. They came to the Deep Green Pool. Oh Mother-o-god! Their hearts were chilled at the sad sight before their eyes. All they saw was the message-bag and the string of sausages that had escaped and swum out of the bag. They were floating up at them like a Tan soldier's guts on the surface of the water. It was a terrible thing to behold – especially for the children. They had once heard from Moll-the-Man (the old scaremonger that she was and always trying to keep them near her at home) that a big dragon lived down there. Everyone kept looking and looking, but there was no sign of poor Dinjo. They knelt down (the children too) and prayed for Dinjo's soul and blessed themselves – to fend each other off from a similar fate. Then, sadder than a funeral, they all traipsed home and back into the real world. No-one had the heart to tell Molly-rattle-the-tea-and-sugar-bag the miserable way in which her son had met his end, and it was agreed by one and all that she'd be given the news that poor Dinjo's nerves had finally given way altogether and that he had been taken down south to the House for Nervous Disorders.

Then some good-humoured scallywags remembered Dinjo's three pet piggies at home, and they wondered wouldn't they be a small bit lonely without his company and was there anything that could be done about them. Even the children laughed nervously as they pondered what would happen next. Of course, in the midst of their sorrow, men were still able to give each other the wink and the nudge for they knew (of course they did) the answer to this solemn question: Dinjo's pet piggies would be dispatched with the long-handled knife before the year was out and distributed on Sunday dinner-plates in time for next Christmas Day.

5

Following his safe return home from the Limerick Hospital, Sonny seemed to be getting himself into better shape as the weeks rolled by. He was (all could see) a good deal more sensible than before. He missed his brother completely. During the nights he couldn't sleep a wink. There was no Dinjo to tuck into bed with an armful of hay and to keep company if he got lonely. He thought he could see the twisted face of his brother and hear him calling him from the depths of the Deep Green Pool.

'Sonny! Sonny! Coom and join me in the green pastures of the Beyond!'

Bit by bit, he began to feel that he too was losing some of his wits and that he was surely about to die and follow Dinjo into the Beyond. But this was not to happen – not for another year or two. Increasingly saddened and lonely, he needed no excuse to spend his days below in Curl 'n' Stripes' drinking-shop, throwing his money in over the counter as never before and bemoaning the loss of his lovely twin brother. You'd see his awkward boots and his bike bumping into each other at any hour of the day or night as he returned to his empty welcoming room. There wasn't even a stuttering fire in the empty fireplace. There was nobody left to argue with, and he felt that even an attack from Dinjo and his rocks would have given him something to occupy his mind with and to talk about. Not even his mother was around the place for him to plague the life out of and leave standing abroad in the pouring rain. He sold all his cows and his dry cattle too. He was rapidly drinking away the price he'd got for them in the market square. It wouldn't be long (sighed the rest of the road) before he drank away the entire blessed farm and the remains of the Wasp's money.

There came a Saturday night when an angry blue-black storm came raging at us from somewhere out in the great ocean, hitting everyone full in the face. All night long it howled and hung over the fields. The older men and women remembered no previous wind with which to compare it – not since the Year of the Deluge and the previous loss of the wooden bridge. Its eerie ghost sizzled and prowled round the back of Shy Dennis's shack. It travelled with the speed of a bullet on across Corcoran's Well. It terrified the cattle, horses and pigs. The little hearts of the crows in their lofty nests were left speechless, and the manic cat that had once foraged the sausages leapt out of its skin above in Sonny's chimney. The children closed their ears from the thunder of it all. They shut tight their eyes from the lightning of it all.

Next morning when the last of this mighty hurricane had drained itself out and had gone on its merry way, all the men ran out to inspect the damage. It had left trees smashed into splinters all over the creamery road. It had knocked out the glass in some of the windows. Sadly, it had brought down a sturdy elm-tree and left it straddled across the thatch of Sonny's cabin, its branches crashing across the top of the chimney where he had recently almost lost his life. It had also cut its way in through the rotten rafters.

The men rushed up and in along Sonny's lane to see what on earth had happened. They crowded into his yard (the children again leading the way) to see the huge tree on top of Sonny's broken-down roof. Nobody had ever seen anything like this before. It seemed a miracle that the walls of the poor man's bedroom were still left standing. Red Scissors and his neighbour, Rambling Jack, broke in through the front door and entered the welcoming room, the rest of the men following. The roof had tumbled down behind the fireplace. The tree's branches had fallen straight down on top of Sonny, landing across his bed and piercing him in the chest. There the poor fellow lay, stretched out on the bed underneath the suspended rafters.

The children ran round the back of the house and peeped in from outside the back window. They saw the huge tree on top of the fluttering remnants of Sonny's torn roof. Through the big hole, the sun was streaming in on the poor man's dead face, tingeing it smooth and soft. And not even a cricket was stirring. They had seen a man with one arm, and now they had seen a man – stone dead. They realized that Sonny was as lifeless as the rabbits on the back of their door and looked just like Saint Francis in the prayer-book with his dark hair and his skin the colour of cream. They knew, of course, that the ghost-of-him was far above them in the clouds of the Beyond.

The men who had crowded into the room smiled to themselves. They realized that Sonny was free from the constraints of his life here on Earth and that he would never be going to the Black North to burn it, that he'd never be lacing his big boots and stamping them down the road to drink his pints of stout, that he had answered his twin's call and gone to keep him company in the Beyond.

The women looked at Sonny's corpse and sighed. There was none of the blue-jaw look of old about the poor misfortunate man, and his ugly bruised scars were gone from him. In death, he was at peace and not a wrinkle left on him.

'Doesn't he look very beautiful with his jetty Spanishy hair and his innocent cheeks like the smooth face of a new-born child?' said Moll-the-Man.

'I never saw him looking better,' sighed By-Jiggery. 'He looks good enough for a church mortuary-card.'

And now, after the recent death of poor Dinjo, the children had been confronted for the second time with the unreal wonder of an untimely ending to a man's life. It brought all manner of holy thoughts into their young heads. They had looked down into the Deep Green Pool where Dinjo got drowned, and now they had seen his brother dead in the bed. Like the grown men, they too knew that his soul was a long way out over Chieftain Hill where invisible winged angels and Dinjo were already welcoming him home. How he got there, they couldn't fathom out. They knelt down outside the back-window, and they made the little ones kneel down next to them. It was a moment when they felt (as never before) a burst of sheer holiness as they prayed with a most saintly vigour for the eternal well-being of Sonny's soul. After that, they trudged sadly down the hill. Battlin' Sal, young though she was and forever having to battle her own corner in life, was traipsing sadly along in the wake of her big brothers.

Late in the afternoon, the neighbours brought Molly-rattle-the-tea-and-sugar-bag up from behind the Hills-of-the-Past to see her dead son. As much as she had cursed him for his ill-treatment of her in the past, the poor woman now sat abroad in the yard, delirious and bedraggled. She rocked back and forth, and she let two fat tears roll down her cheeks. And then she began to bawl like a sick cow pining for its dead calf. She tore her blouse and smashed her head off of the flagstones. The kind friends took her in their arms and marched her away. They entered the house and filled the ass-and-car with her few possessions, including her dowry gift of the grandfather clock that she had given to the Wasp when their match had once been made. Then they shut and bolted the door for the last time.

CLEVER JACK
WENT UP THE HILL

1

In the midst of folk, there had always been fixed times in the year: the time for the daffodils and the time for the skylark in our meadows, the time for the corncrake in our gorse bushes, the time for the pell-mell rains of September, followed by the increasing winds that would rise to full force a month later. A certain Monday evening was now going to be a particular time too – a time for Clever Jack to proclaim himself the biggest villain in our midst. The mountainy men would remember this evening as the Night of the Big News. It was to take place in the welcoming room of Old Titanic and his wife, Be-the-Tair – the perfect spot in which to hold a meeting as important as this, for it was the longest welcoming room that any of us had ever heard tell of apart from Din-Din-Dinny's above in the Hills-of-the-Past.

Moll-the-Man had been responsible for the arrangement. Clever Jack was to go up and spend an hour or two reading the news in his newspaper to our mountainy friends so that they'd get all the latest details about the war and which side was winning and which was losing. They knew that this wretched conflict had been hammering on for a good number of years – even though our own lads hadn't had the chance to go and kill a few German soldiers. They also knew that their women were forever anxious about all the fierce killings taking place across the map, in case they should get a few unexpected licks from the German guns. In which case (they said) they'd soon find themselves laid out cold and lodged in the graveyard.

To get up to Old Titanic's place, Clever Jack had to ride his mare (Hefty) with his little hound (Caruso) trotting along beside him out across the Valley of the Black Cattle and along the side of Growl River. Then he'd have to go on up to Diggledy-doo where lived the High 'n' Dry Men like Joe Solitary and the Lackadaisicals like old Bazeen.

These were the wildest of places where some farmers were a good bit poorer than the rest of the men down on the slopes, with only a few patches of rough reedy land overrun with scrub bushes, their fields at times no better than an abandoned jungle.

The villainous Moll-the-Man was always looking for amusement (wasn't everyone?), and she had informed the men up there that Clever Jack was a well-versed reader of holy books like *The Messenger* and that he had read a number of Zane Grey cowboy novels. Indeed (she said), he was the prestigious reader of any book other than a post office stamp-book and had turned his eyes almost inside out from reading the most recent newspapers that Herald-the-Post was able to get through to him, even going hard at it in the dusk of the evening behind the hay-reek.

Such lavish praise of Clever Jack was just what the mountainy men wanted to hear since they were somewhat ashamed of the fact that they themselves couldn't read the newspapers too well and admitted to her that they hadn't a clue which side was now winning the war. Worse still, they hadn't been told that the war had ended a month or two back. The result was that they were itching for her to bring Jack up and read out the latest events to them.

All was set up. Moll could depend on Clever Jack. The evening's reading would give him (the rogue that he was and with that glint forever in his eye) a chance to distort the truth about the recent conflicts and entangle his listeners' brains with nothing but a bag of filthy lies and a few cleverly embroidered embellishments. He'd be as good as the holy missioner, wouldn't he?

All knew the way things ran – that from inside in the town and up as far as the remote hills, there was a descending scale of literacy, which meant that when it came to reading the newspaper, the literate lads from the town and even those from the slopes were sometimes able to make fools of their less-literate fellows in the remote hills. On the other hand, the hilly breezes (everybody knew this for a solid fact) had always stimulated the brains of the mountainy men so that they were said to have far more brains than the rest of the men and were as gifted as a politician in making up their own lying yarns. The sad truth was that most of them lived too far away from any schoolhouse so that only a few of them had ever had a chance to get to school on a regular footing and as a result had a small bit of trouble deciphering the written words in a newspaper (that's if they ever had the price of one).

2

The Big News Night arrived. It was 6 o'clock, and Clever Jack would be coming in the door any minute now to pay his respects. The room was 20 feet long, and the walls with their many old ghosts, memories and pictures had been newly whitewashed. There were two small square windows as well as the half-door to let in the last few drops of the day's fading light.

A big crowd had already arrived from the depths of the countryside, not only filling Old Titanic's welcoming room but stretching out the door and into the cobbled yard. War-news was very important to them, and there wasn't one of them who wouldn't give his hind teeth to get his hands on a wireless-set so he could listen to the man-in-the-box speaking his words-of-wisdom to them. The only two wireless-sets known to any of them, however, were stuck on the wall below in Lord Elegance's kitchen and in the parlour of Father Honesty in Copperstone Hollow (though Doctor Glasses was said to have put in an order for one). They'd have liked nothing better than make a quick raid on those grandiose establishments and run away with a wireless-set. But for now, they'd have to sit around patiently and wait for Clever Jack to tell them what was in this morning's newspaper.

The clock on the wall was ticking loudly, and the murmur went around that Clever Jack had raced Hefty in across the flagstones and with him Caruso, his famed little hunting-dog. And now they could hear the ring of his hobnail boots striding in across Old Titanic's yard.

Moll ran out to meet him at the gable-end of the house. She tied Caruso to the singletree, ruffling his ear, and she laid before him a big saucepan of scraps and milk. She gave Hefty a few fistfuls of richly-deserved hay. Then she gave Clever Jack a playful little shove towards the half-door and whipped off his cap good-naturedly and led him in under the lintel.

'God save all here! God bless the work!' shouted Jack as he devoured the gathering with his eyes and threw his cap on the nail next to the holy water font.

There was a brief pause out of respect for him and then, 'God save ye kindly, Jack!' they echoed back. In their eyes was a pride in him as they looked at his manly stance. His hair was as rusty-coloured as autumn ferns and was swept back over his left ear like a solicitor's and the dewy frost of the early evening was shining on his face, coat and boots. They were used to observing such items as this in strangers.

Old Titanic dragged his esteemed visitor over to the blazing turf-fire and sat him down at the head of the listeners in the comfort of his own grandfather chair.

Behind Clever Jack and in underneath the hob there was an apple-box from which he could pick out an apple for himself now and then so as to break up his reading spells and oil his parched tongue, but especially to give himself time to think about the next bit of his spontaneous news from the pages of the paper.

He looked around him, taking in the welcoming room and the motley collection of wizened old faces. There was a faint copper light from the oil-lamp wavering its way across the men's heads and making charcoal shadows on the walls. Blue and grey wisps of tobacco-smoke floated raggedly upwards and dissolved in the rafters. So many men (he couldn't count them) were perched in front of him, seated cross-legged in neat little rows like children seen in a school photo-book. He could tell they were as eager as little ones round a burner of curranty rice, their ears bursting to hear the latest bits of news about this wretched war.

'Isn't Jack the fine scholar,' whispered Ned-the-Herd.

'Indeed 'n' he is,' said Old Titanic.

What they didn't know was that Moll-the-Man had grossly misinterpreted Clever Jack's knowledge of books. He was able to read only the three and four-letter words since he himself had barely reached third standard in Dang-the-skin-of-it's schoolhouse.

'Any news – any news?' cried the floor.

'Coom on, Jack! Coom on, blasht ye! Ye're no good at all!' they roared.

'Give us the latest news about the war. What's keeping ye, Jack?'

There were the odd few snorts of phlegm and one or two men wiping the spit on their trousers as if they were making a bargain over a cow in the market square. This was the usual introduction when a stranger came into a welcoming room. For these men seldom saw anyone from down in the valley and were forever foraging for a bit of news – any bit of news at all would do (maybe the pope was dead).

From his perch by the fire, Clever Jack started walking up and down in front of them and showing them one or two little newspaper pictures of the broken-down buildings and the maps indicating where the German soldiers had recently skedaddled home to their mothers and fathers. His brain was working fast for he knew it wouldn't be long before he found himself floundering over the big rocks-of-words which would surely fill up half the newspaper. When that happened, he'd be forced to make up a number of excuses and introduce them to the words 'it goes on to say this . . . it goes on to say that'. The use of this little trick (the '*it goes on to say*' trick) would show his listeners that a wise man like himself couldn't be bothered reading the exact damned newspaper from top to bottom, could he? To do this would take him a blessed week-and-a-half, wouldn't it? Besides this, why should he let his mountainy friends know that he couldn't make head nor tail of the newspaper's longer words? Why should he let his own family down and portray himself as a thoroughbred ass?

Some of the men now wanted to know about the war in Africa. 'Tell us about the Happy-Sinniyans, Jack. How are those lads doing?' they chorused.

Others were asking him, 'What the blazes are the High-Taliyans up to this week, Jack?' And they were soon firing questions into his startled ears from all angles.

Clever Jack got up and waved the newspaper at them. 'Whisht, lads! Whisht, let ye.'

He fixed his eyes on their dreamy faces and then sat down and leant back in his chair. He put on his spectacles and frowned, giving himself the air of a somewhat tragic Greek muse. Then he gave a little cough and spat his phlegm into the fireplace. During this performance, the silence was bursting them all.

He stood up and turned his gaze to the front page, squinting and holding it up to the lamplight, his eyes scanning the print from left to right. This was his moment. He had the sympathy of the entire floor for everyone realised how difficult it was for any man to read the long-lettered words. Not one of them wanted Clever Jack to fail. Not one of them wanted to go home to his wife without the most up-to-date war-news and every sort of encouragement, barring a fist to his jaw, was now given to their smart visitor.

Clever Jack at last started reading about the war's most recent tragedies and began putting fire into his speech, his words lashing out from his mouth like a church fountain. His listeners nodded and winked at one another. Jack was as good as Father Honesty reading from the big missal at Sunday Mass.

He paused for a second before suddenly stamping his angry boots on the floor.

'Will ye listen to this bit, byze,' he cried. 'Several shops and houses were destroyed inside in Moscow last Wednesday. That's what it says here on page two,' and he pointed to the paper. There was a hush in the room. You'd hear a pin drop, and there wasn't even a smirk on the rascal's jaw.

'The Yankee boys climbed over the walls and beat the shite out of the Rooshkees – and he waved the newspaper at them. This bit of information was a sensational twist to the war – the most important victory they'd heard tell of so far. The battle (said he) had been fought to the death. 'The newspaper doesn't tell lies,' said he.

He turned over the paper and ran his finger up and down the next page and squinted in sheer disbelief. 'Holy Moses! It says here (and he jabbed his finger at the page again) that the fight lasted six bleddy hours. Would ye believe that? Six bleddy hours!'

By now, the crowd were spellbound, hearing this fine bit of news – the fact that the Yankee boys had given the Rooshkees a good belting and had won the fight handsomely.

'Cripes, byze, did ye hear that – did ye hear that?' they shouted in a chorus of birdsong. You'd think it was the priest's birthday, as Old Titanic's welcoming room echoed with roars of laughter and mouthfuls of broken teeth. It was a moment of great joy since a number of them had sons in the Land of the Silver Dollar and in their mind's eye, they could see the houses of the Rooshkees blazing right across Moscow. Several of them threw their caps into the air and frightened Moll-the-Man and Be-The-Tair, who were beside the fire making watery tea for themselves from the few grains left in the canister. The fact that the American soldiers had never set foot in Moscow nobody had ever bothered to tell them.

Seeing how his atrocious news was affecting the crowd and the glazed look in their innocent eyes, Clever Jack's heart began to chuckle with suppressed laughter. He called them back to attention, throwing down the newspaper and stamping on it.

'Cripes, byze, listen to this,' he shouted, picking it up again. 'At 4 o'clock last Tuesday (I forgot to read ye that bit)' – and again, his finger jabbed the page – 'a mighty battle took place, and Hitler himself narrowly missed getting his moustache blown off by one of those High-Taliyan bombs.'

'Did ye hear that – did ye hear that?' roared the High 'n' Dry Men.

'Would ye credit it?' roared the Lackadaisicals.

By now Clever Jack's words were falling like hailstones on their ears, and the way he was delivering his news had put paid to any belief they might have had that the war would soon be over. What with the heat of the fire and the excitement and the shouts about each new battle, the place had turned into a hornet's nest, and one or two pipes of tobacco had gone out with men forgetting to pull on them. There was yet another bout of nodding, winking and nudging at the smart way in which Clever Jack was pouring out the news for them.

He slowly turned over the page and scanned it up and down for a second or two before he found what he was looking for. 'Ah, here it is, byze – right here at the top of the page. Early yesterday morning, a house fell on top of Hitler and his bosom pal, Himmler, and it says that his two fine legs are broken in bits.'

He paused to see had the crowd grasped the full force of this outrageous lie, and then he went quickly on reading the next bit before anyone had a chance to question him. 'At any rate, he's inside in a private room in a hospital in South Bang-Bang.'

'Where's that, Jack?'

'A mile or two south of Timbuktoo.'

The room erupted in yet another burst of laughter and cheering. Moll-the-Man and Be-the-Tair blessed themselves repeatedly. For they were very much saddened to hear all this miserable news – especially the bit about poor Hitler's two fine legs.

'Ah, the poor crathur!' they sighed. They were ready to burst into tears from the great amount of wickedness in the world and from the wild men still bent on killing one another. What any woman yearned for (they said) was for all sides to win this blasted war – if only God in His goodness would let it happen.

'Jack! Jack! – read out who's dead,' the men cried excitedly, 'Coom on – read us the names, blasht ye,' they shouted. 'Give us the list! Give us the list! – Go on, do!'

Had there been a blue ribbon for roguery and pure inventiveness, Clever Jack would have won it handsomely. From his lips there followed a gallery of alarming Russian and German names, all made up on the spot by their inspired reader and in words as long as your arm – the Molatoffs and the Hoppensteins and a dozen others.

As they listened to the everlasting list of dead men, the two women were once again a picture of grief. 'Ah, the poor yoong devils, the poor yoong devils!' they groaned. 'May the Lord have mercy on their souls.' And they blessed themselves all over again. The place had turned into a strange mixture – a circus and a graveyard all rolled into one – with the men's bouts of joyful laughter at the thought of Hitler's broken legs and the two women shedding their tears for all the dead soldiers.

The men began to interrupt Clever Jack and his war news. 'Let me speak! Let me speak!' they bawled, each man wanting a bit of the floor for himself to get up and say a few words. The commotion was about to get out of hand and some of them had started to swear, curse and stamp their hobnail boots in anger at the filthy Germans and the savage Rooshkees and at any other foreign race they could think of.

Once again, Clever Jack rose to the occasion. He threw down his newspaper and for several seconds stamped all over it in disbelief. This was met with a hush, and all the necks craned forward to see the cause of his sudden wrath.

'The church taxes are going up again, byze,' he gasped.

Everyone moaned and groaned along with him and, as a result of this inspired diversion away from his war-news, Bishop High-Hat was cursed by one and all into the four corners of Hell.

3

By now, the yellow glow of the risen moon stood above the yard, replacing the thick misty milk on top of Chieftain Hill, and the flagstones shone brightly across the stream. The dusk was coming on, purple and blue and cold and the pine trees screening Old Titanic's haggart had turned from charcoal to black against the sky.

The mountainy men followed Clever Jack out to the stream to wish him farewell. He took a hammer and nailed a big board high on a tree. This was a curious thing for him to be doing. On it, he had written a few scurrilous words. 'The inhabitants of Diggledy-doo are a pack of crazy basthards.'

Underneath this he had written, 'They're nothing but a shower of feckers.'

He was full sure that none of them could make head nor tail of these words. And they demanded that he read out the meaning of what he'd just written on the board. Without a blush to his cheeks, the lying hound told them what he'd written. 'At 12 o'clock next Sunday there's to be an auction of turnips below in Kernel Bootlaces' meadow.'

They were as excited as hell at such a fine chance to go and get themselves a cartload of turnips. The Lackadaisicals said they'd be dressing up in their best finery for such a grand occasion. The High 'n' Dry Men said they'd be trooping off in droves once Mass had finished.

The Night of the Big News was at an end. Clever Jack untied Caruso from the singletree, and he jumped up on Hefty before scuttling from the yard, Caruso again trotting briskly along by his side as he sailed majestically down the lane before tearing down the dipping slope towards the Valley of the Pig.

If you listened, you could hear him whistling a merry tune to himself for he was as happy as a tinker that had just stolen a leg of mutton. Both his sides were hurting from the gulps of laughter coming up out of his throat, and the tears were blinding his eyes as he recalled the long list of scandalous lies he'd told his mountainy friends in his war-news report. It had been the best sport since Black-eyed Suzy (a townie hussy inside at the show fair) had crept up behind the back-tugger (Wiggy-Wagger, it was thought) and pulled his hurling-togs down round his ankles during the last stretch of the tug-of-war, causing his team to fall down in a helpless heap on top of one another. That event *('Ah, lads – that's no sport at all!')* had been accompanied by a bout of robust cursing and swearing ('*the feckin whoor*!') and for poor old Slipperslapper to faint outright at the sight of what she later described as 'Wiggy-Wagger's hairy particles' sticking out from underneath his hurling-shirt.

Clever Jack could picture the look on Kernel Bootlaces' face the following Sunday when he'd behold an army of the mountainy men standing outside his gates and demanding to inspect his turnips. But he knew something else – that if ever his friends from the hills discovered what pure fools he'd made of them, he'd need more than the swift paws of Caruso in his heels to make good his escape, that if they and their blackthorn sticks ever met up with him, his sore skull would have some very different tales to tell. And he knew exactly into which part of his delicate anatomy they'd be sticking their pitchforks if they ever caught hold of him.

NELL PUT ON HER DANCING SHOES

1

It was June. The Hills-of-the-Past had always had its fair share of mischief-makers. But there were times when the mountain slopes saw the other side of the coin, and the fields echoed with innocent laughter and pure joy. It was then that you'd notice how the rascally devilment that was in the hearts of the boys was replaced with this other gentler mood, namely the shy little sighs of the older girls and their shivery longing for a bit of feathery romance during a summer's twilight.

Unlike the boys, you'd never see these girls swinging Old Sam's cat round by its tail and firing it out over the ditch or trying to get up on Red Scissors' wild ass and ride it round the hills. No, these girls were content to spend their afternoons leaning on their elbows, looking out over the geraniums on the windowsill. The little dreamers could imagine a gallant horseman on his shining white steed as he pranced out from the pages of their storybook and raced across the cobbled yard to carry them off to the land of Pleasure. If only . . . if only . . . and they gave a little shudder and shook themselves back into their day-to-day reality.

The days were growing longer and getting hotter, and the girls' hearts were bursting to be off to the season's first platform dance across the fields. Their tingling feet couldn't stay quiet a minute longer. *The woodland fairies* and *the river fairies* (and all believed in their existence) agreed: there was no place on earth as charming and wonderful as the platform dance above in Judy Rag's meadow. It was a trip into dreamland itself. There'd be a crowd of 60 dancers up there, each one anxious to make the most of these fine evenings. For all that was left later on when the summer days came to an end was the great winter

Wran-Byze-Dance in Din-Din-Dinny's long house on St. Stephen's night. The piles of coppers that the youngsters collected from their house-to-house singing for the old folk would allow them to set their skirts a-swirling and their hobnail boots aflame beneath Dinny's rumbling rafters. A fine feast would be thrown in as well. But that was a long way off.

Above in Dowager's house, the day before Judy's meadow-dance saw her young daughters doing more than their usual share of the housework. They dusted the four corners of the rooms with the big goose-wings. They used the little wings for all the more particular work. They scrubbed the welcoming room floor till their knees were red-raw. Then they polished the cups, saucers and plates on top of the dresser till they were as white as a haystack in the snow.

As soon as the housework was completed to Dowager's satisfaction, they took their bowls of dripping and pig-grease down to Abbey Cross to sell to the passers-by or to trade in over the counter at Curl 'n' Stripes drinking-shop for the price of four pennies, which would get them a few lemonades and a contribution to the musicians at the dance.

The boys, of course, escaped all this housework but showed just as much dedication as the girls. They carried their six buckets of water back from the well and chopped the logs for the fire. My-Son-Jack (the oldest of the brothers) looked on approvingly and helped them stack high the woodpile at the pig house wall. He could see his own mind reflected in theirs, knowing how much his young brothers longed for an evening when they could venture like their sisters into the unreal world and escape from the monotony of the house-fire and the ticking of the old clock on the press cupboard shelf.

Wednesday was the evening for the meadow-dance. The girls would wear their one-and-only posh frock, maybe a cast-off from an older sister or a dress made by their mother from a fine garment given to them by one of the rich ladies in the big house. One or two girls had rich dresses (blue, lavender and even pink) from kinfolk living in that heavenly spot across the sea that was referred to as the Land of the Silver Dollar. Dressed to kill, they were sure to catch the nod and wink of every young lad as soon as they made their first few tentative steps round the field's dance-boards.

On the evening before this first dance, the girls knelt down by the fire. They raised their pious eyes to the oil-lamp on the tapestry and offered up their prayers for their brothers since these lads were the proud owners of the shiny bikes that the girls would need for cycling the few miles across country to the dance.

Then they stormed into the big cave room behind the hob and helped My-Son-Jack repair the tyres with the patches, the powder and glue from his yellow tin. When the tyres were pumped up good and hard, they helped him grease and oil the metal parts and made sure to test the brakes for the downward journey home when the moon might be fast asleep behind the clouds. Most girls travelled three-to-a-bike, one on the saddle and steering the handlebars, the other two in turn on the crossbar and carrier.

My-Son-Jack was 24 but could do nothing himself, only cast an envious eye at his brothers and sisters. For, following a kick from the Kerry-blue cow, he had become too stiff in the knees to go and enjoy an evening's dancing. All he had these days were a few faded memories of the rosy-cheeked girls that he held in his arms above in Judy's meadow in previous years.

Tomorrow his brothers would be getting themselves dressed up for the dancing frenzy, then speeding their boots across the shortcut through Lisnagorna Woods to meet up with their cycling sisters. My-Son-Jack had another thought. A year or two from now, each one of them would be flying away from Dowager's nest and taking the Limerick train to Dublin and the cattle-boat across the sea. There was nothing to keep any of them at home whereas he, being the oldest by far, had his duty to do – to stay at home and look after his dear old mother and tend to the little farm now that his father (Warbling Will) was lying cold in the grave.

2

And now it was Wednesday morning, and two of Dowager's younger sons were stripped to the waist and splashing themselves in the freezing yard stream. The girls were fixing up their hair in front of the looking-glass with their hot rags and getting ready their dresses that were laid out on their mother's bed.

The three older boys now jumped in over John's Gate and headed down to the river. Underneath the bridge, they threw off their shirts and trousers and pelted the carbolic soap from one to the other, now and then hitting an unsuspecting daydreamer on the back of his poll with it. Soon they were as clean as a scraped pig. Their laughter and roars echoed out from under the bridge and caught the ear of Fanny Adams above near her Uncle Sam's hayshed. She had just arrived after a breathless 15-mile bike-ride from the far side of town – here for the birth of her Aunt Nora's baby, a most unexpected little gift since Sam was old enough to be put out to grass like an old horse. It was a pure miracle how he'd had the energy to father a child at his age, the crafty rascal.

Fanny stood at the cowshed door, admiring her uncle as he milked his cows and groaned his homemade songs into each cow's ear, encouraging them to spill their milk into the bucket. She couldn't help laughing, for her Uncle Sam hadn't a stem of music in his head and yet was the only soul with brains big enough to memorise the words of every song imaginable. Wouldn't he make a fine solicitor, she thought?

And now she begged him to let her into the bedroom and make herself useful to poor Aunt Nora who was already sweating on top of the bed and gripping the sheets for all she was worth. But her uncle good-naturedly hunted her away from the bedroom scene.

Stepping out into the yard, she spotted little Sing-me-a-song, the eight-year-old daughter of Cackles (Sam's neighbour), as she came hopping out over the ditch, eagerly looking for news of how many more hours it might take for Nora's baby to be born. Fanny was anxious to distract the little girl, and she took her by the hand and led her down the haggart.

'Coom with me, let ye!' she whispered and walked the child off down the field and out over the wire fence at the lower end of Sam's orchard. They strolled on through the pine trees, their feet slipping gingerly over the pine needles. They tiptoed towards the river where the roars of the boys could be heard.

What a sight met their eyes when they got there! They saw Dowager's sons – and with them their friend (Restless Rody) – frolicking around in the river and not a stitch of clothes on them. They were bouncing upstream like a frog on one leg and pretending to be a band of skilful swimmers, although none of them could swim a stroke.

Little Sing-me-a-song let a scream out of her when she saw the boys' nakedness before they turned away and cupped their hands coyly between their thighs.

'Don't bother hiding yeer unmentionables,' said Fanny, 'we've seen them all now!' and she rudely placed her thumb between her fingers and shouted out words of admiration (or was it scorn?) for the attributes of each lad. She was indeed a fortunate young missy to get herself off unscathed before the boys had a chance to lay their hands on her. For if they'd caught a hold of this unseemly madam, they'd have shown her they weren't a pack of soft gentry-folk in their dealings with the fairer sex. They'd have dragged her into the river and introduced her to such mysterious and earth-shaking games as she'd never played in all her life.

That wasn't the end of the matter. What a little heathen this pretty miss and her leering eyes turned out to be. She didn't go back through the pine trees empty-handed but took home

Restless Rody's shirt and trousers and left him without a stitch of clothes to put on.

Not long afterwards, some of Dowager's younger children were playing with their jackstones on the flagstones. One or two of them were trying to draw their mother's face with coloured pebbles from the river when they saw the strangest of sights coming up the road. It was their three big brothers from the river and half-a-dozen sympathetic men from the drinking-shop. They were marching along in a silent huddle. Unbeknownst to these little ones, and hidden away from their prying eyes, was the hapless shape of Restless Rody bringing nothing in the world home with him except his shivery nakedness.

The children stopped their play and scratched their heads. They wondered at such a strange spectacle – a group of men marching along like a bunch of soldiers at this unearthly hour of the day. They could see the group's suspicious eyes peering back into their midst from time to time to see if their prize was safe. What in God's name could these men be hiding? Was it an escaped calf? It could be. Had they brought back a dead crane? Maybe. Was it a deer that they'd just killed with the sickle? They were awfully anxious to get a little peep and find out the answer to this great mystery.

Finally, the men reached the stile outside Sam's grove and arrived at Dowager's flagstones where they came to a halt. There followed a cute little pause which seemed to last for an eternity. Suddenly (and with enough volume to awaken the dead below in the graveyard), the marchers let out a deafening roar and then (the rascals) they ran off over the singletree and in across Dowager's haggart!

Oh me, oh my, oh misery! There in the middle of the creamery road stood the misfortunate Restless Rody, terrified. The little children gasped for he was wearing nothing but his shy little birthday suit and holding onto his private regalia for dear life. The older girls burst out laughing and started dancing round him, poking him with twigs and trying to get a look under his crossed legs. What tales they'd have to tell their schoolmaster (Dang-the-skin-of-it) when asked for their daily news – the tale of a red-faced young man and his fists grasped firmly round his privacies!

3

Bless the bit! It would soon be 6 o'clock, and the dancers would be late if they didn't hurry on. Dowager frantically tried to shoo her girls towards the bikes at the hen house wall.

'Can't ye see how the sun's trembling rays (she was always known for her scholarly words) are already starting to depart from ye? She'll soon be hiding herself out over Galway and the sea.'

Within the hour, the mountain pathways would be filled with streams of young dancers pedalling – faster, faster (the girls) and running over ditches (the racing boys) – towards Judy's platform in the meadow. The gaiety of the music was like a ship's siren calling each of them. Judy, however, would not be able to hear a single note of the fine music for she was as deaf as a post and was 105 years old according to Dowager (who knew all there was to know).

And now she stood with her daughters at the half-door, fussing over their hair and admiring the dazzle of her would-be charmers. She turned proudly towards her boys, shaking her head unbelievably at the stamp of them. They were in their best Sunday jackets and the white shirts with the collars out over the jacket and their hair curved back in a wavy quiff with lashings of soapy water.

She thought how lucky were the girls that they'd hold in their arms this evening and, as though she were blessing the crops in the fields, she gave each of them a good shower of holy water and said, 'Be good and mind how ye go and always remember what I have taught ye – God is always watching!'

She stood on the flagstones and watched them as they set off. 'Look at them daughters of mine,' said she to herself, 'like a crowd of cackling hens, each of them on the look-out for a handsome young cockerel,' and she went back through the half-door, a wise old smile on her lips as she remembered her own girlhood days.

Her younger children came running into the yard and almost knocked her over as they hurried across the stream to give a last wave of goodbye to their big brothers and sisters. There was a mixture of smiles and sadness on their mystified faces. They would do their own share of praying this evening and ask God to hold off the rain in the hope that their sisters and brothers would have the merriest of times doing the heel-and-toe on Judy's wooden boards. In a year or two's time, when it was their own turn to reach a certain age of comeliness, they too would go seek the heart-rending music and do their own tidy dance-steps that'd knock the very strength out of the hills (or so they'd be telling you).

With hearts as light as thistledown, the big girls shot ever onwards, their leggy limbs cycling through the lush countryside. It was steep at the beginning up around Sheep's Cross. More and more dancers then met them at the forge beyond the crossroads where their parents had danced and caroused to the tunes of paper-and-comb and the shy Scissors sisters had played their polkas from inside the ditch.

The hilly lanes suddenly wound upwards, and the girls got off and pushed their bikes when they came to the white cross where Red Scissors' little son had been crushed to death by the mistress's unexpected car on his first day's outing to the schoolhouse.

Once past the Lookout, they got back on their bikes and raced on towards the music, their skirts flapping, and their heads hung low against the breeze coming down through the Lisnagorna Woods. From time to time, one of the bike's chains came off from the inner cranks and a girl's unholy curses would pollute the hills (*'mee friggin' chain – will ye look at it!'*).

The other girls ran to the ditch and brought back fists of sand to cover the chain and cranks and away they went again, the sand causing the chain to grip once more.

In the distant meadow, they heard the swell of the fiddles and button-melodions, and with hearts pounding in anticipation, they pedalled faster than ever. They couldn't wait to throw their pennies into the hat at the field gate.

The meadow was edged with blackened ditches heaped high with smoothed-away quarry-stones. With no coloured lanterns to glorify the dance-floor, the only illumination was the big yellow moon and the dreamy stars and the lofty silvery clouds dancing gaily across the sky.

And now they were there, and they raced out onto the platform, their hearts full of the music and the thumping hobnail boots of their partners, those strange mountainy men in the round-the-house-and-mind-the-dresser half-sets.

Whether the sky was bright or not didn't bother the more experienced girls. Indeed, the darker it got, the better for some of these romantic little dreamers, the music and excitement gradually making them a good bit bolder than their priest in his confession-box would have liked. And as the evening wore on, some of them would go a bit further than their mothers would wish and indulge themselves in the odd bit of shy and slobbery kissing in the darkened corners of Judy's field, whispering words of romance into some poor befuddled lad's ears.

4

This same sunny June, Dowager's older daughter (Nell) was spending her days working from dawn till dusk for Sally-switch, one of the big farmers. She had been doing so since the day she was 13, the time of her father's death, taking on the role of a little slave-girl, no less, and sending home the matchbox with a brown ten-shilling note in it, delivered each month by Red Buckles on his way home from the creamery.

This was her seventh year of hard labour and, at 20, she was heartily sick of it. Indeed, there were times when she felt as old as her mother.

Tonight would be her one and only chance for a moment of enjoyment in Judy's meadow, and she grabbed her dancing shoes with eager hands. She felt almost like a thief, knowing that never again would she be able to escape from her drudgery and the lustful clutches of her drunken taskmaster, not to mention the yard-brush with which his wife (La-Dee-Dah) belted her legs whenever she needed a bit of additional amusement. These two had gone away to sell their racehorses at the Newmarket sales across the sea and would not be back till the following evening.

Nell was to remember this night's dancing for as long as she lived. Before it ended, she'd find her heartstrings twisted into a big muddle at the sight of Patsy Noon and his galloping jig-steps.

In the big house where she worked, lived Tim – known as the silenced priest – no longer allowed to say Mass, the penalty for innocently mismanaging the diocesan funds. He shared Nell's gloomy existence in the rat-infested barn.

As soon as her two harsh taskmasters were on board the ship, he was planning to give Nell the loan of his rusty old bike and send her away to the dance. He knew her daily slavery would again start at dawn when she'd be pulping the turnips and mangles for the two angry sows. This evening's meadow-dance would give her a taste of glory – yes, just this once. Let her life of slavery drown itself in one of the many nearby bog-holes, said he.

Earlier that morning, she had run down behind the hen house where Tim was waiting with a broken bit of looking-glass. He fixed it at an angle on the hedgerow. He helped her unwrap the hot rags that she'd prepared in her hair the previous night, and he carefully twisted her locks into long ringlets. Nell put a little of La-Dee-Dah's powder on her cheeks and a little rouge to her lips. Her heart was all of a shiver as she shyly stepped out of her old calicos and belted on her best Mass frock.

Finally, as though he were Cinderella's very own fairy godfather, Tim helped her smooth out the folds of her lovely dress and made her do a few quick twists and twirls around the yard.

'Nell, my dearest Nell, you look fit to sit at the table alongside Queen Maeve of Ireland!'

Nell gazed at her face in the looking-glass and smiled. Maybe she'd meet a handsome young prince at Judy's dance this evening.

Free! Free! Like a little bird flown from its cage, she raced out from the imprisoning high gates, pedalling like fury across the hills towards the dance.

Half-an-hour later, she heard the music coming at her from behind Judy's cabin, and breathlessly, she jumped off from Tim's bike and threw it on the ditch. She scampered across the meadow towards the platform where the stamping of hobnail boots was already raking the floor as boys and girls embroiled themselves in the mysteries of the dance-steps.

For once in her life she stood there in a trance, gazing open-mouthed at the strange sight and the sound of hammering feet attacking the rickety timbers, at the skill and liveliness of the more experienced dancers, at the feathery fleetness of the younger men as they dashed towards the women and clasped them (*'coom into mee arums!')* to their chests for a final swing.

And then she found herself hurried out onto the platform with the rest of the dancers, and her younger sisters waved excitedly to her from the other side of the floor. They hadn't seen her in ages and were more than excited at the lovely appearance of her.

Soon she was getting a reel in her head from all the spinning and the skirt-cutting swings of the men. One or two mountainy lads swung their young ladies clean off their feet and out over their heads (round and round and round) before dropping them down again, soft and gentlemanly on their tippy-toes. With the laughter and sighs of the women, you'd think a hen was about to lay an egg.

'Why, Badger, aren't ye the wild hooligan!' roared Nancy Slim to her partner, laughing the eyes out of her head.

'Look at Maisy-from-Knockahopple,' said a voice behind Nell, 'her cheeks are as red as a lobster from battering out her grandmother's jig-steps.'

'Look at Danny-be-Quick from Sheep's Cross,' said another. 'So many nails in his boots that the sparks are flying out from under him. A wonder he hasn't set the bench of hay aflame beneath the musicians.'

Nell couldn't stop laughing at the sight of Fatty-Matty whaling into the polka. He was undoubtedly as long in the tooth as her brother (My-Son-Jack) and old enough to be the father of the young school-leavers enjoying their first outing to a dance. His resounding toecaps had splintered the floor in several places, and he suddenly made a hole in the corner where his boot got stuck, imprisoning him there for the rest of the evening (thought Nell), and once more she took a hearty fit of laughing. She hadn't felt as happy as this in donkey's years, and her sisters ran over and surrounded her with hugs and greetings.

Under the oak tree sat the musicians on their bench of hay, flittering their jigs and polkas into the night sky. In the middle of them sat Fiddler-Joe, his bow flying about like an ass's tail. His son was newly learning his fiddle-trade and, with an occasional smack on the head from his father's speedy bow, he kept to his work like a merry young Trojan. Meanwhile, Fiddler-Joe turned his eyes up to the stars as if seeking help from the Almighty. The smile never left his face, and the horsehair kept flying in shreds from his bow. The Sandy brothers (Tom and Tim) had come over from Tracy's Sandpit, themselves and their wimpled squeeze-boxes while one or two girls, barely out of their cradle, were rattling out the rhythm on their knees with their blue quarry slates and spoons.

'Give us the whole of yeer hearts, byze,' the crowd roared, encouraging the musicians to ever greater bouts of gusto. You'd think the players had ten arms on them.

The dancers now took to the floor for the five-part set, and Donie Baloney attacked the floor in great style as he made an advance on Katie Spanners. He had shovels for feet, and though he had all the steps inside in his head, he couldn't get them down into his toes. Before the half-set was over, he gave the floor such a welting that he fractured three of poor Katie's toes.

Then came the ladies' chain, and the girls' frocks swished sinuously, their beefy arms entwining with the men. And once again, the hills were ablaze from the pace and pitch of the music's cadences and the thrashing of the boots and the yelling of the men as the old-fashioned steps were replaced by bits of inventive extemporisation.

Donie came bouncing over the floor on his knees in a desperate effort to impress the broken-toed Katie. The entranced onlookers (*'cripes, byze – will ye look at Donie!'*) sat bedazzled on the ditch, huddled close to one another as they prepared to make their own leap out onto the floor.

'House, byze,' roared Red Scissors, 'if it's mee coat ye want, ye can have it.' And the floor lit up with the glow of his ugly broken teeth.

The women were every bit as lively as the men, and their faces began to glow like roses. They were as light as feathers one minute, leaping here and there. The next minute, they were high-stepping like a troop of plough-horses.

However, such pace could not last long, for who could keep up such unleashed abandonment? They'd be dead before midnight, and there'd be more than a few corpses carried off to the graveyard before next morning's light.

5

It was time for the slow waltz, time for a lad to catch his lady around her trim waist and bring her in close to his heartstrings, time to put a stop to the steam rising up from the dance-floor. And as the pink of the evening drew into the purple of night, and before they completely lost sight of one another, the dancers became a little more studious and a little more cautious. It'd remind one of a horse fair as the men began to inspect the women, and the women began to inspect the men.

Nell's sisters (with a nudge and a wink) could see that Patsy Noon's heartstrings were fit to burst from the force of the arrows Nell fired into him, and Nell herself (poor dear) was as earnest in her own desires for Patsy. The young fellow was wearing his best brown brogues and was dressed in his new sports jacket. He was standing by his bike and staring across the floor at her. His bike was the richest dazzler-of-a-bike she'd ever laid eyes on.

There was something about this lad, but she couldn't place it – not yet. There were handsomer boys, for Patsy's nose was a little too hooked and his ears a little too pointed. But nobody performed the dance-steps with such style and grace as this lad from the Quarries –the tidy movements of his nimble legs, the sudden wild dashes he made in the latest quickstep – and he was to win her heart completely.

Five years previously, his tear-filled mother had sent him to work for Old Gasper, an avaricious landowner in the Limerick Glens.

'Fetch me the coppers from under the gate pier,' he'd say, 'and go to the shop and bring back the Financial Times till

I see how mee money is growing.' Then he'd hand Patsy a few coppers from the heap that he'd stored under the pier.

Like Nell, Patsy at 13 had worked as a pure slave from break-of-day till the dead of night. But from the start, his heart ached to be back home with his mother, she being a sick woman with a damaged heart and his father dead and buried from a fall in the river. At night he cried himself to sleep abroad in the turf-shed where no-one could see him, so soft and gentle was his nature.

A few years later, he could bear it no longer. Slave-driver though he was, Old Gasper had a soft side to his heart as he listened to Patsy's nightly tears and realized how much the lad ached to go home and see his grieving mother. He strode into Slattery-John's shop in town where he bought Patsy a dazzling bike to ride home for the weekend and spend time with his mother. The lad would be able to walk with her to the well and carry back the two heavy buckets of water for her.

As soon as Patsy got up on the saddle of this mercurial machine, he rode like the wind and never looked back till he reached his mother's door. And another thing – he never again returned to Old Gasper with his precious bike, and who could have blamed him? His hours of slavery had well earned him the price of it.

His saintly mother, however, refused to allow his soul (she said) to fry in Hell hereafter. Though it would make a big hole in her late husband's savings, she would pay back every penny for the wretched bike. Enough said.

And now this shy young fellow was piercing with his eyes the blueberry eyes of Nell, admiring her soft lips with the natural redness of sweet cherries on them. And Nell's eyes were piercing into Patsy's. It'd take a horse-and-cart to separate these two young lovebirds.

Once again, custom was seen to take over. For whenever such blossoming romances were spotted, the other girls (never the boys) would steal craftily to the side of the meadow where the bikes were thrown in a heap against the ditch. Out of this muddle of bikes (oh, the little hussies!), Nell's sisters picked out Patsy's beautiful bike and the rusty old bike that Tim had lent her. They untangled the two bikes from the heap and laid them next to each other. Rascally cunning then got to work and to weave its deadly charm. With ream after ream of the nearby fence-wire, they tied the two bikes together, making triple twists in it (good and firm), so that when the dancing reached its sad and inevitable end, it would be well-nigh-impossible for the two innocents to untangle the mess of their bikes. The little devils congratulated each other on having introduced in this way their sister and Patsy to an indescribable degree of intimacy, for these two fluttery hearts would have to spend an age in each other's company in an attempt to free their bikes.

They could picture how the young lovebirds would curse them into Hell for the cruel mischief done to their bikes. They could picture something else too – how their gentle fingers would interlace in their frustrated efforts to untangle the wire. And where would they themselves be lurking while all this was going on? Behind the bushes (the rascals) and holding back their laughter – peeping out at the young lovers breathing into one another's ears, their lips so closely (oh, so very closely) alongside each other. Weren't Nell's sisters the craftiest little rascals ever born?

6

Whilst this match-making sorcery was going on, there was yet another bit of trouble in store. It was for the bike of the Hearty sisters from Growl River. It was always a major job for girls to guard their bike, a bike being the most valuable of objects on earth. One of them had to give the dance-floor a miss now and then and be on the look-out for some mischievous group of boys who'd like nothing better than take turns riding their precious piece of machinery round the lanes and rattling it off of the ditches in an effort to balance on top of it.

And now, such being the rascality of a few earnest lads with no bike of their own (and who had walked the long distance across the hills to get to the dance), the three Hearty girls found themselves tricked into being out on the dance-floor at one and the same time.

In the blink of an eye, three impudent mountainy boys saw their chance, snatched up the bike and had the finest of times riding it around behind Judy's cabin.

The war and the ruction soon broke out. 'Nonie! Nonie! Coom quick! The up-country friggers (*may the devil shit on them!*) are riding our bike round Judy's yard!' They left their dance-partners sitting on their arses in the middle of the floor and raced up Judy's lane where they threw aside their ladylike manners and lay into the miscreants with flying fists. It'd do you good to hear the roars of the other dancers' laughter as they listened to the inventive litany of swearwords and saw the brave boys toppled from their perch on the bike and sent sprawling among the briars.

But before the night was over, these same outraged young ladies and the three roguish mountainy lads would be seen walking arm-in-arm towards the dark corners of the ditch where an odd bout of shy kissing and innocent lovemaking would begin to torment the crows in their nests.

7

You couldn't keep a good man down, and you couldn't keep Father Honesty away from visiting the dancers as they started to leave the meadow. He prided himself on being the guardian of his flock's immortal souls, and now he drove his motorcar to the edge of Judy's meadow where he cut off the headlights and the engine. Armed with his powerful flash lamp (as well as a few mouthfuls of whiskey to warm his heart), this holy huntsman clambered across the ditches, his eyes forever on the look-out for young sinners, and his ears cocked back like an ass listening for the sound of a shy girl's giggles. Ah, cruel lamp man and your prying eyes, what did you hope to find? Would you come across a brazen girl, smoking her father's stolen fags, the cheeky miss? Might there be a bit more, ahem, for your old eyes to see? Perhaps you'd get a glimpse of a young girl's garters or the shock of her bare thighs? Might you and your unseemly flash lamp (God-in-heaven forbid!) spy out a pair of youngsters thrashing the wheat-field of love itself?

The holy man with his personal renunciation of the marriage-bed and his sacrifice of masculinity for the sake of the holy cloth was at Judy's meadow every week seeking out the Devil that he knew from his confession-box lay inside in the bodies of everyone. From the Sunday altar-rails, this sanctimonious squire held up his trusty catechism and denounced the sinfulness of Judy's platform dance and the lusts of the flesh that arose from it.

Alas, though he and his fantasies bemoaned the simple enjoyment of the goodnight kiss, his presence at the end of the weekly dance didn't do him one bit of good. He and his flash lamp nonsense could go drown themselves in Growl River (said the dancers). The poor fellow succeeded only in driving some hot-blooded boys and girls further in over the ditches where they'd continue their intimacy in more remote trysting-places round the neighbouring woods and rivers. Nor was it unknown for one or two mischievous young lovers (had they no shame in them?) to let the priest and his aching soul see what the eyes of no priest should ever have been let look at. And on this happiest of nights, his quest bore no fruit for, on the edge of Judy's callow field, one or two young couples had already strayed to their chosen love-nest to while away a few precious moments smoking their hidden fags and hiding the glow of them in case of the priest's lamp. In the darkness of the field, their hearts were at play, and their eyes had a hunger in them, and their arms entwined in comfort around each other. Their simple few kisses were such that no flash lamp could ever destroy. Their furtive giggles of laughter touched only the nearby croaking frogs while the creamy moon nodded down its face approvingly on their innocence. A few timid kisses (they knew) would never set fire to their souls or land them in the bowels of Hell.

8

There was darkness now around Judy's meadow. It had won its fight with the sparkling stars and the platform dance was over. As bats and owls slipped into the night, so did the dancers scatter themselves across the hills – the boys striding away through the woods of Lisnagorna and the girls cycling back to their yard-streams, frightening the midnight fairies with their downhill speed. They had squeezed the last drop of merriment out of Judy's platform dance, leaving behind them the love-inspired Patsy and his charmer, Nell, with their two knotted bikes and their budding romance. A few little sighs seeped out of their tender young eyes and an almost-sickly feeling of departure flew back into them. They and their whispers (little words of promised love pounding inside in their heads) had to go their different ways – she upon Tim's rusty old heap and he on Old Gasper's razzle-dazzler. Their hearts beat fast, and their pedals spun even faster as they rushed like two small birds to their separate roosts. Patsy headed into the arms of his worried mother who had stayed up waiting for him. She could tell by the glow in his eyes that all was not right with him, and she wondered. Nell continued towards the gloomy gates that would imprison her for another year's drudgery – maybe more.

Patsy would now be her inspiration, and Tim had already drawn up plans for her flight out of Tipperary. She would take her master's best cow to the autumn fair to sell. With the silver coins that Tim had saved for her, she would take a few more silver coins from her master's tobacco-jar. These the old miser surely owed her and would never miss.

However, as she now whisked her rusty bike nearer his gates, she felt nothing but loneliness coming down on her shoulders. She must put aside the wondrous stars and the smiling moon, must put aside the silver clouds and the merry voices of the night-time ghosts that followed alongside her in the roadside bushes. Her world of beauty had stopped with the clock, replaced with her fears for the laborious days ahead. After a few hours of fretful sleep, she would take her sore limbs out to the two angry sows that were waiting to be fed.

And yet (just this once) the platform dance had been a beautiful night for her and worth all the endeavours of herself and Tim. It had been a wondrous night too for her sisters and brothers, their world ablaze with the fires of their laughter. They had jumped out from their home fireside and frightened life itself. Their years of youth would flit away, and one far-off day, they'd have the aches and pains from years of rainy fields and would find themselves hugging the potato-sack close around their backs to keep the warmth inside in them.

Perhaps, as they pedalled their bikes through the hilly breezes, one or two old women in the nearby cabins would turn in their sleep and cock an ear, listening to the tinkling of the young girls' bike-bells. Perhaps they'd hear the laughter and the singing floating on past their windowsills. Perhaps they'd recall the days long ago when they too had pedalled off to a platform dance in Judy's meadow.

'Oh-honey-oh!' they'd sigh. 'Wasn't life grand in them days?'

For the next seven days, the boys and girls would continue to pray that the weather would hold tough, that the moon and stars would not let them down so that once again they could get another bit of heavenly happiness in Judy Rag's meadow.

May the ash-trees come marching down from Chieftain Hill before they ever forget such wondrous nights as this. Blessed be the dance! Blessed be the music! Blessed be the poetry of big boots and swirling skirts and shiny-eyed happiness and the love-light shining back and forth in the youthful eyes of Nell and Patsy Noon.

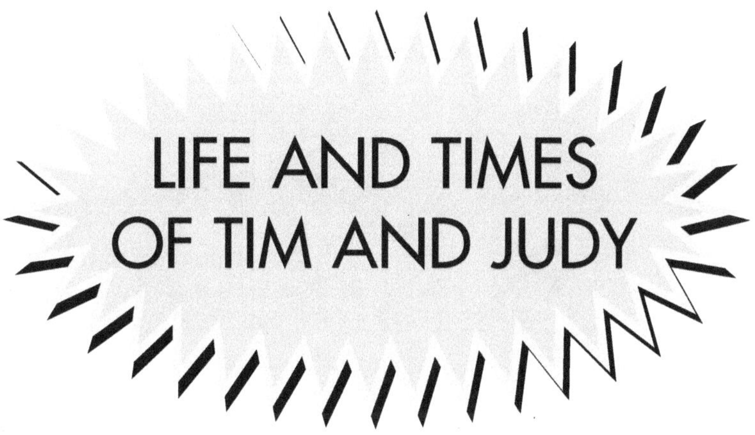
LIFE AND TIMES
OF TIM AND JUDY

1

There were days when Mister Boredom would raise his ugly head, and Moll-the-Man's children, without a backward look and with the hills beckoning them, would cross the stream on tiptoe in case they were called back to do some hefty jobs like bringing back the water from the well, driving back the cows to the rishy field, filling the chest with armfuls of logs, making sure the gate was closed behind their patient ass (Short-Arse) or cleaning out his stable for him.

On those days, the wanderlust of the goat was on them, the invisible spirits awakening in them a new set of adventures, and they scurried up the slope, their eyes all the time searching for the hills ahead in the hope they might reach mighty Chieftain Hill or the place called Fairyland.

There was more to it than this. The most remote river they'd ever heard tell of was the River Sticks, and they'd been told nobody lived further out than this since it was the end of the world. Of course, this was a damned lie. It was the Crown River and lay back behind Bog Boundless, heading on to the Shannon River and Limerick. It was 3 miles away and deep inside the Wilderness.

There were a few old men and women still living their simple lives out there, and some folk would laugh and scoff when they thought of the harsh life in that godforsaken place.

'The last outpost on earth ye'd want to set eyes on,' they'd smirk.

If you were lively on your feet, it'd take more than an hour to walk there – that's if you knew the way between the dangerous bog-holes at the foot of the hills.

This stupendous bit of deception (about the River Sticks being the end of the world) had been spread amongst children from time immemorial and even embellished with a few bits of extra-scary bits – that it was quite close to Heaven and even closer to the fires of Hell. Of course, the adults were always bent on scaring their children, who might be thinking of adventuring too far away from the farmyard and getting themselves drowned in the infamous bog-holes or taken away (said Moll-the-Man) to the Beyond by *the wilderness fairies*.

When Lippy and the rest of the children heard their mother trotting out this same old tale time and time again, they grew sick of listening to her. The idea was now fixed firmly in their minds to go off one fine day and find out where this mysterious River Sticks was. They were not going to be put off a minute longer and if anyone stopped them on their journey, they'd argue their case. Why shouldn't they have a bit of courage like Christopher Columbus in their school-book? Why shouldn't they make their mark on the unknown world? It'd be the greatest challenge yet for their young legs – how they reached the River Sticks – something to tell their own children when their crippled limbs were running out on them later on.

2

So, one Saturday morning they set off to find this great river. They also wanted to see Tim and Judy, the little old man and the little old woman who were known to live so very far away from the rest of mankind. In recent days, Lippy, Philly and Young Jim had got used to helping By-Jiggery save the turf and knew the journey that lay ahead of them and where most of the bog-holes were hidden. Their bare feet would have to travel the rockier tracks to the left of the Eagles' Nest before making an even more-complicated way through the other side to reach the Wilderness.

It was 10 o'clock when the three of them set off (Zeppity and Battlin' Sal were far too young for this adventure).

They had a few warm spuds and hard-boiled eggs in their pockets. They'd have a lot on their minds throughout the journey, trying to avoid attacks from wild unlicensed bulls and any other fiendish monster that might be part and parcel of their mother's roguish storytelling.

On the way, they wasted a good deal of time arguing with each other so that it took half the blessed day to get anywhere near their planned destination. Even then, it was thanks only to their good fortune of meeting a young shepherd boy and his guiding eyes that they at last reached the final lap, which was going to lead them to this wondrous river, the Sticks.

That's when anger and frustration completely took hold of them. For they realized that the river they had set out to find was not the River Sticks at all. Indeed, the laughing shepherd boy had never heard of such a marvellous river, and he must have thought them a pack of eejits. It now dawned on them that Moll-the-Man and By-Jiggery had been making fools of them all along, and it would do a man's ears good to hear the beauty of their curses and the savagery of their oaths – enough to frighten any wild bulls or other monsters brave enough to be venturing anywhere close by. If their prayers were to be heard, neither of their parents would live another day, for they'd be rotting in Hell's fire. To think that the three of them had come all this bleddy way for absolutely nothing and that the River Sticks was nothing but a figment of adults' imaginations handed down from father to son all these years.

And another thing – throughout their long journey, they had been looking left and right with fearful eyes to see if they could spot the two huge eagles in the Eagles' Nest but had seen neither tail nor wing of them. This had been another one of Moll-the-Man's damned lies, the one about these eagles being bigger than a horse-and-cart – eagles that might sweep down and snatch away any would-be little adventurers and carry them off to their nest as a tasty morsel for their growing chicks.

They sat on the ditch and considered their situation. Yes, (they decided) they would have to fight their corner as soon as they got home. And then they began to smile. What amazing lies they would tell the other children: how they had travelled to the edge of the world and how they had seen the mighty River Sticks itself. Yes, if their parents could lie like the ringing devil, it'd now be their own turn to prove themselves better still at this crafty sport of drumming up wild stories, embellishing them with news about huge bog-holes that they'd met on the way and how they had to pull one another out of the deepest pools imaginable and how poor Philly nearly got himself drowned. Yes, they'd cause their parents to faint on the spot when they learnt that a few of their precious offspring had narrowly escaped death out here in the Wilderness.

And then they had another little thought: if they played their cards right, they'd have the sympathy of the entire creamery road and wouldn't have to do a hand's tap of work for the next month-and-a-half (the rascals).

3

As they headed onwards, they were heartened to see tendrils of smoke spiralling out from two small chimneys which told them there was some sort of life out here. A moment later, they could see the river itself, and they were glad. Though it was not the River Sticks, it was by far the widest and fiercest river they'd ever seen. It was the Crown River, and they had reached the little hamlet of Currywhibble, home of the poor flour people, whose flour had always been too poor to sell to anybody else.

They headed on towards the chimney smoke, and finally realised where they were. For on those days when they were drinking tea abroad in the bog, they had often heard tales about the old-timers who lived out here – about Tim Passion and his love for saying prayers, and about his sister, Judy (otherwise known as the Little Red Woman), whose face was well-reddened from the sun and the wind.

Their little cabin was the size of a hen house, and they were as poor as church mice. They had never been a day in school or even seen one. They couldn't read and write their own names.

A great deal of merry scoffing would accompany these stories, for it was always a source of merriment to have someone else to look down on. And on days when the children found themselves sitting on the fallen log in the orchard and sending smoke to the heavens from their grandmother's stolen fag-butts, Lippy was the devil's own at imitating adults and their stories.

'Byze, will ye listen to this,' he'd say. 'Tim Passion and the Little Red Woman are out of bed early this morning. They're taking turns with the hammer and trying to squash a few fleas and paste them to the bedpost.'

With this little tale from Lippy, the orchard would echo with the loud laughter of the other children. Meanwhile, their guardian angels shook their heads and frowned sadly. It wasn't good enough: the little scallywags were on the downward path from their earlier innocence. Instead, there had grown inside them a new feeling of spite.

How unlike these little reprobates were the old man and his sister! Never in their life had they wished another soul malice. Nor would they know how to. Sometimes, their days were bleak when it came to putting food on the table and yet they never once complained. Instead, they greeted the daylight with the fervour of two small birds, as though it were their last day on earth. They finished it on their bended knees, giving an hour or two pouring out their hearts' gratitude to God, asking Him to stop men killing each other on the battlefield, praying that things would get back to what they were like before – especially in those faraway places where many of Tipperary's sons and daughters were earning their bread and were (they felt) in mortal danger of receiving a wartime bullet in the chest or, worse still, a bomb dropped down on top of their heads.

4

Currywhibble was a dreamy-looking place. It had two little cabins, Tim and Judy's and the one belonging to Fat Noolah and her husband, Sad Sam – the sort that a fairy-godmother would love to live in had she small enough wings to get in through the doorway. The two yards were crowded with honeysuckle and hollyhocks and a dozen other wildflowers. It was an absolute heaven.

Heaven, did I say? The children didn't know the meaning of the word. But a week later they'd have learnt a valuable lesson – one greater than all the lessons from their schoolbooks – that Tim and Judy had already placed one of their feet inside the gates of Heaven.

They were the last of the High-and-Dry folk with just a bit of a garden outside the door and a haggart at the side for their vegetables and a few acres of land thrown up against the side of the hill.

The huge departure of folks after the famine was the reason (it was said) why Currywhibble had been left high and dry. And because Tim and his sister were far too old to find themselves partners and produce children, Currywhibble was indeed left high and dry without a child to prolong their race.

Of course, the holy pair didn't just drop down from the sky. Their parents were Hushaby and Holy Devotions, who were already old when people like Dowager were still small children and running around the yard chasing after the chickens, the time that the sad little lady (Victoria, the English queen) was still wiping the tears from her eyes after the untimely death of her beloved husband.

Hushaby spent a great deal of his time trying to get Holy Devotions to put away her worry beads and settle down with him for a night's fumbling under the blankets. But she was determined to rattle off a few more prayers to the Almighty before retiring for the night.

The old man had good reason to push his wife to the doors of the bedroom. In the first 20 years of their married life, they had made one or two feeble attempts at producing a child. It had all been in vain, but they didn't lose heart, having seen the difficulties that their billy-goat and jack-donkey sometimes had in their own awkward attempts to inject their seed where it was needed.

With the wintertime of age creeping into his bones, there came a quickening of the clock in Hushaby's joints, and he continued more than ever trying to get his wife to turn her attention to the centre of the bed and the business of producing at least one little child before they died – or else they'd have to hide away from the rest of the world in absolute disgrace.

Miracles can happen – even in Currywhibble. Though Holy Devotions was nearer to 50 than 40, she nevertheless gave birth to not one but to two children (a son and a daughter), whom she named Tim and Judy.

Her babies (said Hushaby) were a thank-you gift from God for all the holy devotions his wife had offered to Heaven since her earliest days on earth. It reminded him of the gift of a child once given to the aged Sarah in the Good Book. Indeed (said Hushaby) his wife had beaten the saintly Sarah clean out of the field, having been given the double gift of a daughter as well as a son, and she could stand alongside any woman in Tipperary (he said). Fair play to you, Holy Devotions!

Hushaby became a changed man after this double-birth. Whereas previously he pulled his peaked-cap down over his face as though he didn't want to be seen by anybody (the shame at having no child), now he turned himself into a real little turkeycock. He even forgot to say his prayers for a week or two.

On the days when he came down the hill to sell a few cattle, he'd tell everyone that he still had a rustle of blood in his papery old arteries for fathering one or two children. The rest of the farmers smiled and laughed. They slapped him on the back (*'more power to yeer elbow, Hushaby,'*) and followed this up with one or two lewd remarks that were unfit for a priest's ears.

Meanwhile, back in the cabin, Holy Devotions would sigh and smile at her two precious babies in the cradle. 'Isn't God good to us? Isn't God good to us!?' she'd say.

5

But God hadn't blessed with a similar piety the neighbours in the yard below them. This miserable pair were two ringing devils by the name of Worry Beads and the Little Loser. Throughout her lifetime, Worry Beads, when she was expecting a visitor, made sure she was seen on her knees and saying her prayers – out in the yard in broad daylight – clacking away at it with a forcefulness that alarmed not only her few visitors but even the busiest of her hens. However, it was in name only and without a grain of sincerity that she said her prayers. The worry beads might be in her hands, but never (so to speak) in her soul. Even her priest (Father Honesty) was heard to say this was a solid fact.

What artful skills, Worry Beads had taught herself over the years. On days when Holy Devotions went down to Saddleback village for a sack of flour (a sack small enough for her to carry home on her shoulder), this old wretch would lie in wait for her behind a bush. She was the very same as a sly old fox that lurks behind a tree and waits for an unsuspecting chicken to turn up. In her hands were a bucket and a sharp carving-knife.

Holy Devotions would be steeped in her daily communion with the Lord as she trudged her way back towards her yard.

Worry Beads crept up behind her and with her carving-knife cut a small hole in the saintly woman's sack – a hole just big enough to let the flour dribble down into her bucket. Oh, the villainy of this woman!

When Holy Devotions reached her yard, she put her hands to her ears and gave a cry that was nothing short of terror. It must have frightened the waters in Crown River itself.

'Oh, heavenly Jesus, where did all mee flour disappear to? How could this have happened? There must've been a hole in mee sack!' No words can describe the cackling and gloating of Worry Beads after tricking the simple soul out of her flour.

That wasn't enough wickedness to keep herself and the Little Loser quiet. A few days later, Hushaby was sauntering home from the bog with a fine load of turf in his cart. He had saved it with a good deal of sweat and was as happy as a king when along the track to meet him came the Little Loser. Lurking behind and hiding herself under the axle of Hushaby's cart (had she nothing better to do other than falling into the clutches of the Devil?) was that same old sly-boots, Worry Beads.

The Little Loser met Hushaby at the bend of the lane where they spent a pleasant while (as farmers often did) talking about the weather and the crops. Meanwhile, Worry Beads began removing the hasping-pins from the back of the cart and letting down the tailgate. Then she gave the Little Loser the wink. Hushaby, seeing that his neighbour was about to leave him, gave him a merry salute with his ash-plant and went sailing innocently homewards.

Bit by bit, his turf fell softly onto the grassy track where the two villains (God was surely watching them from on high) scooped them up into their sacks.

When Hushaby entered his yard, he found he'd lost almost half of his turf. 'Sweet-God-in-Heaven, where did all the turf we've been saving vanish to? The tailgate must have fallen open on me. How the devil could it have opened by itself?' And once again the yard rang out with the heart-rending cries of the two innocents, turning the place into a right merry orchestra. The hens, ducks, and geese, not knowing what to make of the rackety din, made a speedy retreat in under the hawthorn trees behind the cowshed.

Poor Hushaby and Holy Devotions! – to be treated so cruelly by the crudity of these wretched know-nothings! But after a miserable series of similar misfortunes, they weren't long left in this world for before many years went by (happily, it might be thought), the two old saints went off to meet their Maker in the Beyond. Enough said.

6

Back to the present and the visiting children. The sun was still shining like crystal when Lippy and his brothers found themselves at the edge of Tim and Judy's yard and the wispy curls of smoke belching up out of the chimney. They were sure they'd get a mug of tea and a hot bun or two. That's what Lippy said. They could hear a cow bawling, her udder swollen with milk and eager to come in to be milked. When the milking was over, it'd be time for the old pair to start twisting their worry beads and praying their evening prayers like other folk did below on the slopes.

In faraway France, three small children had said they'd seen the Virgin Mary. They described the sedate look on her face and how she wanted everyone to say a new prayer (the rosary) for the good of the world.

Since that day, the saying of the rosary had begun to influence the lives of every household, inspired by the holy pope, who had sent a message from Rome as far as our own Bishop High-Hat. The bishop had passed this message along to the priests (like our own Father Honesty) – but in a shortened and more modest version.

We were all in a fluster over the pope's message, and we went to church as excited as hell to hear what Father Honesty had to say. We were in for a shock, however, for the kind-hearted priest, having got the gist of things from the bishop, suddenly addressed us in an unusually savage manner and not with his usual words of Sunday politeness.

We saw him stepping out of his pulpit and dancing round on the altar. It was a strange sight to see him gesticulating his arms in a way that would better suit a judge or a solicitor. We wondered had the good-natured man completely lost his senses, had he indeed turned himself into a bit of a missioner?

The only thing (said he) that would save us from Hell and damnation was the power of saying all five decades of the rosary to the Virgin Mary every night. This was meat and drink to our women, and they nodded their heads in fierce agreement. As always, they liked nothing better than to receive a good whipping from a holy man's tongue.

Recent times (said Father Honesty) had been devilish all over the world – what with the war going on like blazes across the map and threatening to *obliviate* humanity (his own estranged word, so angry was he). Closer at home (said he) matters were no better than elsewhere. There was, now more than ever (hadn't the holy pope said so? – hadn't Bishop High-Hat said so?), a need to drive away the wicked spirits that were forever lurking in the hills and valleys? Things would have to change, and wickedness would have to stop. On and on he went. Indeed, it was felt that he was worse than a missioner.

However, he wasn't talking about those hellish spirits who wandered through the world for the ruin of souls. Everybody's knees were already worn raw from praying at the end of Mass against those wicked devils from Hell, and all the prayers (said Rambling Jack) must have beaten the shite out of the Devil by now. Nor was the holy priest asking his congregation to pray for those souls living in Limbo or in Purgatory or waiting to get in the queue for Heaven. Nor was he talking about the poor misfortunate souls that might find themselves standing outside the very gates of Hell.

The men, kneeling on their caps at the back of the church, began to get awfully fidgety as they tried to take it all in. What the devil were Father Honesty and Bishop High-Hat talking about, what were the two of them up to, what were they asking everyone to pray for?

And then it dawned on them. They were asking all the people to pray against a far more wicked spirit than a few of the Devil's miserable legions, asking them to pray against the spirit that was the ruin of many homes and families – namely, the Cursed Drink!

The men, you can be sure, were awfully fond of drinking stout. Father Honesty said it was the *rumination* (his own mixed-up words again as he tried to control his temper) of the entire world. He'd have his parishioners know that it wasn't doing too bad a job here amongst his own flock. The stout and the whiskey from Curl 'n' Stripes' drinking-shop, and that other deadly menace, the potheen that some of the men were making at home, were turning the place upside-down.

By now, he had worked himself into a fine old sweat, pointing out how the drink was driving out and killing every bit of good nature in an otherwise fine bunch of men. And as he spoke, one or two of the sad-faced children began to hang their heads in shame, for they knew that what he said was nothing but the truth – that their fathers could drink the River Shannon bone-dry, that any damned drink would do the likes of them since the thirst was always in their gizzard – to be quenched only when they could get their hands on enough of the powerful stuff.

But their fathers, shy fellows though they were, would have none of the priest's hot-headed talk. At the back of the church, they could be seen shrugging their shoulders and whispering irreligiously to one another behind their cuffs.

'Why wouldn't we be drinking the black stuff?' said one.

'The taste of it is sweeter than buttermilk,' said another.

'The singing and the laughter which it brings with it is a match for the heavenly angels and archangels,' said a third fellow. They were getting almost poetic about it.

Of course, the women knew only too well the way matters stood with some of their men. They'd have one little drink at this shop and another little drink at that shop and just another final one coaxed out of the glass – to smooth the road home. And from their feasts of drink, these men (it was just a few of them, mind you) would become as brazen as hell. As soon as they trudged their tired boots back from the drinking-shops, and as soon as they opened the latch on their door, they were already mumbling bitterly about the gloomy clouds hanging over their lives.

Their wives had no interest in joining them (a thing unheard of) at the drinking-shop door. If these same women were to put on the headscarf and make their appearance at the counter, their men would have been as embarrassed as hell, and their neighbours would be laughing for the rest of the week, thinking that the end of the world had come. And another thing – and this was the most important thing in their eyes – they knew that the women had no interest in rattling the springs of the marriage-bed in midnight frolics with them. Shy though they themselves had always been in that awkward area of their lives, the women had never been anxious (indeed, it might well have been a mortal sin) to throw their clothes to the four corners of the room and make a run at their husband's trouser-buttons. Wasn't it far better (said the men defensively) to forget about these womanly scholars? After all, hadn't their women bamboozled them good and properly when they married them for the sake of the land and its security – and not for themselves and the stuff they were made of? And then these whiskery old lads (now that their stomachs were well-oiled with The Drink) would tap the side of their nose as if to say they knew this for a fact, and it was far better to be filling their bellies with five or six good pints of stout instead of molesting the women in the bedroom. And they banged their fists gaily on Curl 'n' Stripes' counter and called the good man for another pint of the heavenly stuff.

It was only when they were half-drunk or, better still, dead-drunk that a few of these rascals gave a thought to the needs of the bedroom. At this hour of the night, their wives saw the results of the drink. When her man (shy, quiet and hard-working for most of the week) came into the welcoming room, he would become strangely impolite. His bleary eyes brought not a shred of welcome home with him. His wife could see what was to follow when the impudent wretch forgot to take off his cap and hang it on the nail by the holy water font. Instead, he took it into his head to start whaling into the poor woman. Where were the frightened children on these miserable occasions? Deep under the blankets, the flaps of their ears closed (it's hoped). If the turf-fire wasn't looking lively, if the kettle wasn't bubbling for a tasty mug of tea, if there wasn't enough grease in the burner for a healthy mug of soup – the returning hero gave his wife a comely slap on the arse.

This sent the poor dame scurrying towards the bedroom door like a scalded cat. Not wishing to vex her man still further, she managed to calm him down by offering him (*'the useless little fecker,'* she thought) the pleasures of her body. As though a sledge had hit him in the forehead, his wife's beckoning eyes stopped him dead in his tracks and almost made him cold-sober again. And then, realizing what was in her mind, he threw his shirt and trousers to the four winds and pelted her down on the bed. And as she blessed herself and whimpered to God to forgive her, in less time than a cockerel's wink, he engendered yet another soul into Tipperary's hierarchy, the sound man that he was.

7

After the pope's intervention, the saying of the rosary began to take great shape in every house. Back in Currywhibble, however, its delivery in the shape of Tim and Judy was never going to be a match for the more sophisticated praying of the rosary below on the slopes. The two simple souls couldn't be expected to hold inside their heads all the difficult words forming the core of the three traditional prayers – the Hail Mary, the Our Father and the Glory-be-to-the Father. They were at a loss how to comply with their priest's strict orders. You should have seen their sad faces.

That's when Father Honesty decided to come out and give them a helping hand. He'd be getting the usual basket of eggs for his trouble. He was an unusual sight out so far, even though he had travelled once or twice as far as Joe Solitary's door when poor Joe caught a dose of pneumonia.

Realising that the priest's little car would never make its way to the door of Tim and Judy, Joe now came in handy and gave his visitor the best of his mares to ride on out through the Wilderness.

When he reached Tim and Judy's cabin, the holy man startled them with these words, 'What matter if neither of ye have learnt the words of these complicated prayers? What matter if ye can't recall the 15 biblical tales of the Glorious, Joyful and Sorrowful Mysteries of the rosary? Listen to me, will ye? God will reward ye in Heaven the same way he'll reward the rest of us if ye pray with yeer heart and soul rather than with a lot of long-winded words slipping off of yeer tongue.' Then he hopped up on Joe's mare, careful not to damage a single one of the eggs that Judy had given him, and he was out of sight before the two of them could offer him a cup of tea.

Following the visit of Father Honesty, Tim and Judy took to saying their own brand of the rosary in earnest and spent an hour each evening wearing their knees off at the side of the fire. Next morning, after milking their cow, they went rasping at it again.

Not knowing how to pray the long-winded words, they prayed instead with their own uncomplicated ones, feeling assured of support from their priest after he had blessed them with holy water. It was enough to put a smile on the Virgin Mary's face, and the angels too must have gazed down admiringly at the beautiful scene. It was as if Joseph and Mary were kneeling down and praying in their own humble abode in Nazareth.

Tim took down the ass's chains from the back of the door and link-by-link he showed Judy how to count out each of the rosary's trimmings. Fingering the links on the chains was the only way to keep count of how many prayers they were making. If Judy lost her count, Tim would remind her when the decade of prayers was complete and it was time to shout out Glory-be-to-God. These self-composed prayers would become as natural as sunlight to them, and they'd offer them to God with a religious fervour second to none.

They knelt before the fire. Tim started off with a little cough and gave his sister a shower of holy water and nodded to her to start the prayer.

'Judy, avic, let you give out the first smattering,' he urged.

Judy gave her own shy little cough and cleared her throat. Then, taking courage in both hands, she took hold of the ass's chains and began their homemade rosary. With her eyes lowered and afraid to look up (in case God might be shaking his head sadly at her), she wrapped the chains through her prayerful fingers and slowly began to mumble the first words that came into her head.

There was a certain chime and rhyme to them that rang off of the walls. '*Thumpathay, a-thumpathay* and yet another *thumpathay!'* and at each *thumpathay,* she hammered her chest with her fist. This met with Tim's satisfaction, and he gave her a cute little smile across the firelight. He felt there was a powerful sweetness in his sister's sincere attempts to say her rosary. Her voice had an unusual nasally tunefulness in it. And at that most sacred moment, their uplifted souls were captivated with pure holiness.

After that, it was Tim's turn. *'Hangaway, a-hangaway* and yet another *hangaway,'* and he too gave his breast a savage belt at each of his *hangaways.*

These words (short and sweet) would now take the place of the first and second halves of the Hail Mary – brother and sister in harmony with one another. Between them, the rosary had taken on a musical quality which outmatched any dawn chorus of their hens, geese or ducks. Father Honesty would have been mesmerised by the innocent sounds of the humble pair's rosary, and their forefathers' nearby ghosts must have been smiling gently out at them from the four corners of the welcoming room.

The old pair were growing in confidence so that before the week ended, they had developed a certain air of authority in their praying, giving their rosary that little bit of variety – when to hush their voices in reverence to the Lord, when to raise their shouts up high, when to raise their lowly eyes to the rafters.

They began to feel a good bit different as a result of all the new praying. Their faces seemed to shine in the gold of the lamplight and had a gentle composure in them like the face of the bishop. The very walls of their little nest seemed to glow with their ringing tones rather than from the flames of the fire. Of course, their cat (Mouser) became so alarmed at the style of the new prayers that he went off and hid behind the kettle and their aged and deaf hound-dog (Rip-it-up) slept throughout it all even though their praying by this time was loud enough to awaken the dead.

Judy was not used to the jingle of the ass's chains dangling from her fists, and she had a bit of difficulty keeping up the counting of her several chain-links. Her effort at beating her chest was also a distraction. Even the rhyming answers of Tim were fooling her some of the time. Then, after some 30 or 40 *thumpathays* (instead of the expected 10), Tim would grow agitated and pierce her with his eyes across the firelight, indicating with several nods of his head that it was time for her to round off that decade of the rosary and give out the *Glory-be-to-God*.

In the end, he lost all patience with her and let out an almighty roar. 'Blasht yeer hide, Judy, for the sake of sweet Jaysus, will ye give us a blast of the *Glory-be-to-God*?'

The poor confused Judy was in a flood of tears and dropped her muddled chains at being so cursed. However, she managed to croak out an apologetic little cough before letting out a high-pitched shriek of *Glory-be-to-God*.

Tim was then almost in tears of joy as Judy's responses filled the house, and he thanked her over and over again for giving him this fine dosage of the *Glory-be-to-God*. They now felt that their first battle against the cursed drink and the wicked Devil was being handsomely won, that they could now commence the second decade of their rosary.

However, in the middle of this decade, Tim could again be heard raining down curses (the angels put their hands to their shocked ears) on his terrified sister, seeing that she had let the fire splutter and almost die. She had just finished the last of her *thumpathays* when Tim once more interrupted her.

'Blasht yeer hide again, Judy! For the love of the archangel Michael, will ye throw another sod-of-turf on the fire before it quinch on us!'

Judy became a bag of nerves and almost dropped the chains from her fists again. But soon she had the logs crackling and, with the blaze merrily thrashing away, their prayer-making rambled on once more in fine fashion.

Apart from cursing Judy for not giving out the *Glory-be-to-God* at the proper time and not keeping her eye on the fire, Tim was proving to be every bit as sincere and saintly as his mother (Holy Devotions), and the mixing up of his praying and cursing seemed in no way inappropriate either to himself or to Judy. In the eyes of the Lord, he was as holy as any ermined pope, and in Judy's eyes, he was as harmless as the lambs on the green. There'd be no brimstone in Hell for these two soul-mates for God had already marked them out for His own.

8

And now, on this day of the children's visit, the day's milking was over, and Tim crossed the yard with his cow on a rope. The children saw him coming from the shed. His black heavy greatcoat was two sizes too small for him, and it was tied with twine. His boots walked awkwardly as though he had never in his life pared his toenails with the knife. Judy was a step behind him, carrying the bucket of warm milk. She was wearing a cow-dung-stained yellow coat and a pink dress, which had once been red – only washed too often.

A few minutes later, the children stepped across the yard and waited at the side of the cabin. They were somewhat coy and afraid to go in the half-door and introduce themselves. They were unsure what next they should do once the old pair settled in for the evening and the fire was restarted.

They still remembered their previous derogatory words against Tim and Judy, and Lippy was half-inclined to scorn the old pair, not knowing that to be in their company would be an unimaginably great honour. For already, the priests in the town had started to revere Tim and Judy as true saints on account of the innocence and piety instilled into them from Hushaby and Holy Devotions.

The sun would soon be setting, and it would grow dark. Lippy led his two brothers round the back of the cabin and stood there silently. They crouched against the wall and listened as Tim and Judy began their evening devotions. They heard what seemed to be a continuous moaning and wailing coming from inside the wall as the old pair thanked God for the blessings He had sent them this day. Then, to the utter astonishment of the children, came the strange rambling words (the *thumpathays* and *hangaways*) and the unmerciful beating of the old man and woman's fists against their chests at every *thump* and every *hang*.

Tim and Judy were soon well into the high-pitched psalming of their new rosary, their praying voices rising higher and louder by the minute. It was enough to frighten any living soul, and the children could barely keep their stifled laughter down their throats. Among the dark trees, however, *the wilderness fairies* sadly shook their heads at the sight of such sad behaviour. The little rascals had failed to realise the solemnity of these new prayers. They had missed the soulful sanctity and intensity of the moment.

Once more they heard Tim's intermittent curses (*'sweet Jaysus, blasht yeer hide, Judy!')* raining down on his sister's head when she hadn't thrown another log on the fire to keep it going. And then they heard him again cursing Judy (*'for sweet Moses' sake, will ye give us a blast of the 'Glory-be-to-God')* when she forgot to continue counting the last few of the ass's chains and come up with her final *Glory-be-to-God*.

With what feathery feet did Lippy lead his brothers across the haggart to leap their way down through the Wilderness. They couldn't wait for next day when they'd sit on the log in Old Sam's orchard and smoke their fag-butts. That's when the jauntiness in them would come out to play as never before and cause them to mimic this misfortunate old pair.

'Lippy, avic, will ye throw another sod-of-turf on the fire, for the love of the arch-angel Michael.'

'Blasht ye, Philly, ye've let the fire quench again!'

Moll-the-Man must have been wondering had her children seen Simple Simon's ass falling into the well-hole, the children were laughing so much below in the orchard.

'By the limping tinker, Lippy, couldn't ye think of sweet Jaysus on His cross and give us a blast of the Glory-be-to-God?' And so, it went on as the orchard rang with their imitation of the newly-formed rosary. Finally, they ended up marching out over the singletree and solemnly stamping along the creamery road to the tunes of *thumpathay* and *hangaway* and beating their chests at every *thump* and every *hang*.

For a day or two, they continued this new form of amusement at the expense of poor Tim and Judy. Men, taking their ass to the forge or their tanks of milk to the creamery, must have thought that these children had finally lost their minds altogether. What on earth were mothers feeding their children with these days?

9

A few evenings later, it was time for the children to make a second visit and Lippy and the rest of them were back out across the Wilderness. They had brought with them one of their mother's potato-sacks. They went to Fat Noolah's hen house (the house downhill from Tim and Judy's) and stole one of her sleepy hens just as it was going to roost. They put her into the sack (*'that's to keep her quiet,'* said Lippy for she would surely be terrified out of her wits and making her piss).

There were times like this when their mother had thrown a goose down the chimney in order to get her to flap her mystified wings and clean out the soot from the chimney-hole as she tumbled down into the welcoming room. It was nothing new.

As well as the hen, they had brought out a ladder from Sad Sam's turf-shed. Lippy climbed onto the back of the thatch just when Tim and Judy were canting the most serious stages of their rosary.

It was time for a new sport to begin, and Lippy took the hen out of the sack. Then he ceremoniously waved its legs in the air before pelting it down the chimney. The terrified hen lodged in a storm of hot ashes, blinding the old pair's eyes and blackening the cups on the dresser. Utter pandemonium now broke out as the poor creature frightened the daylights out of the unsuspecting Tim and Judy and caused Mouser-the-cat to make a run for the half-door (Tim's hound-dog was stone deaf and slept through it all). This was accompanied by gasps of utter confusion.

'I own to God! I own to God!' screamed Judy. 'What have we done to deserve this – a hen raining down on us from the clouds?' and she began to cry like the Magdalene.

'The Devil take it! The Devil take it! Why on earth should the great God-in-heaven send us the gift of this screaming hen in the middle of our prayers?' stormed Tim. And for once, he forgot to add his curses against God and man as the hysteria took hold of him. The hen had put a stop to their holiness as they ran to rescue the poor creature and desperately tried to throw her out over the half-door. There would be no more thought of saying their rosary this evening.

Sad and bewildered, they took the candle and waddled off to their nest in the bedroom. The children stole round the gable-end of the cabin and flattened their noses up against the window. What were they expecting to see? They took turns to spy on the old pair, each one squinting to see what was going on in the bedroom. It was like a picture or a play about to start.

Tim took off his britches and boots. He kept on his shirt, since all men slept in their day-shirts and never wore a stitch underneath them. Judy took off her skirt and stood in her chemise. The damp sheets of the bed beckoned them, and they hopped into the four-poster bed of their parents. They covered themselves up to their chins with the blankets and greatcoats and rested their heads on the musty pillows. At the foot of the bed, the deaf hound-dog kept watch over their sleep.

It was cold in the damp room, and it was cold in the bed also, and they shivered. In a previous age when winters were harsh, and the turf was scarce, it had not been unusual for a son and his mother or for a brother and his sister to sleep in the same bed and keep the warmth in their bodies from one another's heat. There wasn't a stem of sinfulness in it, and by the time it got to the middle of the night, their limbs would be roasting like hell.

The children were not to know this, having never witnessed it before. So, they waited, and they waited – to see if there'd be any tumbling around in the big bed and whether their ears might catch one or two loving whisperings between the two old souls. Oh, the heathens!

Next day, there'd be a fine day's play-acting for them to perform (the makeshift kissing and coddling) below in Old Sam's orchard if they could now hear or see some of the commotions of Tim and Judy. But all they saw was the innocence of a sister and her brother with their arms around one another's necks and falling asleep in the embrace of their Heavenly Father. And once more, God and His angels and saints smiled down on the old pair. But the Devil himself came to the back-window and gave each of the children a pat on the back, the brazen young devils that they were! The simple, spiritual purity of Tim and Judy still hadn't dawned on them.

Next evening it was time for the scallywags' third visit. Once more, Tim and Judy were steeped in their *thumpathays* and *hangaways*, and Judy was showing how determined she was to keep enough logs on the fire and avoid the wrath of her brother. That's when Lippy dragged out Tim's rattletrap and tied it across the front door with the horse's chains, thereby imprisoning the two old devotees.

He led his brothers to the back of the cabin where it was Philly's turn to perform the mischief. He climbed up the ladder and took an armful of potato-sacks up the thatch and tied them round the mouth of the chimney.

A few seconds later, they could hear the curses of Tim in the welcoming room where himself and Judy and the cat and the hound-dog (who had a very good nose on him) were heard battling against a roomful of smoke, unable to fathom out why the smoke wouldn't go up the chimney.

Tim reached for the bucket of water (not the mere mugful that he used each night to quench the ashes), and he threw the contents onto the fire. Then the pair of them tried to open the door but were prevented from opening it by the rattletrap and chains strapped across it outside. They started to shake with the cold and had no choice but to freeze.

'I own to God! I own to God!' screamed Judy when she tried to force the front door ajar.

'What have we done that God should so punish us?' roared Tim. It was like the story of Job in the Good Book when he was sent several ailments and kept wondering if his latest punishment was going to be the last one.

It was, however, to be the end of the children's shameful sport. It belatedly struck them when they were smoking their fag-butts next day in the orchard (perhaps they were listening to the echo of an angel's voice) that they had done a great wrong and had sinned a great sin. Perhaps they remembered the face of God in their mother's prayer book and how sad He always seemed to be. It wasn't natural for them to be performing such acts as these, and a great deal would have to be done to bring some cheer back onto God's face and put the Devil back in his box.

Tim and Judy weren't as stupid as the cattle on the hill. They saddled up the ass-and-car and after Sunday Mass went into the sacristy to see their priest. They bowed before Father Honesty and solemnly laid their case before him – the chicken raining down the chimney and into the fire, the smoke filling their welcoming room, the rattle-trap across the door almost freezing them to death.

It wasn't long before the wise old priest put two and two together. Next morning, Moll-the-Man heard the roar of his motorcar coming up the creamery road. Without a handshake, the holy man leapt down from his car and marched into her welcoming room. He wasn't the same man that smiled at them most Sundays from the altar but had the face on him that he had reserved for himself the time he spoke against The Drink.

He stormed up and down in front of the children, his face like a cloud in a thunderstorm. He felt like kicking the little arses off of them.

When he had calmed down, he talked to them about Hell and damnation. He talked to them about shame and guilt and how it would take time for these feelings to evaporate from them and how their behaviour had diminished their souls in the eyes of God. They had crossed the bridge between good and bad (he kept repeating). He told them the savage beating that God would give them in the next world if they ever tormented the two old saints again. Then he made them kneel down in the yard.

He brought out from his car a large bottle of holy water (it would have to be a large one) to re-baptise them and bring comfort and peace back into their souls.

By now, they were full of self-loathing and felt very sorry indeed in front of such a great man. They limply hung down their heads and genuinely flickered their eyelids and were chastened. He gave each of them a good dowsing of the holy water, and at each turn of his heel, he called upon the Devil that was hiding in their souls to come out of their bodies.

'Coom on out, Satan! Coom on out this minute, ye scarecrow!' Then he blessed each of them and told them that their contrite hearts and true sorrowfulness had restored them to an unblemished state in the eyes of God and that God had forgiven them on this occasion.

At this, they felt a good deal better in themselves. And then (only then) did he turn aside and give himself a little self-satisfied smile and put his bottle of holy water away. For he too had once been a child. He too had once been a rogue (but not as big a rogue as these little heathens), and he forgave them their recent sins.

'Go and sin no more,' said he. 'Far better for ye to go down to Ducks-and-Drakes and worry the life out of her ould sow who has been threatening to tear the legs off of the little children going to the well.' Then, without so much as a salute, he hopped into his car and went roaring away down the hill.

By this time, Moll-the-Man was in a savage state of anger. She moved at lightning speed to the hen house to bring back her yard-brush and draw blood from her children's legs. By-Jiggery also proved himself unusually vengeful and was already arming his fist with his best sally-switch.

With feet that the best greyhounds in Ireland would be proud of, Lippy and his little army raced into the rishy field and jumped with ease the three-foot wire fence that led into Old Sam's orchard where they fell in a great big frightened heap. They were safe – at least for now.

10

In addition to these rascally moments of Moll-the-Man's children (and they were rare, thank God), there had always been a few wicked adults ready to exploit the righteous. The rest of us were ashamed of these people's niggardly side and their need to hurt old folk, weaker in limb or holier in spirit than themselves. Father Honesty had noticed it, and he had mentioned it in one of his sermons – what he called 'the sour head of greed and covetousness'.

And now again (thanks to the purity of Tim and Judy's souls), this covetousness came running up to Currywhibble like a weasel in the grass. Fat Noolah and her coy husband (Sad Sam) welcomed the Devil in the doorway, and he poisoned them with a dose of jealousy and spite. They had always been as playful as two rats, but now their hatred of Tim and Judy's holiness came spilling out by the bucket-load.

In the grey of each morning, after offering up his day to God, Tim would wash his teeth and the inside of his mouth with the soot from the hob and a mug of water from the bucket. There came a day when garbed only in his shirt, he took himself over to the stream to wash his face with the freezing water whilst listening to the songs of the blackbird and thrush.

Suddenly, he found himself standing on a painful thorn. Whereupon the harmless innocent (and he bare-arsed underneath his shirt), placed his foot on the wall that divided his yard from Fat Noolah's lower yard. He tried to remove the thorn.

Fat Noolah came sailing across her yard to entertain Tim in her usual singalong voice. 'What have ye there, Tim? Is it a thorn? Let me take a look.' The sly old hussy had no notion of helping Tim remove his thorn. From her position in her lower yard, she found herself looking up underneath Tim's shirt and gloating her eyes on the sight of his private regalia.

She ran indoors and beckoned Sad Sam to come out and help Tim remove his thorn. The two of them spent a pleasant few minutes (a sad sequel to their morning's so-called prayers) peeping under Tim's shirt while he was working the thorn out of his foot.

Meanwhile, the saints in the clouds were conversing with one another. 'Men bless their cows. They bless their ass. They bless their horse with holy water before setting off to their daily work. It's with something else, perhaps – the fist-to-the-jaw or the hammer-to-the-head – that other men should bless Fat Noolah and Sad Sam if they ever found out what these two heathens were up to this morning.'

There is nothing so pitiful as hunger and starvation. This had been drummed into everybody's head since the days of the famine. Fat Noolah and Sad Sam had a noble sow which never stopped bawling from morning till night. Its ribs were as thin as a greyhound's.

This cursed sow was a frightening sight and could often be seen dashing through the Wilderness with the fleet movements of a mule, accompanied by its woeful shrieks and its snorting fury. The poor innocent was seen uprooting potatoes and turnips in one field or another for it had to go somewhere to find its food and stave off its hungry belly-pains.

A Monday morning arrived when Judy had washed her bed-sheets and hung them out to dry on the bushes. With nothing better to do, Fat Noolah was looking out the window. An hour later, Tim and Judy set off for the bog to plank another few rows of turf, for the footings were well and truly dried out. By mid-afternoon, the two of them were working like blazes. The daylight was unnoticeably slipping away from them and the pink clouds of early evening were sailing into the blue skies.

At the same time, Fat Noolah, desperate to get her sow a good feed, was unclasping the latch of the old pair's door. As soon as the door was opened, the two wretches let in their starving sow to adorn the welcoming room with her presence.

What a welcome was inside for her! Had the children been there and peeped in the window, they'd have seen how this particular sow dealt with the simplicities of Tim and Judy's cabin. She rushed wildly about, pucking the ring of her nose at the chairs and dishes on the table and almost landing herself in the fire. No longer a sow but a raving bull, she knocked over the pots and pans and anything else that stood in her way. It was (thought Fat Noolah) better than The Daffy-Duck Circus to see such pandemonium.

Then the precious creature knocked down the delf and pewter off of the dresser. Next, she spilt the milk and the spring-water from the buckets and for a finish, buried her head in the sack of flour. The Devil in his home in Hell was warming his hands to see such gallantry in a noble sow. What a miserable picture it was - a sow no longer pink but as white as Daddy Christmas as she pitched the flour all over the floor. There was no greater sin than to destroy a man's flour, the flour he'd be needing for his soda-cakes, the flour that had to last him for half a year's eating.

Mercy-on-us! When Tim and Judy returned to the cabin, they saw the state of the floor and their simple possessions all ruined. Their faces were grey with hopeless grief. They looked behind the hen house and saw the happy face of the sow looking up at them, as contented as a missioner after a mission, and she covered from head to tail in their hard-earned flour.

'Ah-ha! A sow with the staggers!' yelled Judy, her sadness and her anger all rolled into one. For once, she had forgotten her holiness and saintliness.

Tim caught her anger and fanned it. 'Quick! Get the four-grained fork,' he roared.

'Stick it down the impudent sow's throat!' shouted Judy.

'Get its blood!' cried Tim. They were demented to think of their lost flour and the coming hunger that would be upon them. What happened next beggars all belief. To the everlasting horror on the faces of Fat Noolah and Sad Sam, Tim took the four-grained fork, and Judy took the hayfork, and they proceeded to try and kill the murdering sow that had ruined their house.

Fat Noolah and Sad Sam were terrified, getting back a bit of their own medicine for their cruel crimes, and they thought they might be next to get sent to the Beyond with the pitchforks. They hid themselves behind the curtains of their sad little cabin and watched their sow facing up to what would have been its last and fatal punishment had it not had the good sense (when it felt the first dart of the fork up its arse) to run and jump clean out over the wall. It was never seen again (said the gossiping drinkers) from that day to this.

11

Ireland was the land of rain and religion, the land of saints and scholars. And yet these acts of pure unkindliness grew like weeds in the haggart. As Father Honesty had often said when speaking of greed from his pulpit, 'The heart of the mosquito never dries up.'

It wasn't long before men in suits came slyly up the hill from their fertile fields below near the town. They tried to make Tim and Judy sell their bit of land to them and take the road into town now that they were getting on in years. They wanted the price of the land for next to nothing.

Tim and Judy said not a word but went on pouring the milk from their cow into the churn. They loved their cow. They loved their hens and they loved their geese. They loved their land.

'They'll never take my land from me,' Tim whispered repeatedly into Judy's ears. 'I'll give three bawls of the hunger before I take the road to town to die!'

Now that their flour was all gone, hunger and its belly-pains were fast approaching the door. Like hives in the evening sunset, it crept up along the yard and penetrated the four walls of their cabin. As the days rolled on, the dock-leaves stood at their front door, and the scaly green paint on the door fell off in shreds. The rain and the cold winds entered in through the broken windowpanes.

At night the rats became brave, in spite of Mouser-the-cat, and they played peek-a-pooh with him. He wasn't able to chastise the whole pile of them. The mice found themselves a cosy little nest in the remains of the flour-sack. So bold were all these creatures that they ran across the blankets of Tim and Judy in the still of the night while they were sleeping.

Tim was working in his well-loved bit of bog-land out on the heathery hill under the clear blue sky and the reddened clouds where he had gallivanted with his father when he was a child. It was almost time to go home when he tripped and hit his head on a sharp stone. Like a young calf searching for its mother, he tried to rise up. He stumbled again. He who had been as hardy as a snipe all his life was now scarcely breathing. He lay there in the sun, his saddest hour. He knew that Death wanted him.

Harrowed with grief, he wanted to cry out and to bellow, 'Ye'll never take this land from me!' He would die as he said he would, out in the open air on the land that he loved so well, unwanted and unloved by all except his beloved sister, Judy.

When he didn't come back for his midday dinner, Judy took the road to their bit of bog. She found him, sorrow of sorrows, lying there like a useless scarecrow, his glazed eyes looking up at her, and she looking down at him like a frantic bird mourning its fledgling. Tim spoke not a word. Judy wasn't sure if he could hear her speak.

Putting her mouth into his ear, she searched desperately for the right words to say to him. She told him of her love for him. She told him of the absolute love that God had for him. She told him that a better place was now being prepared for him. Her heart was breaking inside in her chest with a love and an aching and a longing, which hurt her ribs more than a punch of a fist.

Tim closed his dead eyes. Judy crossed his two arms. She stayed there a long time praying over him. She gave him the death prayer (The Act of Contrition) – gave it to this brother of hers who had never ever sinned in all his life. He had outlasted the cringing money-grabbers who had tried to steal his land for a price next to nothing. He had indeed given the world his three bawls of the hunger before he died. And the angels came down into the bog and put their wings around him and carried him away with them from all the complexities of this life.

When the other turf-gatherers arrived on the scene, they found his beloved Judy whimpering softly to herself with her two arms around her brother's neck and the spindly bog-land trees looking down protectively on his body in their hoods of green.

Tim's soul was now very far away, and he looked down and blessed his sister, and he called to her from the sunshine of Eternity. And it wasn't many weeks (God rest her) before Judy and her piety heard his call and left the wastelands of life here on earth and came rushing through the skies to meet him.

12

To avoid the painful inflictions of Moll-the-Man's yard-brush and By-Jiggery's sally-switch on the back of their legs, the children promised to go into the confession-box of Father Honesty and lay before him their many misdemeanours. Whatever penitential punishment it took (be it walking on horse-nails or sleeping in the nettles for the night), they'd do it – to please God and, even more, to escape from the wrath of their parents. They were filled with a feeling of utmost remorse.

The following Sunday, it was raining cats and dogs. Indeed, you wouldn't send a cat or a dog out into the yard. The children took the holy water from the font. Moll-the-Man handed Lippy the rosary beads, and off they set.

It was a miserable journey, but they felt that their guardian angel was supporting them on the way. They came to the haggart of Tim and Judy. They felt sad and sheepish and didn't know what to say to one another. They did what the holy priest had ordered them to do as a penance, and they knelt in the soaking rain in a semi-circle. They passed the rosary beads from hand to hand and said all five decades of the Joyful Mysteries. From somewhere above the clouds, Tim and Judy roused themselves and looked down into their haggart at the solemn faces of the children. They smiled, and then they laughed, and the tears of joy rolled down their jaws.

And then a very strange thing happened. The sun kicked the black clouds asunder, and the rain ran away with itself, and a beautiful rainbow struggled in across the heavens, and the children knew that their souls were safe. From now until eternity they promised they'd be as good as gold. Lippy looked back at the vacant little cabin – the well-named hen house.

The others followed his eyes. In that very moment, they realised that something strange was happening to them. They became suddenly filled with a new and inexplicable feeling. It was sheer kindliness, and it rose in a frightening surge throughout their bodies. For this one brief moment in their young lives (if never again), they were as holy as any canonised saint. The sincere love-of-God which Tim and Judy had brought into their daily work, seemed to pour itself down from the heavens on the back of this beautiful rainbow, and the children recognised that all along they had been privileged and enriched on the day they'd started out for the Wilderness and made the acquaintance of two blessed saints in the shape of Tim and his sister Judy here in the hills of north Tipperary. Enough said.

LITTLE DAN AND BATTLIN' SAL

1

School holidays were over, and children's adventures came to a halt as they headed back to the schoolhouse of Dang-the-skin-of-it. On the 3-mile trek, the bigger boys marched the younger ones reluctantly in front of them, prodding them ever onwards with their ash-plants ('get a move on, ye ashy pets, or else we'll be late') and teaching them to recite their singsong tables on the way.

Little Dan (Dowager's youngest son) and Battlin' Sal (the youngest of By-Jiggery and Moll-the-Man's children) were still only 4 and far too young for such an arduous daily travail. Without their big brothers, their mornings would now be dull. They felt sad and lonely with no more mad adventures with which to pass their days. Not only that: even the farmyard animals seemed to be miserable like themselves. The once-noisy hens had lost their acute interest in life, and the ducks and the geese seemed to be singing their shrill songs in a less cheerful manner than before. The crows seemed to hover languorously above the rookery in Old Sam's grove, not knowing whether to take themselves off over the fields or stay becalmed around the creamery road for the rest of the day.

A few days before, these two little ones had been feeling nothing but the joys of life – like the previous Wednesday when they had gone up to Sheep's Cross to witness the grisly pig-killing outside Rambling Jack's shed. The very next day, By-Jiggery had taken Battlin' Sal into town for the sale of some of his cattle. On Saturday, Little Dan had been lucky enough to get down to Abbey Cross with his big brother (My-Son-Jack) and watch the noble antics of the sportsmen and the egg-jugglers at the Daffy-Duck Circus. On Sunday, he had stared down at the dead face of Father Loveless, recently dead and lying as peaceful as a slumbering infant in his coffin outside the town hospital.

But all that was now over and done with. It didn't matter if they weren't as strong as the mighty Lippy – the way he'd been able to use the hurley-stick on the head of the cockerel in an effort to kill him for taking a lump out of Red Scissors' neck. It didn't matter if they weren't strong enough to frighten the fierce gander and send him out over the singletree and into the safety of Old Sam's grove. Any adventure at all would have done the pair of them this morning – even one like the day they were left in tears after giving up the chase behind the bigger deer-footed boys as they climbed the tallest trees or when they went off robbing Old Stroller of his juiciest harvest-time apples. The fact is – Little Dan and Battlin' Sal were now missing the older boys awfully.

2

The morning-time fairies began whispering all sorts of nonsense into Battlin' Sal's ears as she lay in bed. 'There are so many hours in the day and so much you could be doing,' they whispered, 'and every day is moving away from you – faster and faster. It's time you were on the move.'

A little way down the creamery road, Little Dan turned towards the broken-glass window at the back of the bedroom where the moody ass (the Lightning Whoor) was already braying in at him bad-humouredly. A tiny patch of blue sky appeared above the cowshed, and the sun had grown a little bit higher in the sky. It was time for him also to rise up and meet the great big world. He stretched and yawned and turned his steps towards the half-door. Inside him was an inexplicable longing which he hadn't felt before but was yet much too young to explain.

Battlin' Sal said her blessing prayers (with the help of her mother), and she leathered into her duck egg, dipping the spoon of butter into it and circling the salt around in its yellow. Her thoughts, like Little Dan's, were getting clearer by the minute. Beyond her yard-stream, the creamery road seemed to shine silvery, as though laughing and beckoning her to follow it. The laurel bushes at the singletree leading to Old Sam's grove sparkled and also seemed to call out to her. The ivy climbers at the haggart-stick joined in, hoping to welcome her out amongst their natural finery. But, like Little Dan, she was still unsure of these unusual impulses calling her to do something a bit different.

She sat in the clay near the yard-stream, and with a twig, she continued to draw the image of what she believed her future schoolhouse would look like. The only tall buildings she'd ever seen were the church in Copperstone Hollow and the creamery at the fork of the Limerick road. Surely a schoolhouse was as big as either of these?

She still hadn't moved but lay down at the tree-stump, watching an old beetle rolling a ball of dung across the flagstones, just as in earlier days she had watched the golden caterpillars crossing the road at dinnertime. She smelled Hammer-the-Smith's ancient tractor spluttering down the lane at Sheep's Cross and wondered what it must be like to sit on a tractor alongside the big man. In the meantime, a crowd of flies followed the progress of the beetle and the ball of dung, and the ants came out from their home in her little tin mug and darted around behind the flies. That's when a shadow appeared above her. It was her best friend, Little Dan.

There were some marked differences between these two little souls. Little Dan was on the frail and fragile side whereas Battlin' Sal was round and sturdy. Her skin was brown as a berry whereas Little Dan's was as pink as My-Son-Jack's spuds. His hair was flaxen and his eyes a robin's egg blue, whereas Battlin' Sal's hair was black as a crow and her eyes as dark as laurel berries.

And now the cold sunlight glistened on the new arrival, and the little boy's presence was as fresh as a daisy, banishing the gloomy air around the little beetle-watcher. The sky also seemed even bluer than before as Battlin' Sal took a good look at Little Dan and Little Dan took a good look at Battlin' Sal. How fine a thing it was to have a morning visitor! The newcomer was carrying a purple bellflower that he'd plucked from his mother's garden, and he handed it to Battlin' Sal. The two of them then walked down along the side of the thistle field.

There was a moment's silence as they weighed up the need for adventures to enliven their day. Neither child was sure what they should do for they were still just two frail children – that's what they were – looking for those past days spent with the happy faces of the older children. The gallant sun had begun to come across Fort Dangerous. It would soon be blinding their eyes and, like the road and the bushes, it too was beckoning them.

It was time to stop gazing after an old dung-beetle or twig-drawing an imaginary schoolhouse. It was time to give themselves up to higher thoughts which would lift themselves away from the loneliness they'd both been feeling.

They had heard tell of another world – a world that lay out beyond the bog road and the Hills-of-the-Past, out towards the mysterious purple hills and the awe-inspiring Chieftain Hill that rose up to the sky and looked down on the glassy sparkle of the Shannon River. Like Battlin' Sal, Little Dan was beginning to feel *the morning-time fairies* telling him to get a move on and go seek this great big mountain and see what fine fun they'd have when they got to the top of it.

They had heard the sad story of Balaraggin's yard and the green door that was covered with his dying blood – a sight the older children were forever talking about. And now, for the first time in their lives, they were listening to this deafening call from outside their world. Children in bygone times had heard this same call too. It would be the greatest adventure since sailors had sailed the seven seas. They would tell not a soul. They remembered the way Lippy and his brothers had bragged when they came back from Currywhibble after braving the incredible bog-holes in Bog Boundless – how, like ravenous wolves, they had eaten an entire apple batter between them – how they had spent the evening posturing in front of the younger ones, telling how they had fought with the fierce unlicensed bulls beyond Growl River, how sailing across the dreamy skies they'd seen the two wild eagles that had their nest in a hollow cleft near the summit of Chieftain Hill – eagles that could carry off a man and devour him in one gulp! That's what they said (the bleddy liars), and they had filled the heads of the younger children (of Little Dan and Battlin' Sal especially) with new and unfulfilled dreams.

3

Before they set out on their mighty adventure, our two small heroes ventured on a bit of childish knavery, which would (they hoped) absolve them from any feelings of guilt they might have. They collected two big bunches of bright wildflowers from Simple Simon's ditch and filled out these fine nosegays with a few artistically-arranged dock-leaves. Battlin' Sal handed her bunch in over the half-door to her mother that she might add the finishing touches to her bedroom altar.

'What a wonderful child you are to be thinking so dearly of your mother,' smiled Moll-the-Man. ('What a rascally child you are, to be planning an escapade beyond the Hills-of-the-Past,' said her guardian angel).

Little Dan ran home and placed a similar bunch on Dowager's bedroom altar before she got herself back with the cows from the bull-paddock with My-Son-Jack. Then he raced up the road to start out on his great big adventure. What tales they would have to tell when they returned triumphantly at the end of the day! Imagine the stunned faces of Lippy, Philly and Young Jim when they heard the wonders of their adventure!

They had another little thought. Just as big men looked up at the stars and wondered how far away they might stretch, so the two of them wanted to know what were the depths of the hills and mountains, and who were the people who lived out there, and where did the two huge eagles have their nest, and what lay beyond the Valley of the Pig and the Valley of the Black Cattle, and what was on the other side of mighty Chieftain Hill? Their heads were full of it.

'Why,' said Little Dan, 'there must be more and more hills and mountains.' They were old enough to realize that, in the end, they could go no further than Ireland, for they would then come to the ocean, and that was the end of the whole world.

Bedad-sez-I and his friend (Lowry) were the most famous adventurers that anyone on the creamery road had ever heard tell of. They'd been told how the two great men once walked out past Galway and had their photos taken in the stormy waves without a stitch of clothes on, how these photos sold in their thousands the length and breadth of Galway, how they'd come home and said, 'We can die in a peaceful bed this blessed night now that our two eyes have seen the great ocean.'

4

The children started up the road towards Sheep's Cross.

The wind was hushed at the sight of them, and it tried to give them their first warning. 'Poor innocent children!' it whispered, 'Ye don't know what ye're doing. Take care! Take very great care!'

Then the branches bowed down towards them and gave them a further warning. 'The bog road is a place of many twists and turns,' they whispered. Then the little birds followed along behind them, shrieking their loudest chitter-chatter – another warning. But the two little adventurers paid no heed to these warnings. Nothing was going to stand in their way. And then the tattered clouds scudded away from the growing sun's heat and began to tell the news to one another – about the two impending adventurers and the great big journey their brave little hearts had started out upon.

'Coom on, blasht it! Let's be attacking these damn mountains,' said Battlin' Sal, imitating the only language she knew – that of the grown-ups. Sadly, they hadn't given a single thought to the worries anyone might have over their whereabouts, desiring nothing but to see all that Lippy and his brothers had seen – the bloodstained mystery of Balaraggin's yard and (above all) mighty Chieftain Hill. If good fortune prevailed, they would find themselves greeted by the fairies themselves, for the hills and the mountains were the realms of Fairyland. Any fool knew that.

They scampered on up the slope, not stopping for wild strawberries or blackberries. They would soon arrive at the first hills, and beyond that, get to Bog Boundless and Growl

River, and beyond that, they'd reach mighty Chieftain Hill. They were sure of it.

It was getting on into the morning, and as yet, no-one other than the hens and the swallows in the turf shed had seen them stealing away. Dowager and Moll-the-Man would think they had gone off to play in the cubby-shop, for they had never before ventured out on their own – even as far as Sheep's Cross. They were near it now, and they knew they'd recognize Hammer-the-Smith's forge where they'd seen him shoeing the ass and had admired the heat of his fiery furnace.

Their feet had now stopped running, and they stopped and looked back. They waved goodbye to their two farms and to Fort Dangerous and the leprechauns who hammered nails onto fairy shoes. They began to pant and puff a bit. There was still time to go back home if they wanted.

They had reached the crossroads, the place where Shy Dennis's dead mother had come back from the grave in her ass-and-car to collect her best cardigan for her journey to the Beyond. Once more, they tiptoed by and never gave the shack a single look.

The little breezes persistently scurried after them, and the little birds followed them from bush to bush. 'Go back!' they frantically tweeted. 'Go back! Go back! Ye wobbly-headed children.'

Ahead of them, a dark threatening cloud sailed by like some forlorn ship crossing the sun, its dark edges reddening as it drew near them. By now, they should have heeded the many warnings being planted inside their heads, but (ah, the incautiousness of these brave little souls) they thought they could roam the world outside their own safe bit of paradise. The sun in the morning sky was still only middling high, and they had already walked a good stretch. They had yet to feel the full force of the noonday heat when there mightn't be a puff of air left to breathe.

They had reached the fork of the road, and a difficult choice had to be made. For a second, a bit of panic crept into them and told them to run back home. To the left of them was a little donkey-lane, almost covered in briars. They knew it was no use stepping down that way. The road ahead of them led towards the Valley of the Hollows and to Tipperary Town, far to the south. There would be no mountains to climb on that road. The road to the right (and weren't they the lucky children to have guessed it!) led straight into the Hills-of-the-Past and eventually to Bog Boundless.

They took this road and marched on to the Valley of the Pig before reaching Red Scissors' spring-well. They knelt on the slab, cupped their hands for the trickling water and drank avidly. They looked to the left and then to the right, in case one of their demons (the Holy Terror) might dash out at them and put them in his sack and sell them at the fairy fair. To comfort themselves, they gathered a few old crab-apples lying round the scabby trees near the well. They'd be two hungry savages before the day was out.

Close by, they heard the hooves and snorts of Rambling Jack's red bull stamping pace for pace along with them – he on the inside of the ditch and they on the outside and only a few feet separating them. They wondered whether there was a gap in the ditch once they'd reached the end of the road and if this huge bull might rush out and pelt them with his horns so high in the air that they'd sail out over the hay-sheds and land in the eagles' nest and be eaten alive – even before they had a chance to have their great big adventure? They were now terrified.

They passed the bend, and the raging bull (thank God) was nowhere to be seen. They were high enough in the hills to look back at the creamery road behind them. It was as white as a bone. In front of them were further hill-slopes and countless trees with their leaves twinkling in the sunlight. But already there was sinister laughter in the depths of those trees where new and wicked spirits were inviting them to come and shake hands with Mister Danger.

They had reached the Valley of the Black Cattle and heard the squeals of Ned-the-Herd's pig as he was sent flying out from his pigsty so that Ned could clean out the dung from his sty and inspect his shape for next morning when he'd be killing it. They prayed they'd be home in time to get the pig's bladder and race with it round the blue-button field.

They heard a rifle shot echoing over Old Stroller's hayshed and knew that another young rabbit was bleeding and at death's door. They thought of the suffering of Rambling Jack's big pig and the suffering of this little rabbit. They remembered other sufferings too, for the men were always teasing them (getting them to curse and swear) about the sufferings of older children at school and how their own two little arses would soon be getting a fine thrashing from the sally-switch of the school-mistress for not being able to recite their tables. They believed that this very thing was happening to the bigger boys this minute, and they felt it would teach the rascals not to go stealing Old Stroller's gooseberries and not share them with smaller children like themselves.

They came to the gate looking out over the field where a mysterious stranger strolled by one summer's evening and asked the hurlers could he join their sport. These young lads soon witnessed his unbelievable wizardry. They were told that he was no mere mortal but a demon hurler from a kingdom beyond the grave. At sunrise next day, the hurlers ran to the priest's door to ask his blessing. He blessed their hurley-sticks and sent them away with a few buckets of holy water.

They went up to the hurling field and sprinkled the bucket of holy water in the four corners of the field. Little Dan and Battlin' Sal had heard the tale of this strange ghost-hurler a hundred times whilst sitting round the bedtime fire and now they began to shudder and quake – to think that this ghostly hurler might still be in the field inside the ditch and ready to waylay them at a moment's notice. Maybe he'd be sitting on the very next gate, smoking his pipe and shaking his sides with laughter at their childish impudence in walking so far from their own yards. Their legs now grew fresh, and they devoured the road at a most admirable speed.

The morning was turning to noon, and the hill-slopes were rosy with the growing efforts of the sun. They couldn't be too far away from Bog Boundless (they thought) with its carpet of purple heather. They had seen it not only when swimming in the sally hole, but the time they were bringing home the turf in the horse-and-cart with By-Jiggery.

And now they recognized the furze bushes with a buttercup yellowness beginning to show on them. They recognized the ditches too, dripping in the purple, pink and orange of the foxgloves and honeysuckles. The road had turned into a grassy lane and then became a donkey-track with neither a nest for the crows nor a cartwheel track or an ass's footprint to be seen anywhere. The sun played foxy games of hide-and-go-seek with them – one minute appearing above the rusty remains of a long-forgotten cowshed, the next minute disappearing just as suddenly where the tall bushes intertwined.

They were tired by now, having walked their legs off, and they sat on the grass by a gate at the edge of the track. Opposite them was the deserted shack of Old Moonshine, and the yard was a mass of thistles and weeds. The vacant windows seemed sad and lonely whereas, years before there had been children's voices gladdening the hearts of all. A stray wildcat peered out at them from the top of a rusty tar-barrel and looked bemused at the sight of two strange little visitors, but the cat couldn't tell them where next they'd be – at Balaraggin's yard and his bloodstained door.

They soldiered on. The track changed to sloppy mud, and their bare feet and legs took on the colour of tar, and the nettles and thistles grew more and more densely on each side of them. The fairy-folk inside the bushes shook their gloomy heads, and a flock of windy birds suddenly flew out over the ditch and scudded off to the safety of their nests in the fields below them, frantically indicating that they should follow them back to their homes (there was still time) and that nothing but impending darkness lay ahead.

'For the love of sweet Jesus, go home. Ye have reached the Land of Mystery, and there's no room here for small people like ye.'

Neither of them wished to admit that they were afraid. Trampling through the nettles and slapping their bare feet through the bindweed, they continued along the track until it became no track at all. Was this really the end of the world? The two of them could have cried out their fears if only they were old enough to put them into words.

'Oh, that we had been let follow the older children down the road to school. Oh, to be leap-frogging and playing tag in the school field around the bridge. Oh, to be running along the sunny banks of the stream among the pine trees and paddling under Echo Bridge.' All they could hear was the whispering of the fairy-folk penetrating into their frightened hearts and the sinister sounds from snoring ghost like Balaraggin close at hand. If only God would help them. If only He would forgive them for deceiving Dowager and Moll-the-Man and setting off to find Balaraggin's yard and the top of Chieftain Hill and driving the two poor women clean out of their minds with worry.

5

At last they were at Balaraggin's place, and they went inside the yard where Sally (his dead mother) had driven back her ghostly ass-and-car with its rattling chains. They half-expected to see her pouncing out on them and attacking them like a cat playing with little mice. She might put them in her suitcase along with the few possessions she'd come back to take with her and carry them off to the Beyond. But they saw nothing, only the greenflies wandering aimlessly about in the sunshine and singing in the light.

They sat among the briars near the ruins of the dead man's pig house. Next to it was his lopsided hayshed with its rusty roof fallen to the ground like a box-player's bellows and it covered in ivy and dock-leaves big enough to wipe a giant's arse. Round the edge of the yard were the shadows of bony trees and overhanging thorn-bushes, all black and gnarled with age. The yard was covered in nettles and mallows, and straggly dead poppies peeped out between the cracks in the cobblestones. They had never before seen a place like this, and the eerie silence was overpowering.

They gazed at Balaraggin's sad-looking cabin, a grey cobwebby ruin like the hayshed and leaning to one side. Its rafters were open to the heavens, and sickly-looking ferns grew out of the thatch and chimney, and more of them peered out from the broken windows where once there grew boxes of glistening geraniums.

Maybe the ghostly shadows of Balaraggin and his mother were now looking out at the two little wanderers standing there in their yard – a yard that had once been full of glossy hens and geese and the shouts of Balaraggin and his mother, a happy yard once full of their echoing laughter, like their own yards back home.

As if in a dream, the children walked towards the doorway. They had heard the bigger boys' tales of Balaraggin while eating their potato-skins on the ditch. They knew about his cut-throat razor and his dying screams and the tears rising up inside in him and the unforgettable sadness inside him after the death of his mother when she left him behind her, staring thereafter into the miserable darkness of his fireless chimney-space. They knew how the sad man was seen rambling along the moonlit donkey-tracks, drifting from field to field under the pale stars and slowly losing his mind – gentle and kind one minute, cruel and hurtful the next. Hadn't he chased Old Moonshine with the four-grained fork the time the old villain suggested Balaraggin was trying to take his young wife away and carry her into his own bed? And yet, at other times (when Old Moonshine was sticking the black knife into one of his pigs), hadn't Balaraggin gone down to that yard and prayed on his knees for Old Moonshine to spare the poor pig's life – the pig that had never hurt anyone in all its innocent pig's life!

And now the mesmerised children were at the frightful door itself, gazing at the green paint hanging down in long flakes the length of the broken slats and the huge blood-spatters now turned brown, and they were terrified at the sight of it.

This very minute the older children might be reciting their poems far off in the schoolhouse, but these two little ones were now feeling what no book of poems could ever seep into their souls – a sense of utter bewilderment and astonishment. Sunlight had disappeared from their hearts. Darkness and sorrow for poor Balaraggin had taken its place. It was all too much for these two small children to take in – as though they had drifted into the ancient past itself and were listening to the sadness of its music. Around them stood suggestive shapes (but not the spirits of laughter and dancing), and it felt as if these sad spirits were peeping out at them from the withered trees. They might even meet Balaraggin's ghost, the razor in his fist, or hear the sound of his mother's ass-and-car and the rattling chains of her ghost coming across the yard to greet them. They squeezed each other's hands tightly, not knowing whether to proceed on their way or run back home (that's if they could ever find the way again). However, their curiosity held them a little longer, and they tiptoed in past the bloodstained door and into the most uninviting welcoming room in the world, its whitewashed walls all yellow and crumbly, not like their own walls back home.

Inside the doorway was Balaraggin's woodpile, the grass growing up through the woodchips. They made their way across the stone-slabbed floor beneath the overhanging webs of giant spiders. On the wall was the Sacred Heart picture that protects all homes but had failed to do so the dastardly night of the sad man's death when it was most needed. On the nail beside the picture was Balaraggin's rosary beads. They looked around, but there was no sign (thank God) of his cut-throat razor. On the dresser were his mother's hat and cane and her big black boots. They could almost hear the click-clack of her ghostly footsteps as she walked around in her bedroom.

The older children had boasted of their own bravery and had told them how they had climbed out their bedroom window in the dead of night to take the long walk up to Balaraggin's yard, how they'd stood in the moonlight and looked at the bloodstained door before bravely putting their hands down along it – told them how they'd heard not only the rattling ass-and-car and the chains of Balaraggin's mother but heard her opening her press-cupboard drawers in search of her best cardigan for her journey to the Beyond, how they'd seen her ghostly face after she got drowned in Bog Boundless and the unutterable sorrow in it as if it was her doom to spend eternity searching vainly for this cardigan and her other belongings to take away with her in the ass-and-car. A year or two later, they might have told them about the rascally poachers who had played their love-games with her abroad in the fields and fathered Balaraggin himself.

The children's hearts were by now chilled by the icy coldness of Balaraggin's welcoming room, not a single friendly angel to give them a bit of courage. Were any children ever as lonely as this?

Moreover (and now they remembered), they had heard tales of the Wild Witch of the West and could now feel her presence all around them. They had no wings on their legs to help them escape if she came swooping down to seize them and swallow them up. Hadn't many another child been snatched away by the cruel spells of this wild witch? That's what they'd been told. Their childish laughter had disappeared, and huge tears came streaming down their faces.

They stumbled out from the welcoming room and sat in the yard. It was 2 o'clock (the hottest time of the day), and the sky above them was as hot and livid as a bruised eye. Their tears continued to glisten their faces, and their two sets of tightly-gripped fists joined them together like glue. They staggered through the gateway and left behind them the ghosts of Balaraggin's hens and geese and the ghost of Balaraggin when once he was a boy, sitting on his youthful chair in the yard alongside his mother, his concertina resting on his knees. Which way were they to turn? They were sure they were at the end of the world.

6

Lost! Lost! That's what they were. Lost in the heart of the hills. Lost in one of the most forgotten places on earth with not even the song of a blackbird to raise their spirits. Far from their own warm fireside, ravenous with the hunger, their spirits knocked clean out of their bodies, and they sat down to die. Nobody would find them. They were so very young to be dying like this. What was it like to be dead like Father Loveless lying in his box, like Rambling Jack's pig lying in bits in the barrel? It must be a terrible thing. There'd be no more By-Jiggery, no more My-Son-Jack, no more Dowager or Moll-the-Man to chide their little backsides with the broken leg of the chair for their devilment. There'd be no more Lippy or Philly to whom they could tell their tale. They would never get the chance to stand on top of the mighty Chieftain Hill or see the two wild eagles. They feared that these same eagles were now looking down at them from their nest and thinking how these small people had the damnedest impudence to believe they could ever come and visit them on top of their high mountain. They closed their eyes and waited for these eagles to swoop down and fly away with them like they did with the new-born lambs and to carry them out over the ocean.

At last, they knew that Lippy and his brothers were a pack of filthy liars and that not one of them had ever been as far as this. They believed that they'd reached Fairyland where the fairy-folk of their storybooks spent their days beneath the thumb of the Wild Witch of the West. She might be hovering above them this very minute with her broomstick and her army of banshees and boodeemen waiting on her every beck and call.

This day, however, was never going to be quite like a storybook for at this precise moment (the lowest moment in their lives), the Wild Witch of the West was in a nearby field gathering twigs and furze bushes for her fire. Her legendary fierceness was nothing more than a sly old myth spread abroad by the big people to prevent their children wandering too far from the yard. She lived all alone and was more to be pitied than feared.

There had been a time (long ago) when she had been the loveliest young girl and had danced the shoes off of her feet at every crossroads-dance in the hills. Her beauty had spellbound the hearts of many young men, including the youthful Balaraggin.

The day came when the Land of the Silver Dollar sent her the call, and she crossed the seas like many before her. Then the time came for her mother to die and pass on to the Beyond and leave her father behind at the fire, alone and crippled with pains in his knees and an ache in his heart.

She returned to comfort him. And soon, she earned her witchy name as a result of her extraordinary powers in curing the sick of their various ailments. She took to farming her father's land with gusto, as good as any man. She'd carry out bundles of hay on her shoulders to feed his cattle in winter's harshness. She'd follow behind the speeding plough with the horses in early springtime. She'd tram the hay and with her rake would trim the reek in the haggart at harvest time. She'd bawl after her lost cow or goat and chastise her mule when he got himself trapped in the briars.

That was many years ago. She was now too old to work the land, and the hardships of farming were 1000 miles from her, thank God. With the death of her beloved father, she was mistress of his land and had all that she ever wanted from life – her few simple strolls through the silence of the hills, her cottage with the one solitary rose bush blooming its redness in summertime, and her yard which she kept as clean as the driven snow. The land she had sold to the Forestry.

To keep her company in the long hours of the night, she had her beautiful parrot that she'd brought home from the Daffy-Duck Circus with its tail-feathers as long and golden as any cock-pheasant. She had given it the charming name of Goldshit.

And now she heard the sobbing tears of Little Dan and Battlin' Sal, and she stood in her tracks as though she'd heard a goose just caught by a fox. She let fall her bundle of twigs and in her long black skirts hurried to the children, jumping out over the ditches. When they saw this little old woman with her sharp-hatchet face and her bewitching eyes towering above them, it seemed as if she'd stepped out through the walls of the universe.

They knew it – they had come face-to-face with the Wild Witch of the West! The fireside stories of the witch's black pot and the boiling water and the little children eaten alive – these very stories had finally come home to roost, and they wrapped their arms around one another in unimaginable terror and prepared to meet their death.

'Lambkins! Lambkins!' sighed the old woman, and her voice was as welcome as a shower of summer's rain. One minute they were about to meet their death. The next minute they found they were in the presence of their very own guardian angel and their tears took flight. If they were ever to get home alive, there'd be no need to boast how they saw buckets of Balaraggin's blood spattered round his yard. Instead, they'd have the tale of all tales to tell – how their lives were spared by the Wild Witch of the West herself! By now, they had got back all their courage. This was no ordinary witch from the pages of a storybook – a witch who might put them in her pot and gobble them up. They could see the tears in her eyes, feel the tender love welling up inside her as she spoke.

'What have the saints in Heaven brought me this fine day? God-sakes, what a holy fright ye lost souls gave me!'

She reached out her healing hands and stroked away the tears from their cheeks. They threw themselves into her arms, and she wrapped them in her apron, her sympathetic coils of hair around their faces. She almost devoured them with her hot breath before guiding their weary footsteps down the lane, out over the stile and into her yard.

Her cabin was as clean as a new pin and surrounded by apple trees – enough to be eating for the rest of their lives. They entered her welcoming room where a bit of coloured matting covered the cobblestoned floor. They remained huddled together near the half-door, still unsure and ready to make good their escape at the first sign of danger. The Wild Witch of the West lit her oil-lamp and her candles in her candlestick holders. With the lid of her sweet-gallon, she blew up a blaze underneath her furze bushes and threw bits of candles into the flames till it blazed up cheerfully and soon warmed their hearts.

She beckoned them shove in from the half-door and sit by the blaze of her fire. Her cheerfulness banished the last traces of their fear. With a dishcloth, she wiped the black mud from their legs and the tearstains from their eyes. Soon she had the kettle singing on the crane, and she poured them out a mug of tea with a slice of currant-cake, which they pounced on as though they hadn't eaten a bit since Lent. She gave them mountains of bread and jam and then wiped their sticky fingers and faces using the dishcloth once more. No king or queen could have been treated with such cordiality.

The surprise of all surprises then followed when down from the chimney flew the squawking parrot (Goldshit), who had been asleep on a blackened stick that stretched across the upper hob, half-ways up the chimney. In the brightness of the firelight, they could see his magnificent colours (unlike anything they'd ever seen before) and realized how he got his name and how his beauty contrasted with the withered features of the old woman. A strange whispering conversation (like a long-drawn-out litany in some foreign tongue) now took place between the parrot and the Wild Witch of the West. And for the next few minutes, Little Dan and Battlin' Sal might as well have been back in Balaraggin's yard or above on the moon.

Thanks to the old woman's coaxing, Goldshit was no longer afraid of the children and sat himself on a lower perch by the side of the fire. He edged from one end of the stick to the other to make himself more comfortable and to warm his feathers but, bit by bit, he began to sway, and his dreamy eyes began to close till he fell sound asleep. His dignified dreamland was soon shattered when he overbalanced and fell from his perch, landing with a scream into the middle of the fire.

Such a commotion then filled the room that it must surely have been heard back at Sheep's Cross as Goldshit staggered out of the hot ashes like a drunken old man, his feathers scorched for the 100th time.

The Wild Witch of the West got herself into a thundering rage and (losing her gentle voice) swiped at her dazed parrot with her dish-cloth. 'God-sakes, will ye look at Goldshit, that shitty little article – he's at it again!' She chased him round the floor with her tongs as though she would beat the daylights out of him. 'He'll get himself burnt to a cinder,' she said. Then her mood changed, and she laughed till the tears ran down her jaw. Goldshit could hardly have escaped from her for he was trapped at the half-door where he looked very foolish and dazed.

This merry little game between the parrot and the old woman was played out a number of times during the next half-hour. The children had seen little birds caught in winter cages in the yard for them to look at before setting them free to fly away. But the sight of the magnificent Goldshit sitting on a black stick under the hob above the blazing fire and then falling asleep and tumbling off his perch and landing in the hot ashes and then struggling with the blazing sods of turf in the fire and the Wild Witch of the West chasing him round the floor – this was something that would stay with them forever.

Sensing the ever-present danger of Goldshit falling into her skillet of cabbage, the old woman continued to chide her pet.

'Is this what I reared you for?' Finally, she picked him up in her arms (all the time fondling and stroking him) and marched him off to his cage in her bedroom. She put a towel around the cage, and he became quiet as a mouse for the rest of the evening. She took her lid from off the burner and waved it at her young guests.

She shook her head and sighed, 'That bleddy old eejit, Goldshit – what a nuisance-of-a-bird he is these days!' Then she looked down into the depths of the burner. 'I have often been tempted to put him in the pot and boil him with the spuds and cabbage.'

Like all grown-ups, she was a terrible liar, for Little Dan and Battlin' Sal could see how dearly she loved her beautiful Goldshit and how afraid she was of ever losing him in the fire. They could also see that by falling asleep and all the time tumbling off of his stick, Goldshit must be very old and have very poor balance. They felt he was as many years on this earth as the old woman herself.

7

In spite of the layers of currant-cake and the bread and jam, in spite of the comical antics of Goldshit, the two little children had become aware of the sun beginning to fade in the sky and an increasing darkness creeping its way in through the half-door from the overcast trees of the haggart. Fairy voices in the yard were whispering to them to hurry home before the late afternoon turned into evening.

The Wild Witch of the West sensed the growing uneasiness in their empty eyes. She knew it was unusual for children to spend the day running around the secret haunts of the countryside but even worse for these little ones to be seen roaming round the world in the dark. Why hadn't she thought of it before? Poor Dowager and Moll-the-Man would be out of their minds with worry, thinking how their children might be lost and unable to find their way home. Waiting at the half-door, their eyes would be grainy from looking out for them and wondering if they had got trapped in a bog-hole or caught in the briars inside Fort Dangerous. They'd be combing the dykes and the thistle field in search of them. By-Jiggery and My-Son-Jack would be running in panic along the banks of the river in a demented search for them.

The old woman went to the half-door. The tops of the hill-slopes were shot through with the last of the red sunset. The pine trees were painted with the sun's very last rays, and her own dusky yard was almost hidden in the inky clouds of night-time. She put on her coat and old bonnet against the chill of the evening. She took the two of them by the hand and hurried with them to the orchard. She climbed into the nearest tree and twisted several apples and threw them down. With their pockets full of apples, they were as excited as ever they'd been and even more delighted when the good creature said she'd walk them back home.

She threw a mug of water onto the fire so that the place wouldn't catch fire when she was gone and that Goldshit wouldn't get himself burnt. She closed the front door and put the key in the geranium box. The three of them (the wind filling their chests and their feet scarcely touching the ground) set off for the Hills-of-the-Past and home. Not another soul was stirring – just the three of them and their echoing feet thumping down the lane and out onto the road. The little explorers were more than glad of the old woman's company as she knew all the lanes and roads like the back of her hand. When darkness came, she'd have the eyes of a fox to lead them down past Sheep's Cross and out onto the creamery road.

The watery moon had risen from its hiding-place behind the pine trees. The children went skipping their way ahead of the old woman, and she could hardly keep up with them since the wings had now returned to their feet. They could see the town's blue gaslights sparkling merrily in the darkness of the valley below. The ghostly whispers of *the night fairies* encouraged them, and a trace of merriment (even though they were sick with tiredness) warmed their hearts. Oh, to be coming home! Oh, to be no longer lost! What tales they'd have to tell! What great big lies they'd have to tell! Tales of Balaraggin's ghost, who had stared out at them from his window and how they heard the rattling chains of the ass-and-car and how Balaraggin and his mother were seen having their tea in the haggart and how the two ghosts took the scrub-brush and wiped away the spatters of blood from off of the green door. The lies would come trotting out of their mouths for the next week-and-a-half!

Dowager and Moll-the-Man (By-Jiggery and My-Son-Jack too) had already worn away their knees from saying decades of the rosary on their beads. They had prayed to Saint Anthony (the patron saint of anything lost), and he had listened to their prayers for, with both their ears cocked, they at last heard the bare feet of Little Dan and Battlin' Sal staggering in across the flagstones.

'Ye little fairymen – what on earth kept ye – where on earth have ye been till this hour of the night?' The two women, their faces red with pleasure, their eyes full of happy tears and their arms outstretched, ran across the yard to meet the mighty ramblers. Dowager wrapped her locks of hair around her little man, and Moll-the-Man lifted Battlin' Sal to the sky. They were like two old hens that had found their lost chicks.

The Wild Witch of the West (the children's saviour from the mountains) came puffing and panting in the gate and (for what seemed an absolute age) herself, and the two women were seen whispering excitedly. The conversation was far above their heads, but the children could see the agitated frown-lines crossing the faces of Dowager and Moll-the-Man and their fingers twisting and fidgeting continuously. Then (what none of us had ever seen before, for physical affection had never been demonstrated among our people) Moll-the-Man and Dowager grasped the old woman in their arms and hugged her half to death. She was startled and confused by the hugs, and she wiped a little bit of tearful wind from the corner of her eye. She had saved the lives of these two small adventurers for, without her timely rescue and the currant-cake and the bread and jam and the distractions of Goldshit, they might well have found themselves dead or carried off by the two wild eagles.

Turning to the children, Dowager and Moll-the-Man explained in words of crystal clearness the terrible dangers that could have killed the pair of them – the unseen fairy creatures and the wild unlicensed bulls and the two wild eagles. The shamefaced little adventurers (having been at first more than joyful to be home) were almost as unhappy now as when they'd been thinking of the boiling cauldron supposedly bubbling in the cabin of the Wild Witch of the West. And they vowed with all their hearts they'd never go rambling again.

Moll-the-Man invited the mountainy woman to take a cut of her soda-cake and a mouthful of tea, which she politely refused. Instead, she placed her hands on the children's shoulders and gave them a last fond look from her loving eyes, to be remembered forevermore as it flew from her eye and into theirs. Prodded by Dowager and Moll-the-Man, they shook her hand in gratitude, knowing that what had started out as a childish adventure had almost turned into a terrible disaster.

Then (almost abruptly) the Wild Witch of the West's black figure turned roundabout and, like a lively puff of chimney-smoke, she swooped away out the half-door and was gone! Her black skirts rustling, she hurried back towards her Land of Mystery and not once did she look back. The last the children saw of her was at the shoulder of the road near Shy Dennis's shack where she got sucked away into the Hills-of-the-Past. They could hear the echo of her boots behind her as the last twilight melted into night and the day finally closed into cloister-quietness. This old saviour of the day would be tired and weary, and (sad to say) she'd be feeling as lonesome as a lost lamb before she reached her front door and Goldshit.

Inside, in Moll-the-Man's welcoming room, the plates were laid out, and there was a fresh smell of the melting juices of cabbage, boiled spuds and turnips. Little Dan and Battlin' Sal licked their lips in anticipation. In spite of their feasting at the table of the Wild Witch of the West, they were so ravenous that they could have eaten a bag of horse nails, their appetite having been stimulated by the cold air which always fills the mountains, but more so by their unadulterated fear throughout the day. They emptied the plates and washed the food down with two or three mugs of milk, followed by further mugfuls of spring-water.

There was a moment or two of silence in which they realized what they had done. To have caused such worry and anxiety to Dowager and Moll-the-Man and the two big men and not to have let anyone know or sought anyone's permission before setting out on their foolish quest – this had been their first great sin, and Father Honesty would have to be told all about it (said Dowager) in his confession box a year or two from now.

It was the end of a memorable day. Dowager took Little Dan out into Moll-the-Man's yard and waved a hurried goodbye. Moll-the-Man and By-Jiggery closed the half-door and the big door behind it, sending away the darkness. The lamp and the candles were lit, and the rosary beads were taken out for prayers.

Dowager had to carry Little Dan the short distance down the road. She filled her warming-jar with hot water from the kettle and (something she had never done before) she placed it not inside her own blankets but in the sheets of her little son's bed. He crept gratefully into his nest, and for once, he forgot to say his prayers at his bedside. He was soon in a mountainous sleep.

A minute later, My-Son-Jack came in after fruitlessly searching for the children. He gazed down at his sleeping little brother and thanked God for this day's miracle. Then he went out to ease himself before retiring for the night. He listened again to the gentle sighing of the winds through the haggart pine trees and watched the clouds climbing across the moon. Inside, in the welcoming room, the night had given way to the dancing firelight, and the warmth of safety and comfort had returned.

Behind the Hills-of-the-Past and even further beyond (in the heart of her untouched wilderness), the Wild Witch of the West was struggling onwards the last few strides. She entered her yard and looked up at the millions of stars across the black heavens, so very far away. They seemed to be winking down at her, acknowledging the noble way she had saved the lives of two small souls. Wearily, she opened her door with the key. The rescuer of young lambkins was back in the peaceful quiet of her comfortable little nest. She was back with Goldshit, the droopy companion she could always depend on. She lit the yellow oil-lamp, and it threw a petal of cheerful light around her welcoming room. Later, she merged herself down into her small bed beneath her five blankets.

'God is good! God is great!' she sighed, and soon she melted into the black pool of a blissful sleep, her forefinger resting on her motionless lip.

In the long-winded days that followed, it seemed as though the entire population of Tipperary was full of the news – how two small children met the Wild Witch of the West. Lippy and his brothers were fit to burst with rage, so great was their envy. Nothing could ever again compare with the bravery of this daring adventure into the realms of the Wild Witch of the West. Not since Adam and Eve had there been so great an expedition, and to think that Little Dan and Battlin' Sal had come back alive to tell the tale of it!

For the rest of the week, their exaggeration and downright lies ran away with them as they told every blessed soul (in a language that stuttered in fits and starts) how they had almost reached Galway and the very gates of Heaven and the ocean itself. Even the mighty Chieftain Hill and the splatters of blood on Balaraggin's green door had to take second place to all their tales.

For many days to come, two small children were seen parading up and down the creamery road, their chests sticking out like a pair of proud turkeycocks. But, back in Balaraggin's yard, if you had been up there and found yourself looking in through the bars of the gate, it was a far different story. Just inside the gate, you would see two little streams of yellow poolie, where Little Dan and Battlin' Sal (our two frightened little wanderers) had severely wet their britches.

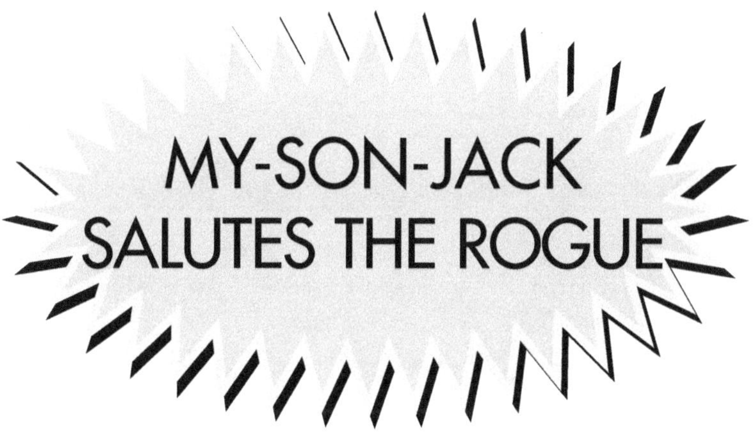
MY-SON-JACK
SALUTES THE ROGUE

1

My-Son-Jack rubbed the sleep from his eyes. As early as five o'clock (long before any cockerel crew or a beam of light had slipped through the window) he was lying awake underneath the blankets, listening to the incessant rain coming in from Kerry and in across the woods of Lisnagorna and making its dreary descent among us. The black night would soon be carved open, and out of it would come the dawn and after that would come the various sounds of the little birds in the trees, and the farmyard fowl would join them a minute later, chorusing faster and faster even before leaving their roost. Then the daylight would lighten and throw a white sheet across the back wall of the big cave room that separated himself from the hen house. And only then would the cockerel (Rampant) crow and crow until he was as hoarse as an old drake.

Half-an-hour later, Dowager was seen disappearing out the half-door, even before her son had time to reach for his britches on the bed-rail or put his nose out the bedroom door. She was just in time to watch the faint light of the moon disappearing and taking with it the half-hearted stars. Such precious moments as these were the best time in her daily life. She was just like her sentimental son and loved these unreal mysteries in her world – the times when she was on her own and in her private small fairyland of half-hidden shapes among the surrounding trees, when she was listening to the lively music of her yard's ever-rolling stream, now heavy with flood-water from the black night's rain.

She emptied her piss-pot onto the ash-pit behind the pig house and waddled down the yard towards her hen house. She removed the big stone that protected it. She carefully inspected and counted her 30 hens and her 12 ducks (her geese slept in the cowshed these days). The hens were well-used to her arrival and greeted her sleepily as always, and the ducks muttered their annoyance and un-tucked their heads reluctantly. Neither the fox nor the weasel had come to greet them during the night, and the old woman blessed herself as usual.

Making her way back to the welcoming room, she noticed how the blackbirds and the jackdaws were already making a day of it, scuffing with their beaks amidst the yard's debris. Not to be outshone by the likes of them, the little robin was giving air to his own energetic notes in among the silver spider-webs on the pig-house fuchsia bushes. Even before Dowager had reached the half-door, those hitherto unfriendly ducks had beaten the hens to the yard and were already dabbling their webbed feet in the stormy waters of the stream.

She almost bumped into her big son, who had, at last, made his way guiltily in and out from the pig house gap at the upper end of the yard and was carrying on his back a sack of logs, twigs and thorny bushes for the day's first fire. The two of them went in the half-door silently, and with the broken bits of candle, they started to tend to the fire. And then My-Son-Jack took the two buckets to the well for the first of the day's six buckets of water.

Today was going to be the day when he would see to his rods and tackle and his jam-jar of fresh maggots. He had made plans for a day's fishing-trip with his young brother, Little Dan (20 years his junior), and to add to his education. From the moment he woke up, his mind had been full of the fine fishing the two of them were going to do. He'd make sure that Little Dan's shoulders would carry his own small fishing-rod, cut from a hazel-tree before they reached the bank of the river.

Following the night's non-stop rain, the river would have lost its smooth-sliding look and be swollen to the gills with flood-water from the Hills-of-the-Past as well as the odd branch from trees trying to hold her back. The brown trout would rise to the surface to get themselves a breath of fresh air, and our two fishermen would be there at the river's edge to greet them with their fishhooks.

The art of fishing and My-Son-Jack were inseparable, like two sides of a windowpane, and he loved nothing better than to sit on the bank of the river and look down at those big brown trout and see the way they looked back up at him. He loved the closeness of the hunter and the hunted. His mother would never go short of a bite to eat as long as he could slip his rod and line into a river.

There were times, however, when he went fishing in places where Mother Nature was not their mistress but where the laws of Lord Elegance prevailed – inside in the privacy of His Lordship's ornamental lake where he saw the finest of trout during the early evening when the mayfly and swarming midges were at their busiest on the lake's surface.

This present week, he'd been down at the graveyard paying homage to his dear father (Warbling Will) and kneeling on the spot where the good man had been buried. Over the last ten years, it had always been the same story – to the day and to the hour, if not the minute. At 4 o'clock, he'd kneel on the grass with his prayers and rosary beads, making this a private pilgrimage to the man who had been the best of fathers before coughing up the last bits of his liver inside in the hospital at that very hour (4 o'clock).

Always the finest of singers, he had sung his last farewell verses (*The Bird in the Gilded Cage*) to the doctors and nurses that gathered at the doorway. The other patients rose up from their beds and drew near his bedhead to hear him sing his last quavering song. The only thing missing was his battered old concertina that would lie forevermore dusty above the hob back home. It would have broken any man's heart to see such sorrow for the loss of so fine a father and husband as Warbling Will. Enough said.

Having paid his respects, My-Son-Jack tore himself away from the graveside and hopped in over the wire fence leading to Lord Elegance's lake. He stood there alone with his thoughts, looking at the black Japanese swans sleeping beneath the willow trees in the last of the day's sunshine. He gazed at the pintail ducks and the foreign-looking geese from Canada and Egypt and watched those huge trout as they leapt dolphin-like into the air in their search for the plentiful gnats. He smiled to himself, for he knew something none of these trout knew – that the greatest of all the trout was a fish called the Rogue. Rambling Jack and Dowager's brother (Saddle-the-Pony) had seen this monster-of-a-fish (perhaps the two of them were just a little bit drunk) leaping a foot out of the water and with a size on him the length of your wellingtons (they said). The Rogue, however, didn't live in Lord Elegance's lake but a mile up along the river.

2

Little Dan was playing with his coloured cards on the upturned ass-and-car in the yard. He knew nothing about this great big fish or the fact that this very afternoon his big brother would lead him a mile upstream through the tangled reeds to that secret cavern known as the Big Hole where the Rogue held sway over his minions.

Although he was looking forward to this fishing encounter, My-Son-Jack couldn't get the thought out of his head – how this cunning rascal-of-a-fish had broken Saddle-the-Pony's best hazel rod to pieces. He knew he'd need a wrestling arm's strength in his own struggle with this mighty fish, that it was a battle he simply had to win – for the sake of his little brother, his new fishing companion.

He had been planning a long time to take the little fellow on this fishing trip and feel the refreshing breezes of nature seeping into him from all the majestic scenes he'd be seeing along the riverbank. The little lad would carry home the echo of the river's music and fill his bedtime dreams with pictures of the muddy trout that spent their lives playing beneath the water's surface in the Big Hole. But first of all (and with the sun trying to eat away the last of the mist), the cows had to be milked.

Even before he could reach for his coat, Little Dan had already loosened himself from his sleep and into his wellingtons at the half-door. Before Dowager had time to get to her two sons and dowse them with the holy water, the morning breezes were already washing their two cheeks as they headed down the creamery road under the gloomy trees and on towards John's Gate and the bull-paddock. Though My-Son-Jack loved to walk barefooted through the morning grass and feel the dew between his toes (a sure cure for corns and bunions, he said), there was no time this fishing day to take off their wellingtons and let the coldness climb up their legs, no time to look up at the battle between the clouds and the sun.

The big man was thinking how his cows hadn't yet eaten all the mushrooms that had grown overnight amidst the spider-webs, thinking of his mother's big frying pan too. He was thinking of one or two fine trout lying on their back in the middle of that same pan, and the dab of butter and plenty of salt thrown in around the fish, and the melting juices of the fish mingled with these bull-paddock mushrooms and the whole meal washed down with a mug of hot milk and pepper. It put a smile on his face. He sat his little brother in the shelter of the oak tree. The cows were stirred out of their dreamland and came loping towards them.

As soon as they had closed the gate, they led the lazy-eyed creatures up the road and into the cowshed, their breath pouring out of them in a fog of steam. In no time, the milk was streaming into the buckets of My-Son-Jack and his mother. The two rascals kept Little Dan busy, hopping from one leg to the other, as they laughingly squirted streams of warm milk into his face. Now that his other big brothers and sister were all at school, his mother got the little fellow to say his counting numbers while she was milking (he was well past 100 by now) and a few of his *God Bless* prayers and to repeat his former nursery rhymes and maybe sing a verse of *I have a bonnet trimmed in blue*. The longer he went on singing (said My-Son-Jack), the more milk they'd get from the cows. Then they drained their heavy buckets through the muslin cloth and into the tank, and the three of them went back to the welcoming room.

3

The children of Moll-the-Man and By-Jiggery had always been fond of My-Son-Jack. What a fine healthy bunch they were, an air of the tomboy about each of them. The youngest child (Battlin' Sal) was not old enough to take the 3-mile trek to Dang-the-skin-of-it's schoolhouse whereas Lippy, Philly, Young Jim and Zeppity had their heads down on the desk every blessed day trying to get the sums and dictation into their heads. But this was Saturday, and they came padding in across Dowager's yard and up through the pig house gap where My-Son-Jack was chopping up logs from the wood-stack. They watched him laying siege to the timber. By now, he had worked himself into a great ball of sweat.

Seeing them, he stopped to wipe his brow. To tell the truth, he was enjoying his work far more than he would have imagined when he'd staggered out of bed earlier in the day. He piled some of the smaller logs into the arms of his little brother and Battlin' Sal and told them to fire them in under Dowager's stool near the fireplace. She would now be able to keep up a blazing fire for boiling her spuds and cabbages (he said) and for feeding her two pigs and the fowl.

There was a great big heap of sliced logs lying higgledy-piggledy in the sawdust. The older children, anxious to get their teeth into more work, rushed over to My-Son-Jack. He gave them a few weighty armfuls and told them to make a wood-stack near the pig-house wall and show him the mettle of their arms. It was a job they got to grips with only too well.

As a reward for their labours, he took from his pocket a package of fags. They were made of stronger tobacco than his usual Woodbine fags and stronger too than the fag-buts that children everywhere stole from their father's canister to smoke in Old Sam's orchard.

He laid two of the fags on the chopping block and with his penknife, divided them into four halves. The boys sat down beside him against the pig-house wall with their arms folded across their knees. He lit up the four fag-halves and handed three of them to Lippy, Philly and Young Jim, keeping the fourth one for himself.

The boys energetically puffed and coughed on their strange new fags. They watched the fag-smoke rise up in lavish plumes and float off over the wood-stack in little wisps. From time to time they sucked their cheeks inwards and breathed in and out through their nostrils like My-Son-Jack. In spite of themselves, they were soon swallowing huge heaps of smoke. They closed their eyelids as if nothing strange was happening to them, but their eyes began rolling round in their heads. My-Son-Jack (the rascal) was chuckling to himself. But he capped off the morning's smoking (for his heart was as soft as a bog) by teaching them to make wide circles with their lips and form smoke-rings. They were soon making bigger rings than himself. The art of smoking had turned out to be a tremendous success, and everybody began to laugh, and the little ones clapped their hands excitedly.

4

The gathering at the woodpile was suddenly interrupted by the clanging of Moll-the-Man's tin tray against her flagstones. In times of emergency, this tray was her natural weapon, acting as a warning for her children to hasten home at rabbit-speed. Sometimes it was just a ruse of hers – to put an end to her rascally children galloping all over the countryside and to bring them back for the most mundane of tasks such as shovelling out the dung from the stable. But they had already dealt with this task the day before last, and the stable was as shiny as a church window. However, it still needed a few cartloads of ferns from Bog Wood to make the ass's stable-bed as comfortable as Lord Elegance's.

With a skip and a jump, Lippy led his brothers back home from the woodpile and out into the thistle field where their dull-blinking ass (Short-Arse) was chewing his way through a few choice nettles. With the reins and blinkers safely on him, they returned to the yard.

They backed him in under the shafts of the ass-and-car and harnessed him tightly with the bellyband. By-Jiggery had made the sharply-pointed stakes for the four corners of the car, and he carefully handed two sharp billhooks to Lippy and Philly to use when the time came for them to cut down today's heap of ferns.

Before they could head off to Bog Wood, their mother ran out after them and fingered the sign-of-the-cross on their foreheads and also on the head of Short-Arse before he made his sluggish way out of the yard. They left Battlin' Sal behind and took their way down the creamery road.

Bog Wood was one of Lord Elegance's private realms. The ferns were more than plentiful in there, and the children could bring home load after load on poor old Short-Arse. Like His Lordship's ornamental lake, Bog Wood was a place forbidden to everyone. In the eyes of young Zeppity (who had never been down there before this day), it was another secret part of childhood fairyland.

Once September came round and the season of hay-and-wheat was finished, and all that our men had to think about was killing the pig and worrying about the harsh winter ahead and the job of warming the family fireside - that's when Lord Elegance would open up Bog Wood to everybody to go and collect their kindling and chop up the fallen branches.

However, it was still August, and one or two farmers (including My-Son-Jack) were making stealthy raids on it after dusk and loading up the ass-and-car with as much ferns as they could. Their animals' winter bedding would be made a bit more comfortable by topping the usual rough corn-stalks with this soft touch of Lord Elegance's greenery. With all this urgency about bringing home the ferns, you'd think it was a palace that men had in mind for the likes of their animals!

5

Meanwhile, having listened to Saddle-the-Pony's dispute with the Rogue and the way the monster had broken his rod, My-Son-Jack was anxious to make tracks to the riverbank with Little Dan and make him aware of the importance of a fishing day. He was sitting at the breakfast table and swallowing down a huge mouthful of bread and butter and licking clean the edge of his knife when he harmlessly let slip how there was a fish of monstrous size living in the Big Hole less than a mile from Echo Bridge – a fish that none but the mightiest of hunters could ever try to catch. Then came the solemn pause in his voice and after that came the great big lie when he told his little brother that he had made several attempts at catching this fish but had failed every time.

'This monster is called the Rogue, and he's the king of all the fishes in Tipperary,' said he. He gulped down his tea without so much as batting an eyelid.

'We must catch him! We must!' yelled Little Dan, jumping up from the table and forgetting the spoon in his upturned egg.

'And let me tell you this,' went on My-Son-Jack, 'three fine hazel rods this wicked fish has smashed on me (and this was an even bigger lie), and he is well-named the Rogue. Last year he damned near pulled me into the Big Hole and was about to swallow me when Saddle-the-Pony came and rescued me in the nick of time.' There wasn't the trace of a smile on his rascally lips. He should have been performing on the Dublin stage. Was there ever a man in all Ireland who could lie like My-Son-Jack?

Little Dan saw My-Son-Jack get up from the table and go into the big cave room. He reached behind the bedpost for what he called *the medicine* – his two hazel rods, just in case one of them was to get broken by the huge fish. His little brother forgot his other daily niceties, such as feeding the ducks and hens with his mother and trying to draw a picture of her face on the flagstones. Everything else was cast aside, and his little heart was pounding like a rabbit's.

He clutched at his big brother's sleeve, 'Ye'll let me go fishing, won't ye, Jack?'

The big fellow gave him an unusually threatening look. 'I might take ye with me, I just might – but only if ye're as quiet as a mouse.'

He saw the fretful trace of doubt creeping into Little Dan's face. He bent down gently and threw him up on his shoulders and spun him round and around the room. The little lad finally knew that they were both going on this very special fishing-hunt – a great big hunt for the king of all the fishes inside in the Big Hole and that it would be a glorious day's outing.

Dowager was standing beside her two sons. She was thinking (just like My-Son-Jack) about her big frying pan and the trout and the mushrooms that were going to fill it.

She followed him into the big cave room and threw open the lid of the piano (Old Harpy) that Lady Friendly had bequeathed her on her deathbed and which nobody ever played. Inside the lid was where she stored her icing sugar and her nutmeg and other spices, as well as her flour. She pulled out a large satchel. She blew the dust off of it and wiped it clean of its flour-stains before handing it to Little Dan. She had been planning to use it as a future school-bag when he'd be trotting off to join up with the other scholars.

'I'm relying on you, mee little hunter,' said she, 'to fill this great big satchel with the silver-bellied trout and to bring them back to me this evening.' Her little son was only too ready to obey her commands, and he snatched the satchel from her. He knew what he would have to do – obey his big brother's instructions at all times so that they'd catch the king of the fishes, and My-Son-Jack knew that they'd need the patience of a saint if they were to snare the Rogue and a few of his fishy friends. How else were they going to fill a great big satchel like the one Little Dan was now going to carry?

6

Beyond the woodpile and close to Simple Simon's ditch, there was a pile of stale manure that had been gathering from as far back as anyone could remember. Each springtime, My-Son-Jack would skim the top off of it and fork out the sharp-smelling matter and shovel it into the horse-and-cart before taking it across the fields for spreading. This monstrous slimy mess was known as the African Sink, and its blue mire stank to high heavens. It was rich, however, in the number of oily maggots deep down in its middle. Little Dan had been warned never to go near it. If he climbed up on top of it (said Dowager), his two legs would be swept out from under him by a family of wicked spirits who were far deadlier than the boodeeman, and he'd be sucked down into darkest Africa (wherever that was) and be swallowed up by the Monster-of-all-monsters, the Devil. A child of almost four didn't need to be told this story more than once!

From the haggart-stick, Little Dan stood looking at the African Sink, holding onto his mother's hand with the grip of death and watching his big brother at work. My-Son-Jack had brought out a large jam-jar, and he drove his four-grained fork repeatedly into the dung around the edges of the African Sink, trying to bayonet his way through its fermenting fumes and find the best possible maggots for this day's work.

Finally, he saw what he was looking for (a huge heap of maggots), and he picked out the longest and thickest ones. Some were blue, and some were pink like the chickweed blooms amid the little farm's potato-stalks, and they glistened and wriggled around his wellingtons. He soon had a big pile of them.

'Food for the line that's going to hook the Rogue,' he laughed, thinking how these maggots would herald a rich day's fishing for himself and Little Dan.

The jam-jar began to fill up nicely with his selected maggots. He looked across at the little fellow and showed him the wrigglers swarming like the pile of twisted rabbit-guts whenever Dowager was cleaning out her rabbits at the front table.

Meanwhile, she was kept busy chasing away the inquisitive hens that had followed her out from the yard and were scurrying round her son's wellingtons in search of the odd maggot he might let drop.

If there was one thing Little Dan feared (apart from a long list of leprechauns, boodeemen, and Fort Dangerous), it was the sight and touch of a maggot. At potato-picking time, his big brother was up to his usual devilment, pelting maggots at him when he least expected it – simply to hear him pour down on his head those foul curses that he'd learnt from the visiting card-players. Then the row would rise up as the pious and holy nature of Dowager attempted to prevail against her big son.

'Is it for Heaven or Hell that I'm to rear this child? How can I make a saint out of him if this is the way ye're going to blackguard his innocence?'

And now, seeing how the little dreamer had wandered off from the African Sink towards the safer puddles and how he was gazing down into the reflections of the clouds, the wily rascal picked out the juiciest maggot and fired it at Little Dan's head. And whatever bird, hen, duck or insect happened to be nearby, they were surely frightened out of their lives by the sheer profundity of the curses (*'feck! feck! and feck ye again, Jack!'*) that the little fellow rained down on the head of his big brother. And while My-Son-Jack had a pain in his side from his fit of laughter, Dowager was far from amused ('Will this bleddy eejit ever learn to watch what he's doing – himself and his stupid maggots?'), and she walked away in disgust.

My-Son-Jack put the jam-jar of maggots into his coat pocket. He checked the flexibility of his two rods and also his tin for the soundness and suitability of his fishhooks.

Ruffling his little brother's curls, he took him by the hand and said, 'Let two-men-of-us go hunt the trout and bring back the king of the fishes to Dowager and put a smile back on her angry face.'

However, there was something missing (Little Dan's fishing-rod). My-Son-Jack noticed one or two dark clouds appearing over the little fellow's eyebrows.

'Did ye make me a fishing-rod?" he asked. His big brother was stung by his own forgetfulness and assured him that he'd have a fishing-rod before they were at Echo Bridge. After a quick dash of holy water, the two hunters set forth and headed for the Briary Stile, which would lead them to the river and the Big Hole.

7

Meanwhile, Moll-the-Man's children were busy too in their quest for ferns. They had got as far as the entrance to Bog Wood. They spent the whole time looking anxiously around them to see if Lord Elegance was about to spring out and seize them by the throat before they could open and replace the wire fence behind them. Zeppity and his vivid imagination began to see several changes among the trees.

He believed that messages were being passed along from tree to tree by the woodland fairies. 'The children are coming! Short-Arse-the-ass is coming! They are here! They are here!'

His big brothers set to work, and (as with their handling of My-Son-Jack's pile of logs) they were soon showing the stout mettle in their arms as they stacked the ferns higher and higher in the ass-and-car, filling the four corners first. Quicker than you'd think, they tied the reins criss-cross over the finished load and led Short-Arse out to the Easy Tree – the tree where children from days gone by made their first attempts at tree-climbing when they were coming home from school.

A few paces away from them flowed the majesty of the river, beckoning them to come down and cool their aching bodies. Thanks to the floodwater that followed the recent rains, the river was deeper than usual and had risen even higher than Lippy's knees. They took off their short britches, and the four of them began paddling about in their shirts underneath the echoing bridge and its dappled shadows. It was like a bit of paradise to them, and it wasn't long before they started cupping their hands and firing water into one another's eyes. Then, in case their shirts got soaking wet, and their mother had to lay into them with the yard-brush, Lippy gave the order to remove these obstacles. And without a stitch of clothing on them, they entirely forgot their good manners, making grabs at the privacies between one another's legs before falling in a heap and screaming abuse and foul language to the heavens above. What Short-Arse-the-ass thought of all this rude rascality has never been recorded. Asses were never so impolite as this.

Old Slipperslapper, with her ass-and-car, was crossing the bridge on her way home from town when, suddenly, the boys ran out from their hidey-hole and saluted her most regally. They brazenly showed her their backsides before giving her dazed old eyes the full manifestation of their private regalia. The poor old soul clung onto her bonnet and almost died of fright at this manly gesture. She gave a fierce lash with her ash-plant to the misfortunate back of her startled ass (Flat-foot) and sped on.

It had all been laughter and smiles up till now. But even in these children's newly-found paradise, a touch of boredom was likely to creep in and raise its ugly head. The children recalled the story of the biblical baptism of Jesus that had recently been taught them at school.

Lippy shouted out, 'Hey, Philly! – it's time for Zeppity to get himself baptized in the river Jordan,' and he made a sudden rush at his delicate little brother. Philly, sensing that this was going to prove a bit of further amusement, joined in with his older brother. They took a leg apiece of their terrified little brother (you'd think Zeppity was a turkey's wishbone!) and tipped him upside-down above the river. You could hear the little fellow's shrieks above at Sheep's Cross.

'One – two – three!'

They ducked his head repeatedly under the water and held him down for as long as they thought fit. It was a miracle he didn't drown, what with the gallons of water he was swallowing. He must have had half-a-dozen fishes inside in his belly!

'Ye basthards! Ye basthards from Hell!' was all that poor Zeppity could stammer as he eventually freed himself and fled from the river. He snatched up his shirt and britches and, not bothering to put them on, raced up the road in the direction of his home and his saviour – his mother. With blinding tears running down his cheeks, he fled past Slipperslapper and her ass. This second bout of his nakedness ruined her day completely, and she'd be sitting up in the bed for half the night thinking about it.

My-Son-Jack had been busy cutting Little Dan his first fishing-rod from a clump of hazels at John's Gate when he saw the hasty flight of Zeppity. The little boy had the look of a demented pig after its slaughter.

'The basthards have just baptized me in the river Jordan,' he cried. He was shivering from head to toe with cold and fear. My-Son-Jack helped him into his britches, and Little Dan helped him into his shirt so that Zeppity was decent-looking enough by the time they'd finished with him. But his little heart was still trembling like a lost lamb when Slipperslapper and her averted eyes raced on past, her whip still leathering into the confused back of poor demented Flat-foot.

'Ye'll get a fishing rod, Zeppity. I'll cut it for ye meeself if it's the last thing I do,' said My-Son-Jack angrily. 'And I'll tell ye something else – ye'll spend the rest of today fishing with the two of us. By God-in-Heaven, won't yeer lousy brothers be the scalded cats when they see ye coming into the yard this evening and the fine fishes ye'll be bringing home to yeer mother and father?'

By now his brothers realized the terror they had struck into him, and they called a halt to their river merriment. In silence, they put on their shirts and britches. They led Short-Arse out onto the road and headed up towards John's Gate. They were just in time to see three noble hunters lightly tripping down the hill towards them in the shape of My-Son-Jack and Little Dan and ('do our eyes deceive us?') their little brother, Zeppity. Without so much as a look or a word, the three fishermen past them by. Zeppity (how quickly children seem to forget their wounds!) was no longer shuddery but had a fresh smile on his face and held his nose in the air. As soon as they reached the Briary Stile, My-Son-Jack turned around and shouted up the road.

'Ye'll be wetting yeer britches tonight when By-Jiggery gets a hold of ye. Yes, by God, yeer legs will be red raw from the fine belting he'll give each of ye.' Such steely talk was uncommon from a kind-hearted soul like My-Son-Jack. But it was no laughing matter the way they had half-drowned their little brother and the poor child not yet old enough to defend himself, and he vowed he'd never offer them a single one of his half-fags again.

All the children's good work in Bog Wood now counted for nothing. The shame-faced crew struggled sadly up the road and into the yard, their eyes staring down at their toes. They were just in time for the bit of dinner and the loaded plates of champ and mugs of milk.

Whilst they were coming up the road, they had had time to think about what they'd done. No fools, they had made a pact with each other. Lippy would do all the talking when asked by their mother where on earth their little brother had gone to.

Lippy coyly explained how poor Zeppity had fallen backwards into the river while they were pretending to give him a religious baptism the way Jesus had once been baptized. With the delivery of this bit of news, his brothers had to smile and wink at each other for Lippy had hit the nail on the head. Their mother loved Jesus more than words could say, and she'd be as pleased as punch with this biblical tale-of-events.

'And where's he now?' she asked.

'He's below at the river and gone off fishing with Little Dan and My-Son-Jack.'

'Aren't men awful eejits,' she muttered to herself, shaking her head. 'Surely My-Son-Jack knew better than this – that it was time for the poor lad's dinner? I'm surprised at him. Zeppity will be starved-to-death by the time he gets home.' Without another word (which could have complicated matters a good deal further and reveal their act of treachery), the children heaved a sigh of relief and raced through their plate of champ and milk. Moll-the-Man cleared the table and picked out the two largest spuds she could find from the skillet pot and cut them into quarters. She added a plate and a knife and a fork and a small bottle of milk, and she stowed them in her shopping bag.

'Go down to the river, let ye', said she, 'with these spuds and milk and see that yeer newly-baptized brother is well-fed and watered.'

At this, the rascals gave her a vigorous nod-of-the-head, and she smiled at the readiness of her good-natured children to make amends for their thoughtlessness in letting their little brother go off fishing without them. Little did the simple soul know that her children had made a complete ass out of her.

Before they reached the half-door, she added, 'There's to be no roaring or yahooing whilst ye're down at the river (do ye hear me?) for ye'll have to be as quiet as the grave if ye want My-Son-Jack to catch his fish.' Again, the heads nodded spontaneously. And then their mother had a second little thought, 'Who knows, ye might yet be able to redeem yeerselves from the worry ye've caused me in losing Zeppity, ye might even bring back one or two little fishes for the frying-pan.' The children couldn't wait to get out from under her feet, and they ran towards the yard at considerable speed. They had escaped their mother's wrath.

8

Meanwhile, onwards towards the river tap-tapped the other three merry sets of fishermen's feet. The two-men-of-us were carrying their fishing-rods on their shoulders, and Zeppity was carrying Little Dan's big satchel for holding the fishes. The master and his pupils were now enjoying the almost-poetic essence of this soul-calming day. The bushes were still wet with the night's lodged raindrops and looked like pieces of diamonds. The sky was light and blue, and the clouds had been scattered away by the high winds.

They passed Old Stroller's field-gate where the ghost of the slain woodcutter (Larry Cash) would sometimes appear and frighten the dancers coming home from the platform dance on summer nights. They had reached the Briary Stile. They heard the river brawling long before they could watch her fighting her way towards the mill to meet up with other rivers.

My-Son-Jack knew every inch of this river – all the little turns and twists and the deep rocky pools and sally holes. He knew the clear shallow stretches and the little sandy beaches, knew the spots where (undisturbed by any other mortal) you could sit down with your canister of tea and hang your legs out on an over-reaching log across the water and eat your fill of hazelnuts and blackberries. He knew those rare shady parts under the remote oaks and beech trees where no man (other than Rambling Jack and Saddle-the-Pony) had ever clapped their eyes. These were places on other days where you'd see him sitting on the shiny side of his waistcoat and shivering with delight as he conversed with those river fairies (the ghosts of his ancestors) who forever seemed to accompany him on his mystical rambles into the heart of nature.

One at a time he took the little boys' hands and led them up onto the stile. The far side was covered with nettles. He jumped down and grasped them in his fists so as to clear a path for the children to get through. They eased themselves over the wire fence, and he swung their legs (and their unsuspecting shrieks) out over the nettles. From where they were standing, they could see the two pillars of the bridge above their heads where children returning from school on schooldays would often look down at their own reflections. How privileged (thought the big man) were the two little fishermen to be standing here this Saturday afternoon and watching the river's silken curves. Ahead of them was the little tributary stream that flowed down from both their farmyards. Back and forth leapt My-Son-Jack across it, carrying each boy over amid their further shrieks of laughter.

They knelt down and cupped their hands and drank the clear water. The real journey had begun. They were on their way to the innermost haunts of the river, leaving behind them the creamery road and the world as they knew it. The ghosts of former fishermen came out to greet them from Old Stroller's ferny field and beckoned them on towards the mysterious Big Hole.

The children walked in front of My-Son-Jack along the green fringes of the river, listening to the rustling sounds of the spiky ferns, which were so tall that the little fellows felt almost lost. A few yards away from them, the fishes were playing amid the swaying rushes and darting around in their underwater kingdom.

Men had rarely come this far up the river. At the height of summer, however, a few of the older boys might come here in secret to find a bit of paradise and bathe in the sally holes. The big girls might come here also at other times. It was a clothes-free place, full of frivolous fleshy glances on those hazy afternoons – a place to which boys might scurry down amongst Old Stroller's cattle and sit amongst the hidden oak-trees on the river's bank and steal scandalous looks at the fleshy young girls bathing without a stitch of clothes on. In a similar way, girls might go down and spy on the boys to see what they were made of. And then you'd hear the screams of recognition (the girls) and the folded arms and cupped hands (the boys). Was such unbridled laughter and such cursing and swearing ever heard tell of before or since? The poor little fishes hid themselves deep in the rushes, deprived of all their heavenly peace and quiet.

Little Dan slipped out of his sandals and handed them to his brother to hold, wanting his bare feet to feel the grass. So intense were the young fishermen, that their heads were almost falling off as they gazed around.

My-Son-Jack thought it best to hold them by their hands and keep them away from the edge of the water – in case Zeppity got himself baptized all over again. With this hilarious picture in his mind, he couldn't help from quietly laughing to himself.

The children had never been so far along the river, and My-Son-Jack told them they were near the Big Hole. How much better (he thought) to spend a day here in the wilderness, journeying to the Big Hole and swallowing the song of the river and its scenery. It was much better than squeezing their shy little shoulders (when the time came) into the back benches of the schoolhouse and singing their droning tables. It was much better to be learning from nature than all the knowledge drummed in between the ears of other children at the hands of Dang-the-skin-of-it with his lofty poetry.

He stopped dead in his tracks. They had reached the Big Hole. His heart could have danced a jig when he thought of the many trout carousing around in rings, paying their respects to the king of the fishes. The three fishermen leaned down and peered over the edge of the pool, its ripples shining like a hundred silver coins. Perhaps the Rogue was looking up at them. Perhaps he saw the eyes of these fantastically-shaped giants looking down into his eyes?

My-Son-Jack placed his rods against a tree. The little birds kept breathlessly still and wondered at the three strange fishermen entering their world. Death was nearby (they knew it).

My-Son-Jack scraped away some broken sticks from under his feet and brought a few clumps of musky ferns and laid them on the ground. He settled the children into their new hidey-hole on the bank and made them as sheltered and comfy as could be mid the long-shadowed trees where no wind or rain could get at them. They sat there obediently and wondered what was going to happen next.

My-Son-Jack looked back at them and smiled. They were sitting stock still like two young stags on the shiny lining of his waistcoat, far enough from the fishing-hole to be safe from his flying rod when the time came to fish. He felt the impish eyes of the *river fairies* peering down at him from the gap in the treetops where the hazy sunlight reflected itself in the yellow wrinkles of the pool. He was lost in his dreams of the river's greatest treasure (the Rogue), and for once in his life, there wasn't a word out of him.

9

Leaving behind them By-Jiggery to fork out the ferns from the ass-and-car and deal with Short-Arse's stable, Lippy, Philly and Young Jim had made their way in over the Briary Stile and in next to no time they had reached the Big Hole. They hid themselves a short distance away from My-Son-Jack, not knowing what to expect from him. They couldn't stay there watching like fools, and they plucked up courage and gave a few coughs. Tentatively, they held aloft their mother's shopping-bag on a stick as a peace-offering to Zeppity and their old friend, Jack. They emerged from the ferns.

'We've brought ye some spuds, Zeppity,' they whispered, remembering their mother's warning not to disturb the fishes and seeing My-Son-Jack with his finger on his lips. 'We're sorry for baptizing ye in the river and the trouble we caused ye. We've brought ye a bottle of milk as well.' The list of their sorrows went on and on. They knew when to make the right crestfallen gestures and hold their heads low (the crafty little actors).

It didn't take much to soften the heart of the big fellow, and he shoved Zeppity forward to take the shopping-bag with the food in it. The reunited brothers now felt a bit more comfortable in themselves and sat cross-legged on the sheltered bed of ferns. Once again, My-Son-Jack smiled on them like a loving father. They looked (he thought) like they were back in Dang-the-skin-of-it's schoolhouse, preparing for the great schoolmaster's lesson to worry its way down into their heads.

But it was Saturday, and it was fishing-time. All eyes were fixed on My-Son-Jack. They could sense the growing excitement oozing out of him and the thoughts in his mind

– to catch the Rogue and fish him out onto the bank and into the satchel and have him on the dinner-plate in the evening. His silence throbbed like a sleeping infant, and they wondered if the same silence filled the watery souls of the fishes.

My-Son-Jack cut himself a squid of tobacco with his penknife and rolled it round in the palms of his hands the way his father used to do. He lit his pipe, and the honeyed smoke filled the children's nostrils as they watched him drawing in jaw-filling puffs of smoke beneath the lid of his pipe and banishing the flies, a number of which were by this time out and about.

He had a great deal to consider. After the night's heavy rain, this was the best time to fish. The trout would be full of false confidence and sink down to the bottom and hide themselves from the eyes of man. The longer they stayed below the surface, the more their eyes would become unfamiliar with the increasing sunlight, and the younger and more innocent trout would be more likely to take his bait of maggots, being unable to recognise the line and hook when they first came up to the surface to greet the light.

As soon as he'd captured enough fishes to put in the satchel, he'd let the children join him fishing. Meanwhile, he'd fix their two little rods deep in the mud of the bank. Later on, he'd put a few maggots on their hooks and help them throw their lines.

With his leathery fingers, he skewered one or two maggots onto the hook and stepped into the freezing water and onto the boulders around which the river spilled. He could sense the thumping hearts of the fishes as they heard the soft thud of his wellingtons.

'Here comes Man. Here comes our greatest enemy. Here comes his inevitable rod and line.'

My-Son-Jack looked along the edge of the pool at the bubbles around the gleaming stones where the inexperienced trout danced through the blades of the rushes, and the water chuckled playfully and avoided the strong tumbling currents at the centre of the Big Hole.

'Before this afternoon is finished, these young numbskulls will dance to a far different tune and find themselves on the end of Little Dan and Zeppity's fishing rods,' said he to himself.

He continued to gaze into the heart of the Big Hole where that great fish himself and all the older lazy-eyed fishes were looking up at him and giving him the evil eye, their tails no longer swaying, their bodies no longer dancing, their very souls frozen in time. They knew that the mental battle of wits had begun – the battle between Fish and Man.

Suddenly, My-Son-Jack heard the plop of a solitary trout rising up from the far corner of the pool. He looked towards the spot and got ready to cast his rod. A rustling bird warned the unwary trout of the line's perilous approach, and it scurried away to join its comrades behind the protecting tussocks of grass at the far edge of the pool. My-Son-Jack followed it with his line.

Now came the waiting. Then came the hoping. Then followed the uncertainty and frustration. The children saw the change in the big fellow's face as the tension built up in him. He was thinking of nothing but this single runaway trout, and swift action was needed if he was to snare his first catch of the day.

What was going on in the mind of this poor trout? One minute he was making a desperate dart for safety and trying to reach the reeds and hide. Next minute (thanks to his hapless irresolution – or was it his poor eyesight?) he found himself turning back towards the savage hook and its mesmerizing feast of maggots.

My-Son-Jack's rod suddenly grew taut. The runaway fish had caught himself on the hook! It looked back helplessly at its comrades in the reeds. The children sat bolt upright and watched. They saw My-Son-Jack yank out a fine, white-bellied trout – the end of its unrestricted liberty. They slipped down the bank where they saw the speckled fish thrashing about on the end of the fishing-line. With a flushed face, My-Son-Jack took the fish off his hook and threw it high up the bank towards the children. For a few seconds, it tumbled about like a lump of jelly in a vain attempt to flop back down the bank and get itself into the river.

Little Dan picked up the slippery fish and with Zeppity's help, fumbled it into his satchel. A moment passed, and then the two little fishermen nearly jumped out of their skins. The dead fish seemed to have come back to life – twitching and fluttering about inside in the satchel with the final hammering of its little heart. That's when they felt the true horror of the fish's death – felt the last seconds of its precious life. There was going to be no more playfulness for this misfortunate trout, no more races up and down the river towards Echo Bridge. This very evening, this young fish would lie on the burning frying-pan together with the delicious bull-paddock mushrooms.

My-Son-Jack fixed another maggot on his hook. Not once did he give the children a look but continued to puff-puff on his pipe for he was absorbed in his efforts to penetrate the mind of the Rogue and understand the thoughts inside the great fish's head when he must have seen the rod and big wellingtons above him. Perhaps in former days, this great fish had seen a certain fisherman in his dreams, had seen the fisherman that one day would come looking for him – the fisherman that would prove to be the fiercest of all threats to his life.

But luck and good fortune had always been on the Rogue's side. He had the finest of hiding-places in the Big Hole and had always avoided racing away with the younger fishes through those bright green runnels and rushes. Like the older fishes, he spent most days resting peacefully, sleeping for hours in his cavernous palace behind the rocks. However, not even this mighty fish could sleep away the whole of his days, and when the early evening's light came calling him, he'd be forced to rise up for his daily feast of midges and gnats. This was a fact, and the big fisherman knew it.

But there wasn't an ounce of fear in this mighty fish and, though he was certain of his own importance, he was never rashly over-confident. In many ways, the Rogue and My-Son-Jack were much alike, and the big lad felt that this battle with the king of the fishes would not be easy to win when the evening light drew them both inevitably together.

10

Bit by bit the fishing satchel grew fat with more and more trout. The children were kept busy running up the bank to catch the somersaulting fishes that tried to roll their way back towards the river. They threw them into the satchel Zeppity was carrying. He felt them twitching helplessly about in its dark depths and couldn't help shuddering.

It was time to call a halt in this battle with the fishes, and My-Son-Jack climbed up the bank. He took Moll-the-Man's shopping-bag from the shade in the ferns and gave it to Zeppity. The big brothers looked at their little brother as he unwrapped the spuds and, though they had just eaten their dinner, they had the appearance of avaricious dogs. My-Son-Jack also took out the doorstep sandwiches that Dowager had wrapped in layers of newspapers – the bread and dripping ones for himself and the bread and butter and blackcurrant ones for Little Dan. And again, there were the sad-looking eyes of the older boys, whose daily soda-bread saw butter but never a trace of blackcurrant jam on it.

My-Son-Jack led the children a little way upriver where they sat and acted as if they had nothing better to do than while away the day without a care in the world – just like the fishes themselves would now be doing, thinking that the fisherman had gone off home.

'Young fishes,' the big man shouted back at the Big Hole (for there was no need to whisper this time), 'we're off home now, but we'll be back tomorrow.' Under his breath, he added, 'We'll be back a lot sooner than any of ye think.'

With the children, he went further along the bank of the river. He knew a few rocks dotted beyond the bend and an overhanging branch of a tree where they could sit and dangle their legs above the water and wiggle their toes in the pebbles.

He bade Lippy, Philly and Young Jim lie down by his side while Little Dan and Zeppity leathered into their bit of dinner and milk. The children sat there quietly, listening to the bubbling song of the river. My-Son-Jack finished his sandwiches. He stretched his arms behind his head, gazing round at the serene hills and the changing patterns of the clouds and breathing in the fresh breeze that whistled down on him through the treetops.

A little lethargy had crept into the children's spirits, and they soon dozed off into the lost land of their innocent dreams and were thoroughly at peace with the world and its solitude. My-Son-Jack smiled down at them.

It was time to return to the Big Hole. He put the milk-bottle away and wiped his mouth with the newspaper before leading the children back for his stealthy battle with the Rogue. Now would follow the finest fishing the children's eyes would ever see – the song of the rod and the cunning of the mighty fish, and they each prayed for the death of the Rogue.

My-Son-Jack put a few maggots on the children's little rods and showed them how to study the pool with their eyes and search for their trout. He helped them cast their lines as far out as they could. Lippy, Philly and Young Jim looked on rather helplessly, their spirits long chastened following their previous baptism of Zeppity.

Little Dan and Zeppity soon became part of the river, and their eyes glittered with concentration. Was this the day when they'd catch their first fish? The fact that they had the best maggots from the African Sink, coupled with their newly-acquired patience, meant that they finally caught a fish apiece.

It was a picture to see their astonished eyes as they whispered, 'I've caught a fish! I've caught a fish!' And My-Son-Jack made sure that each fish wasn't so large as to pull the children back into the river and perform yet another ceremonial baptism on Zeppity as he helped them yank their precious fishes out into the air.

The two new fishermen stumbled up the bank and helped each other hold down their still-living fishes before throwing them into the satchel. This day was an almighty triumph for them, and even Lippy was forced to throw up his hands in admiration and raise a smile to his lips.

11

Daylight was passing. My-Son-Jack tipped the rest of the maggots out onto the newspaper. He selected six of his best blue-heads (all fat and juicy) and wrapped them round in a ball like twine before skewering them firmly onto his hook. What a feast was in store for the Rogue! He took a last look inside the satchel and counted eight fishes in all. He was now hoping to catch the king of the fishes and keep him for himself. The children could picture him hopping down to Curl 'n Stripes' drinking-shop later that evening and showing off the greatest prize of all time to the mesmerized drinkers. Those starry-eyed old men would be talking about it till kingdom come.

He cast his rod back over his shoulder and whipped it out into the centre of the pool. The cunning crows woke up on their dreamy branches and with their cries warned the fishes that danger was nearby in the shape of the line with the blue-headed maggots – in the shape of the fatal hook and Man. My-Son-Jack kept asking himself a number of questions: had he cast his line too soon? Had he cast it too ungainly? Had he cast it far enough out into the pool?

Down, down, down swam the Rogue, all the while eyeing the line. His minions swam down alongside him. They rested on the sandy bed and avoided any noise they might make against the stones. Unreal was the tranquillity as My-Son-Jack stood frozen on the bank, the very same as a heron. Likewise stood the children and the ghosts of previous fishermen and the feverish river fairies that forever live on the river's banks. They were all thinking of nothing but the Rogue and the man – and the battle.

Something like fear had taken hold of each child for only Rambling Jack and Saddle-the-Pony had ever seen the Rogue or knew how monstrous such a fish might be. Maybe he was huge enough – maybe he was savage enough – to drag My-Son-Jack down into the Big Hole and drown him. Maybe he'd have jaws big enough to gobble him up in one great gulp (thought Zeppity). And they blessed themselves and gave the Rogue new and imaginative powers of his own.

Lippy whispered that the Rogue might make a rush out at any moment and devour them up – one and all – and Philly swore that even if the Rogue were to die at the hands of My-Son-Jack's rod, he'd be sure to come back as a ghost that night and haunt the daylights out of every one of them for the rest of their lives.

The unsettled sun continued to drag itself along into the late afternoon. The children were just as unsettled as the sun, not knowing if they were about to see the end of the mighty fish's life. There followed the quick action of the mighty fish. And then there followed the even quicker action of My-Son-Jack and his line. And then they saw him laughing to himself as his line sprang taut.

'I have snared ye at last, mee beauty,' he said, and his smile was as blissful as a little child with a bag of sweets. This was followed by a most peculiar look in his eyes – a look of remorse and (could they believe it?) a look of sympathy and sorrow for so mighty a fish.

'Ah, mee most beautiful fish!' he cried when he saw how the Rogue had been tempted by the amounts of juicy blue-headed maggots rolled round in a ball on the hook. His jaws were irretrievably embedded on the hook, but there was a great deal of life still left in him as he struggled and thrashed the surface of the river in an effort to escape with his life. A curse on that blasted hook! It was what he had always feared. It was what his clever mother had always warned him against when he was a young fish.

A minute or two later, the children saw the rod bending into an unearthly curve (almost to the point of breaking) and then they saw the final trust as the line sprang back in a quiver. And then they saw the upward trust of the rod into the air – and an enormous fish sailing aloft with it.

Were children ever before so enthralled by life and its mysteries? However, they gave a sigh of pure relief when they realized that as monstrous in size as this mighty fish was, he was nowhere big enough to devour even Little Dan – let alone drag My-Son-Jack down into the Big Hole.

Then Lippy, Philly and Young Jim began to have another little thought to themselves, and it was a wise one: might not the boodeeman and the king of the leprechauns and the Devil himself all be just a number of tall tales told to frighten the lives out of innocent children like themselves? But they kept these wise thoughts to themselves and told none of this to Little Dan or Zeppity. After all, they themselves had had to put up with all these damned fears long enough.

In spite of the look in My-Son-Jack's eyes and his mixed emotions of happiness and sorrow over the great fish, this was the time for the mighty creature to die. The mystery of it all: one minute, swimming about in the river, the next minute, flying through the air and wrapped foolishly round the branch of a tree where the line had pelted him and swinging about like an old clock's pendulum.

They crowded underneath the body of the Rogue and gazed up at him. My-Son-Jack stumbled frantically up the bank towards the fish – to see its size first-hand and compare it to the flagstone sketch made by Saddle-the-Pony. It was indeed the Rogue. And then . . . the eye of the big fisherman looked into the eye of the big fish, and the eye of the big fish looked into the eye of the big fisherman. The children saw it all. Fishes were meant for the frying-pan. Fishes were meant for the delicate blending with a handful of mushrooms from the bull-paddock. Above all – fishes were meant for a man's belly. One thing was sure and certain: fishes were never meant to be returned to the river. It was a thing unheard of in the history of all Tipperary.

There followed a moment which was pure magic for a child to behold – a moment of acute sorrow and joy – a moment when My-Son-Jack reached out his hand towards the mighty fish. It was almost too much for the big lad's heart to withstand. Carefully and slowly he freed the Rogue from the hook, almost reverently touching his poor hurt jaw.

'Ye great big fish,' said he as he lifted the king of the fishes down from the tree. He stepped carefully down the bank and gently placed the Rogue back into the Big Hole.

The great fish looked back up at him and circled around for a moment or two on the disbelieving surface of the pool. It was hard for the befuddled eyes of the children to take it all in. The king raised his exhausted head aloft as though he were saying farewell to Man. It was an unspeakable and precious moment – a moment of pain and relief for Fish and Man, a moment of such privileged personal intimacy between the hunter and the hunted that no other human being should ever have been allowed to stand and witness it. And then the great big fish sank down into his underwater kingdom and was gone.

12

It was time to depart. My-Son-Jack climbed up onto the bank. His eyes were misty with his tears, and they were difficult for him to hide. He picked up the satchel of fish and retrieved his rod and line. He swung his rod over his shoulder in an effort at manliness and led the children towards Echo Bridge. Unlike him, the children's hearts were light and airy, thinking of the great day's fishing that had been done. They were anxious to tell Dowager and Moll-the-Man all about the Rogue, but My-Son-Jack warned them not to tell a living soul about the battle – the battle that his rod had just won, the battle that his heart had just lost and how he had let the great big fish get away with its life. He'd be the laughingstock of all Tipperary.

They reached the echoing railings of the bridge. The peace of the fishing day had ended. The secrecy of their magical world was again marred by the sight of the cattle in the bull-paddock and they bawling to be milked. They made their way over the Briary Stile and out onto the creamery road, My-Son-Jack lumbering along and the children scurrying ahead with their tales to tell. At John's Gate, Little Dan said goodbye to the bigger boys, and My-Son-Jack gave them their two fishes wrapped in newspaper. Their heels were soon out of sight as they raced with their prize on towards the avid smiles of Moll-the-Man and her outstretched hands.

The two fishermen walked across the bull-paddock and picked up the pink-gilled mushrooms, as many as they could find. My-Son-Jack peeled each one from the centre to the edge to see if they were good enough to eat, and between them, they filled their pockets. The big man led his cows out through John's Gate, and they trudged up the hill-slope. They crossed the flagstones and were just in time to see the moping hens following the ducks into the hen house, leaving behind them their dusty beds under the hawthorn bush.

The pulse of the day was now gone, and the sky's wine-colouring had rolled down through the last of the day-clouds. Spears of gold, bronze and red added to the over-painting of the dying blue sky but already the grey and navy clouds were sailing in over Lisnagorna Woods.

Moll-the-Man's children were tired out from the long day, and within an hour, they had sunk down into their own sunset and were lying in their settle-beds. In the darkness of the bedroom, they said farewell to their day's bit of paradise.

Dowager gutted the two fishes and washed them in the cold yard stream. It wasn't long before the frying-pan was got out and sent sizzling with plenty of butter and fat from the dripping-bowl on the press. Little Dan and My-Son-Jack had gluttony on their minds, and their stomachs were turning over with the hunger. Their nostrils were soon filled with the sweet and succulent smell of the trout and mushrooms and the salt and onions and buttered mashed potatoes. It'd put a smile on the walls of the welcoming room. Soon the three plates were empty and wiped clean with a sop of bread as the last of the trout-meat was wolfed down. It was a pure joy, and Little Dan felt like a prince.

He had scarcely time to finish his meal, so many were the tales he had to tell his mother, all of them greatly exaggerated as he threw his arms out wide to indicate the size of some of the fishes he and Zeppity had caught. Not a single word did he utter about the mighty king of the fishes and the way My-Son-Jack had placed him gently back in the Big Hole.

Night entered the yard and peered into the welcoming room. Dowager lit the oil lamp and the two candles. The three of them knelt down in a ring and said their fervent prayers to guard them from the boodeeman and the other wicked spirits that rambled through the world for the ruin of souls. My-Son-Jack raked up the ashes, and they each took the holy water from the font to protect them in their sleep. With the two candles, they headed to the left and to the right – Dowager to her little anteroom and the two-men-of-us to the big cave room next to the hen house.

My-Son-Jack blew out the candle on the corner of the tea-chest, and Little Dan snuggled down under the cover of the blankets and wadded quilt. He shivered deliciously in the damp musty sheets and wrapped them round his ears. He put his two small feet in between My-Son-Jack's legs and rested his head against his chest.

The darkness of the big cave room seemed to be piled up in the four corners, and the stars shone dimly in through the broken-glass window. The moon tangled itself amid the trees of the haggart, and the faint glimmer of curly black clouds showed where the cowshed was, and the wind shrieked on the hen house galvanized roof. Being so close to his big brother, Little Dan felt very brave and believed that he could take on a great big lion if he ever saw one.

My-Son-Jack lay awake for a long time. It had been a good day's fishing – a load of dead trout and some of them already eaten. But there were many more trout (thank God) swimming happily this night beneath the rushes of the Big Hole, and he was already mulling over in his head another fishing trip with his little brother. He wrapped the little fellow tightly to him, protecting him from the wind and the rain and the boodeeman.

All the children had learnt a great deal this memorable day. They had seen into the gentle soul of the big lad. The Rogue was once again swimming safely in the Big Hole. This mighty fish was thinking (you and I might like to believe) of Man and his great kindness – of a particular man, who had gently lifted him off of the hook and had reverently placed him back in his home. The king of the fishes swam happily among his minions, deep in his kingdom in the moonlit silvery pool.

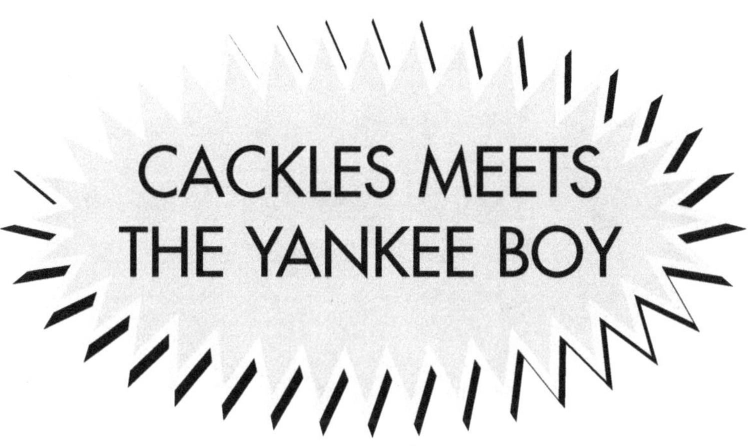
CACKLES MEETS
THE YANKEE BOY

1

Everyone knew that there was the laughter of the hyena, but it could only be found elsewhere in foreign climes far away. Men and women had the laughter of the hen after she had laid an egg amongst the nettles and dock-leaves abroad in the haggart, where you'd have the devil's own job finding herself and her egg. One would think it was the very first egg she'd ever laid, the laughter she came out with. But better than that, there was Cackles, and her very name will tell you what a peal of laughter she had inside her blouse.

'It's louder than the Angelus Bell in the church tower,' said Dowager.

'Cackles can make a cat laugh,' said My-Son-Jack. This would leave any child wondering what it was like to see a cat laughing. There was something new for children to learn every day.

'She's like a 100 hens laying their eggs at one and the same time abroad in the hayshed – that's why she cackles so much,' said Dowager. That was supposed to be the end of the matter. Wouldn't any child know that this bit – the bit about the 100 hens – was just another damned lie, like those tales about the Wild Witch of the West?

Cackles was nearer to 50 than 40 years old. Her husband was Johnnie-tackle-the-ass, and he was the centre of her good nature and devotion. Johnnie was 70 and forever tackling his ass and going off in the direction of Bog Wood for yet another cartload of ferns. That's how he came to get his name.

Dowager (who was always nosey and forever peeping out the front window on tiptoes to see who was passing by) would watch him speeding down the creamery road, and she'd turn to My-Son-Jack and say, 'Johnnie, avic, go and tackle the ass and bring a load of ferns.' These words turned into a regular singsong expression of hers. Of course, she didn't mean My-Son-Jack to head off to Bog Wood (like Cackle's good man) and bring home a load of ferns: she wanted him to roll up his sleeves like Johnnie did and go out the pig house gap where there was a pile of timber waiting for him to chop into logs and bring in for the fire.

Between Johnnie and Cackles (miracle of miracles, now that he was 70), they managed to produce one of the loveliest children known anywhere, and the name of this child was Sing-me-a-song. She had dimples on her cheeks, although all children had these. But then she had dimples on her wrists, and she even had them on her elbows and on her knees so that some men thought that Dimples might have been a far better name for her.

The years went by all too quickly, and Sing-me-a-song was growing up just as lovely as nature intended her to be. Time and again the old pair did their best during their tumbles in the four-poster bed to give her a little brother to play with. But they were far too old for this sort of play-acting. It was high time for Father Honesty to come and tell them to give up trying. Even the biblical Sarah had produced only the one child as late as this in her life.

But a year or two later, to the astonishment of everyone (not least to Cackles herself) the good woman had another birth. Without the visitation of Black Bess, the nurse, she gave birth to a pair of premature twins, crossing and uncrossing her legs on the welcoming room floor while her good neighbour (Freckles) did the best she could for her.

But (oh and alas) the little dears were dead as soon as they landed on the blanket, and Cackles was out of her head with grief and didn't know what to do. She'd let no-one near them. With her own spade she buried them as deep as she could in the family grave, tearfully covering them with a huge heap of laurel bushes. Then she ran back home and lay down on her bed and cried and cried herself to sleep. God help her, she stayed tied to the bed for a week-and-a-half, leaving Johnnie-tackle-the-ass sad and alone and scratching his old head. Would she ever again take up her habit of laughing and cackling?

Although the twins were gone before they'd had a chance to give her a few little smiles, there came a growing compensation for Johnnie and herself whenever they looked across the firelight at their lovely little daughter. Even before she hit the road for Dang-the-skin-of-it's schoolhouse, Sing-me-a-song turned out to be the sweetest of singers, and her songs made her the life and soul of the creamery road. In the course of time, her sad parents put aside the cause of their grief and started to realize (thank God) where their true happiness lay. The laughter of Cackles was once more restored to her, and it filled our valleys and hills whenever she listened to Sing-me-a-song singing.

The little girl would clear her throat with a mug of spring-water from the bucket behind the door. Then she would trot out *No-one to welcome me home,* a song that made everyone weep with its sentimental journey of an old man coming back from the Land of the Silver Dollar. She'd follow this up with *Why are you loitering here, pretty maid?* or *Dim in the twilight I wandered alone.* The other children could stay listening to her for half-the-day as though they had nothing better to do with themselves. How on earth did a little child like her keep stored in her head all the big words that were in these songs?

'God must have given her a dozen brains,' said Rambling Jack and the women, passing by on their way to the well, wondering was there a child anywhere on earth who had so many brains floating around inside in her head.

She had already developed a gap between her two front teeth. Such a gap was said to be the birth-right of anyone hoping to live beyond a hundred years of age. But the gap in Sing-me-a-song's teeth had another consequence, for it gave her the gift of the double-whistle (like the one you'd make by whistling on a piece of card), and it was as though two people were whistling inside in her mouth.

For hours on end (and with Moll-the-Man cursing her children for not coming in to their tea), Lippy and the rest of them sat on their heels and listened to this strange whistling of hers. One would pay good money at the Daffy-Duck Circus to go and listen to it.

So, instead of going off paddling in the river and bringing back coloured stones to draw with – instead of climbing over the wire-fence and half-kicking to death Old Stroller's two pet dogs in his yard – the children now preferred sitting in the ashes of Cackles' fire and listening to Sing-me-a-song at her whistling.

As important as a few young adventurers had become in the eyes of everyone else after their memorable visits to Tim and Judy or the two toddlers' adventures with the Wild Witch of the West, it was now admitted that Cackles' daughter and her melodious gifts beat Lippy and his brothers, Little Dan and Battlin' Sal too, clean out of the field. She held the creamery road in the palm of her hands.

There were times when the older girls would come up from the Kill and follow Sing-me-a Song down into Old Sam's orchard. They didn't give her a moment's peace and kept her sitting on the fallen tree and pestering her to open her mouth and roll her tongue so that they could find the reason for her mysterious whistle.

Wasn't that what children had always done whenever they found a dead thrush – opened its beak to see how on earth so small a creature could come out with its wondrous music? Sing-me-a-song (the good-natured child that she was) patiently opened her mouth and twisted her tongue so that they could see the source of her split-whistle. But, no matter how they leaned down towards the inside of her throat or tried to twist their own lips and place their tongue at the back of their teeth to copy her double-whistle, they never got the hang of its unique mystery – until finally, they saw that it was the gap between her two front teeth that was the cause of it, and they gave up trying to copy her and went home dejectedly.

For a day or two, they had other things to occupy their minds. Philly brought home a dead crane and asked Lippy to cut open its belly with their mother's good scissors. After all the snipping was done, they saw several small fishes wrapped up inside in its guts. They were just as puzzled as they had been with the thrush's small beak and all the beautiful notes of music that it had once sung. How could a crane have held so many fishes inside in its belly? They had no answer. This brought them back to the same question: how on earth could Sing-me-a-song's teeth have taught her the double whistle, and what was so special about the gap? They were one and all enthralled.

2

Every child went bare-footed even when they had to have boots on their feet for the schoolhouse. They slung them round their necks until they were within a yard of the school. Only then (because they were forced to do so) did they put them on. They were far happier to be in their bare feet where they could run around like a pack of wild hares. But that didn't stop them from frowning about the fact that Sing-me-a-song had no boots to wear. She'd be going off to school in a year's time and would need to get into the habit of covering her feet with boots.

They got it into their heads that they should try and get her a pair, and they started parading the length and breadth of the creamery road till they finally found an old boot. It was a shade too big for a five-year-old child, being the leftover of a passing tinker-woman. They spent the whole of May searching for a comrade for that old boot till, in the end, Lippy found an ancient wellington in the dyke at Red Scissors' well-hole. He cut it down to size with By-Jiggery's penknife and then, together with the boot which they had stuffed full of moss, it made a fair enough pair of boots for our little heroine to put on and step out in.

Philly asked his mother for the blacking-tin in the bottom of her press, the green tin with the lovely face of the black racehorse on its lid. Then he gave the wellington and boot a good rinse in the yard-stream. He dried them out on the ditch and gave them a polishing that would befit a racehorse. The children (making sure that the little singer was nowhere to be seen) gathered round and wondered at the new boot and wellington that lay shining like the sun.

It was time for the ritual. They marched Sing-me-a-song down to the well-hole and, with a degree of ceremony and pomp, handed her their precious gift. It was their reward for her being the finest singer and whistler they were ever likely to listen to. That's what they said.

Cackles missed little Sing-me-a-song when she started off with the other children on the daily 3-mile trek across the fields to Dang-the-skin-of-it's schoolhouse. But the good woman's loneliness didn't last long, for who should come running home to her in a great big flurry – back home again from the Land of the Silver Dollar – but Jimmy-the-Yank. He was Cackles' favourite nephew and had come back to keep her company.

'But only for a short while,' he warned, for he had a lot of serious business on his mind (he said) and would have to go marching off again in a few weeks' time. Cackles was impressed.

From the moment he arrived, Jimmy was full of bustle around Cackles' yard – yet all the while looking back over his shoulder as though he were expecting to see a mad bull leaping out over the ditch and tossing him into the air.

The children were left wondering why he had come all this way across the ocean and why he'd be leaving them just as quickly. Those who had previously gone out to the Land of the Silver Dollar had seldom, if ever, come back. It was as if they'd got lost in a bog-hole or were lying below in the graveyard. And, if indeed, any of them ever did make the return trip, it was only their sentimental dreams that had forced them to come back in their very old age – with a small Yankee pension and a hatful of dollars in their back pocket, if they were lucky.

Their return proved to be no happy-ever-after tale for none of these old prodigals could settle down when they came home to the Old Dart (their word for Ireland). The friends of their youth were resting in an early grave, thanks to all the rheumatic pains that our damp climate had given them – or else they'd been sent down (a good few of them) to the House for Nervous Disorders to have their bad nerves looked at. And these never returned home either. A few more of them had been shipped off to the County Home amidst the hypocritical tears of their children. Enough said.

The return of Jimmy was a bit different. It took only half-a-dozen pints of Curl 'n' Stripes' stout to be poured down his neck for him to give out the news that all wanted to hear – why he'd hot-footed it back home. It was then that he took on an almost god-like stature among the neighbours, the children especially. He said he was a man on the run ('ah, the poor devil,' said the women) from a bunch of Yankee hoodlums, men who'd have liked to have tasted his blood after he'd embezzled them out of a few crates of their finest whiskey.

When the rest of the drinkers heard this astonishing tale below in Curl 'n' Stripes' shop, you should have seen the way they slapped his shoulders. 'Fair play to you, Jimmy!' they shouted, 'if only you had thought to bring us back a few crates of the hot stuff for ourselves!' And Curl 'n' Stripes' drinking-shop rang with laughter.

Jimmy had always been a prime boy, but he was in the direst danger now. What was he to do? Where was he to go? He couldn't go back across the ocean. The gangsters would give him a right royal welcome (he said) and put a bullet up his arse.

In the meantime, the children were left scratching their heads at the sight of him. They'd never before seen a young man like Jimmy. The bishop in his high hat was one thing, with the red robes that he wore at their confirmation. But Jimmy was an entirely better sight to be gaping their eyes on: a man on the run and a mad pack of gangsters from the Land of the Silver Dollar soon to come steaming over the ocean and make pig's meat out of him. Maybe the entire population of Tipperary would have to go to war with them and get out their old pitchforks for the protection of their lovely Yankee boy.

The days rolled on into weeks and months, and the children grew more and more in awe of their new hero. It gradually came out that he had stolen a good deal more than a few crates of whiskey: he'd stolen a suitcase full of the gangsters' dollars. It was for that reason that he could ape the great showman when he stepped down from the train at the town's railway station.

The children compared their own raggity clothes with his silk suit and his garish tie and his sparkling brown brogues, not to mention the new moustache sprouting from under his nose. They were damned if they too wouldn't get themselves off to the Land of the Silver Dollar one of these fine days and get themselves a rich set of togs like his.

To see him step out into the blue-button field was the wonder of wonders as he carelessly threw off his expensive coat. The children made a grab for it and spent ages feeling the lovely silkiness of it in the hope of finding a few dollars dropping of their own accord out of the pockets.

Jimmy took off his rich shoes and his herringbone socks and challenged them to a running race. It was easy for him to be challenging the likes of these poor scholars. They could see the get-up of him. He had muscles all over his chest and shoulders and more of them coming out from his two ears, and he towered a foot above Lippy, who was the tallest of the bigger boys. The children all lowered their eyes shamefully and admitted defeat, even before the race could start.

'Coom on, ye little whoors!' laughed Jimmy. 'I'll lay ye down ten of these crinkly dollars that none of ye will be left in the field once I've finished with ye, and I'll give each of ye a 10-yard start in a dash to the rotten tree.'

Before anyone had a chance to clear their throats, the speed of him had taken him almost as far as Curl 'n' Stripes drinking-shop door, and to the astonished eyes of all the children, there wasn't even a puff out of him – he hadn't even broken sweat!

After this performance, he led them out into the haggart, casually leaping out over the five-barred gate as he ran on ahead of them. It couldn't be denied – he had already established himself in the annals of north Tipperary for all time. That's a fact.

3

Cackles brought in her armful of washed sheets from the bushes for a final airing round the fire. As she waddled in and out from the half-door, her nephew stood looking across the yard. He was thinking – thinking awfully hard. And then he shook his head. The savage rains (as with Freckles the previous year) had flooded his aunt's stream during the last few weeks. By now it was half-ways up her yard. It would soon reach her half-door if there was another downpour, and she'd be trapped for days on end and wouldn't be able to set foot across the flagstones and get her sausages and black puddings from the shop to feed him.

Cackles too was thinking – thinking of the previous plight of Freckles and how the good woman's new tar-barrels had been laid side-by-side to make a tunnel for the waters pouring down from the hills.

She was now dreading the next few days. Unlike Freckles, she had no tar-barrels to tunnel the waters of her stream and was resigned to her sad fate. She could see the stream coming in the door and onto her welcoming floor, soaking Sing-me-a-Song's settle-bed.

Herself and Johnnie-tackle-the-ass started twiddling their rosary beads in great earnest. They felt heartily ashamed of themselves. They remembered the Great Deluge a few years ago when it had emptied the contents of their cabin and sent them gaily floating down the swirling waters to be swept away in the river. There was every chance it was going to happen all over again.

'How the hell could Cackles get across the swollen stream and down to the shop,' quizzed My-Son-Jack, 'unless we can teach her to swim across the stream and get herself out onto the road?!'

Jimmy stopped thinking. By now, he had the answer to the problem. 'Like Freckles,' said he, 'we'll have to bury the wretched stream before it's too late. That's what we'll do. What need have we for the silver beauties of the stream's galloping waters or the heavenly music that she brings, if we're all to get drowned by her?'

We all gasped, realising that Jimmy had become quite the poet after learning such rocks of words across the ocean, and Cackles blessed him over and over again. He was the saviour sent from Heaven, and Jimmy gave her a reassuring little smile.

The very next morning, he tackled Johnnie's ass (Raggity) – this time not to go and get a load of ferns for them. Lippy borrowed Dowager's ass-and-car as well as her ass (the Lightning Whoor), and then the two ass-and-cars headed off for town.

They arrived at the railway station and told Neddy-the-Stationmaster they needed eight empty tar-barrels that were lying around, old and useless and forever tripping him up. He gladly helped them load them up onto their two ass-and-cars.

Jimmy and Lippy balanced them (four apiece) onto each ass-and-car, Neddy all the time scratching his head and wondering if Jimmy was going to form a new musical band with the tar-barrels. Might he be performing at the show fair next year?

Armed with their prized load, Cackles' two heroes hurried back home in a tidy procession, the two important-looking asses and the sound of their tar-barrels rattling in the ass-and-cars. Numbers of staring children followed behind them as far as the sheep field and wondered who on earth would want so many useless old tar-barrels?

The next day brought in the sunshine. In Cackles' haggart, a crowd of men came together and rolled up their sleeves. There were Hammer-the-Smith and Ned-the-Herd. There were Joe-the-Jinnet and even one or two of the Jugpussers and the Lackadaisicals from out over the hills. They had brought with them their forks, shovels and spades. They had sledgehammers, sickles and scythes. They had wheelbarrows and several bags of cement from the Yellowstone Quarry. They had buckets and hosepipes for the transportation of the stream's water.

They leaned on their implements and studied the stream from the safe distance of the haggart where they had placed the tar-barrels in a neat little row along by the hay-reek. Behind them stood Johnnie-tackle-the-ass, Old Stroller and My-Son-Jack keeping an eye on the children, who had come from all over the place to see the work. There were several children on show: Sweeney, Golly, Bucko, Patches and Cull from Fiddler-Joe's yard and Lippy, Philly, Young Jim and Zeppity from By-Jiggery's yard. They were all keeping their eyes fixed on the proceedings. The younger ones (Battlin' Sal and Little Dan) remained standing behind the big men's legs. They were full of excitement, never before having seen so many tar-barrels. They wondered what sort of article the men were going to make with them and might they be making a contraption with wheels on it and turning them into a train or a tractor. They weren't sure.

Cackles brought out a handful of rosary beads that she'd collected from the neighbouring women. She handed them out among the men to pray for the success of the tar-barrels, and they all bowed their heads solemnly and began mumbling the second part of the Hail Mary in response to Jimmy and Cackles' opening salvo.

Finally, the children understood what was happening: the men were going to make a big tunnel through which Cackles' stream would be carried along and tipped into a mighty waterfall below in the dyke before rushing on into Old Sam's grove.

You wouldn't believe the way these heroes set to work. The children had never witnessed such a sight before: the warding-off of the waters with a makeshift dam from Simple Simon's ditch, the stream raging itself down alongside the creamery road and into the ditch instead of into Cackles' welcoming room, the new trenches that the men's picks and shovels were making faster than a hen that had made up her mind to lay her first egg, the meticulous measuring of the straight line for the tar-barrels and the bucket-loads of fresh cement.

In the end, there was no sight left of a single tar-barrel because all of them were now buried beneath the cement and the sods of grass piled high on top of the cement.

The work had been completed with the speed of light, the men all the while laughing and telling yarns and swearing good-naturedly and cursing one another's mothers and forefathers for giving birth to such a useless article as the fellow next to them. And then they all traipsed back to the haggart, feeling a need to celebrate the birth of the newly-tunnelled stream.

They dug their fists down into the buckets of stout and liberally consumed several mugs of the black stuff. There'd be a second need for a few more decades of the holy rosary in the evening when the women would ask God to help them in their everlasting war against the damned drink and the huge amounts of it that their men were forever downing into their bellies if given half a chance. The whole day was as good as a circus, and nobody would ever forget it.

4

It wasn't over yet as the afternoon suddenly came upon them. It was now the turn of the children to show the men what they were made of and to celebrate the baptism of the tar-barrels in their own childish way.

The men sat down and looked on. They lowered the galluses of their britches and let their bellies (well full of the drinking medicine) hang out over their trousers like a sow's paunch. They waved their hands authoritatively and gave out instructions for the start of the children's races in Cackles' nettle field. They ordered the children to set up twigs and long sticks for the start and finish of each race. They took off their own socks and tied them around the children's ankles for the three-legged race. Then there were the wheelbarrow races and the hop-step-and-a-jump and finally the pelting of the heavy rock to see which of them could put it hopping off of Old Stroller's hayshed and damage his eardrums some 50 feet down the field.

In the meantime, the little ones were lining the banks of the stream near Old Sam's dyke, waiting for the arrival of the new waterfall. When they saw it coming out of the tar-barrels in a great big gush, they jumped up and down and gave a tremendous cheer that you'd hear a mile off. The speed of the stream was immense.

It was time for the men to gather armfuls of flaggards and make flaggard-boats and pass them round amongst the children. They assembled the younger children half-ways down the field where the bend gave the stream a chance to drop their new flotilla of ships into it. The race could now begin.

'Ready! Steady! Go!' yelled Jimmy. The children let slip their boats, and the bigger boys raced hell-for-leather down the field to see could they beat the flaggard-boats that were now sailing speedily down the stream – each of them vying to be first to reach the wire-fence at the end of the field. The men and the children were all in their heaven.

Yet still, the day of the tar-barrels hadn't ended. The last of the fun was the hide-and-go-seek. This was the best time of the day when the children, after relishing all the memories of what they had been seeing and doing, looked out over the haggart-stick and pined over the last of the reddening sun beyond Corcoran's Well. They could hear the little birds achingly calling to one another, telling their news of the day as they settled themselves down in the trees for their roost. They could hear the faraway yelping of the vixen and the frightened responses of Galloping Gret's turkeys as they scurried up into the pine trees behind her hayshed.

Everyone (old and young alike) now scattered themselves everywhere, looking for good places in which to hide from their seeker. One or two climbed on top of the haystack or on top of the turf and logs in Johnnie-tackle-the-ass's two barns (the one for the ass and horse, the other for the four calves) or hid themselves in the upturned rattletrap.

Then came the best part of hide-and-go-seek – the absolute silence, as though the world was standing on its head or had come to an end. There wasn't even a single giggle out of anyone – a frozen moment in time. Would the seeker discover them in their remote hiding-place? Would they be caught and made a fool of before they could reach the safety of the home-tree? The waiting in their lair and the listening for the approaching footfall was sheer agony, and they nearly wet themselves with excitement.

The women would never be caught acting so childishly as their men (the big eejits). But the men and the young girls and boys were spinning their own fairy-tale webs through the charms of the early evening. The men and one or two of the older boys had other things on their minds (the rascals) and made several playful attempts at lifting the older girls' dresses to catch a glimpse (*'they're lavender*!') of the colour of their knickers. The squeals of the girls ('*Go 'way – ye pack of basthards*!') was mixed up with their own unladylike brazenness, for they were just as mischievous and lascivious as the men.

Some of the younger boys got in on the act (*'aren't ye the dirty little whoors!')* and copied the men and made a grab at the skirts of some of the women, who were at least ten years older than themselves.

Ned-the-Herd pinned the beautiful Nora down behind the haystack near the hen house and wouldn't let her go till she offered him a big wet kiss. With her eyes closed and her mouth quivering, she was only too ready for such a forfeit, but (the devils that these men are!) he tiptoed away and left her standing there like a pure fool with her lips puckered up and her expectant eyelids flickering as he ran off down the haggart, followed (a minute later) by her angry curses ('*Ye whoor-of-all-whoors!')*. His sides were hurting him from his sudden gales of laughter.

But *the sad-faced fairies*, who hide themselves in our trees, streams, and ditches are never satisfied with a crowd of merrymakers, and they were now lurking close by. Fiddler Joe's eldest son (Sweeney) had been hiding a long way away from the rest of the children, down behind the blackcurrant bushes. He was not alone. With him was the shy and breathless Noolah (Madge Roundabout's youngest daughter). The lad was clumsily trying to whisper in her ear (oh, the cheek of him!) how much pain he'd recently been suffering as a result of all the love he had for her till Noolah's eyes were starting to glow. She felt as high and lofty as the overhanging elm trees, for she'd never heard such words of love spoken to her before.

The magic of the day, however, was punctured suddenly by Sweeney's tragic screams. The leprechauns in Fort Dangerous must have hopped out over the ditch to see who had been maimed or killed. For as soon as this dreamy young lover and his dewy-eyed temptress thought they might be discovered in their hiding-place, they ran like hares in a bid to reach safety and escape the outstretched hands of their seeker, Hammer-the-Smith. Sweeney had almost reached the home-tree when he tripped over Ned-the-Herd's discarded shovel and landed in the heap of new briars that Johnnie-tackle-the ass had placed against the back ditch to keep out Simple Simon's cattle.

As soon as his screams were heard, the games had to be stopped as one and all came to stare at the damage done to him. His innocent face was a river of blood. It reminded everybody of the sad face of Jesus with His crown of thorns. Indeed, Sweeney had the self-same sad look of Jesus except that when the pain was inflicted on Jesus, He had held onto his usual dignified composure and didn't shatter the ears of Jerusalem with screams like Sweeney.

Johnnie-tackle-the-ass had been sitting on his stool at the half-door, smoking his well-earned pipe. He had not taken part in the evening's amusements. What would a man of 70 want chasing after a bunch of young women and lifting up their skirts to see what was underneath them?

Since the death of his little twins, he and knickers had bidden each other a fond farewell, he'd have everyone know. But when he heard Sweeney's roars, he found the energy of his past youth and leapt up from the stool. Like a rabbit after the gun is fired, he ran behind the ditch where the briars were and reached into their depths and caught Sweeney by his heels. He dragged him through the air for 50 feet, down to the new waterfall and shook him the way you would a dead fish.

The rivers of blood began to disappear from Sweeney's face as old Johnnie dried his wounds with bunches of fresh dock-leaves. He called for a bundle of laurel leaves and vigorously rubbed the juice of them onto the young lad's face. This (his grandfather had once told him) was the best of cures for staunching the blood. Finally, he brought out the goose's quill and his bottle of iodine to complete his work. He knew that before the first star rose in the sky, Sweeney's face would be as good as a new one.

All now went quietly home, tired and worn from all the day's excitement. They were well-satisfied with the many proceedings and would make sure to thank God in their night prayers for the gift of the tar-barrels tunnelling Cackle's new stream away from her yard.

Nor did they forget to say a thank you for the healing hands of Johnnie-tackle-the-ass. When the children closed their eyes for the night, they knew that they had found a new doctor, one that would compare well with Doctor Glasses and in the days that followed, whenever they got an unhealthy cut or a thorn too deeply embedded in the soles of their feet, they would shout, 'Go fetch the doctor!' Everybody would make a beeline for Johnnie-tackle-the-ass's yard, for they knew that he was as good as any doctor when they needed his laurel pastes, his quills and iodine. Doctor Glasses wasn't going to make a shilling out of them for months to come. Indeed, Johnnie-tackle-the-ass had become almost as sacred as their famed bonesetter (Fingers Jack), who dealt with any breaks to the arms and legs of the men.

Cackles smiled with pride to think that the neighbours had found a master doctor in its midst in the shape of her own sound man, and in her mind, she all but canonized him.

5

In the following days, when the shovels and the men were gone away and when life had returned to normal, Cackles continued to be a subject for the road's attention. She laughed on her way to the creamery, and she laughed on her way to Mass. She laughed when she was abroad in the bog, and she laughed when she was pelting the spuds into the ass-and-car above in the wind on Freckles' Heights. She laughed when she saw that Sweeney's face was made new again, and she laughed and put her hand to her chest when she realized she was the proud owner of a new tar-barrelled stream.

From time to time, when she noticed some passers-by, she would call them in the gate and put her ear to the ground and listen for the echoing sound of the water running through the tar-barrels. And they'd catch her laughing all over again when she led them into her haggart and hopped out over the ditch to inspect the mighty new waterfall as it hissed out into Old Sam's dyke below her.

'God is good! God is great!' she'd say.

But the time had now come for Jimmy (the tar-barrel engineer) to pack his suitcase and take to the high road. He was no fool, and he made the wise decision not to take the ship back to the Land of the Silver Dollar. It was too hot a place for so young a soul as himself, and he was too young to go back there and meet his death.

He wrote a few lines to his brother (Matty) in the Land of John Bull. He still had enough money stashed in his hip-pocket to take Cackles and Johnnie-tackle-the-ass on a trip yonder with him and wanted to show them the fame and the beauties of that great big city.

Sadly, Johnnie-tackle-the-ass would hear none of it. 'I'm too old for this sort of adventure,' he sighed, and he waved Jimmy aside. Indeed, he was terrified of the speed and the roars of the Limerick train. He'd also heard dramatic reports of the sea's mighty waves and their pitching and tossing from shore to shore. The mere thought of it made him sick in his stomach. He had always had a weakness in that bit of him (he said).

Jimmy and Cackles took the holy water and set out on their great big adventure. They reached the big city in less than a day-and-a-half. They found themselves well-suited to the many glories that were to be seen there and, with Jimmy's dollars itching to escape from his pocket, they had themselves a merry old time of it. Cackles felt she had landed on the moon.

A day or two later, she got herself up into the dome of the Great Cathedral and walked round its Whispering Gallery. She toured round the statue of the Great Sailor in a place she called Travel-car Square.

After two long weeks, she returned in a triumph that the pope would have thought fitting only for himself. Before her return, however, the poor woman had been forced to say farewell to Jimmy and leave him behind in a greasy lodging-house in the dirty backstreets of London.

Back home, she held several audiences in her welcoming room and told her amazed listeners of her wonderful trip to the king's palace.

It was then that the lying tongues of the old gossips gave themselves a right good airing. They reported that Cackles had been to see the king and his lovely queen, that the king had taken a real shine to her, that he was more than pleased when she told him of the stream and the tar-barrels. The queen (they said) laughed politely when she heard of Sing-me-a-song and her double-whistle. They were now building up steam. The king (they said) told her he would write to the little whistler and invite her over for tea and a slice of his soda-cake. All this news went on for the next few days – better than a circus – the way these old gossips went at it and spread it around. Oh, the lying hounds – the heathens that are bred along the creamery road!

6

Now that she was back home, Cackles was seen to be a different woman from the one that had set sail with Jimmy. She hadn't become as proud as you might have thought or grown too grand in her ways so as not to talk to her neighbours. What was it then? She had lost most of her gaiety, and her renowned laughter was seldom if ever heard. Hadn't Johnnie-tackle-the-ass warned her not to be making a fool of herself and taking on such an arduous journey? Cackles had listened to none of his pleas. She knew better than him as always.

Now, however, she knew how wrong she had been for the excitement of such a lengthy trip had been too much for her, and she began to feel a strange foreboding rising in her chest. She told no-one.

She was a week short of 60 and had laughed her way throughout life more than anyone else had ever laughed. However, just as some women work themselves to the bone (even to the point of death), so it was with Cackles. She had worn herself to a thread from her travels.

There was one more trick left in her, however. When the fuss of her first few days back home had died down, she summoned the children from up and down the creamery road into her yard and showered them with presents that she'd brought back for them with Jimmy's dollars. The rusty bowlee-wheels and the box of coloured buttons and the sock-balls, and even the pig's bladder, could all go and bury themselves in the river from now on.

In the following weeks, she spent hours telling children her stories of the great big city across the water. In fact, she was beginning to believe all the tales spread about her and how she had seen the king and his lovely queen a number of times. Her tales grew and grew till the children believed that Cackles was sick and tired of having to go and take tea with the sad king.

A month after her return, Cackles was abroad in the yard and watching the antics of Sing-me-a-song as the child attempted to do cartwheels among the hens. Suddenly, the children heard a little cough and after that an almighty crash. Cackles had given her last burst of laughter, and she fell down in the yard. There she lay, close beside the invisible stream that continued to flow underneath her feet.

Sing-me-a-song ran to her mother and gazed down into her glazed eyes. Her heart racing, she leaned over the dear soul. 'Mother, Mother, dearest Mother, can ye hear me?'

The old eyes blinked. The old hands reached out towards the child, and the child felt the last squeeze of her mother. Then (what sort of heavenly angel must have taken hold of Sing-me-a-song's soul?) the little girl began to whistle. She whistled a tune that not even she had heard before. The other children stopped to listen. They jumped down from where they were swinging on Old Sam's gate and rushed back to Cackles' yard where they saw the poor misfortunate Cackles stretched out on the broad of her back. They saw Sing-me-a-song and heard the whistling-music pouring out over the face of her mother. It was as if the saints and angels had come down from Heaven and entered the body of Sing-me-a-song, causing her to soothe away these last few moments of her mother's life. All the ghosts of Cackles' ancestors were standing nearby and watching the sadness in the yard. They were pouring their own strength into Sing-me-a-song so as not to let childish tears flow out of her eyes – for her to go on delivering her unearthly whistling.

Johnnie-tackle-the-ass came in from the barn and walked slowly down the yard in a daze. He knelt down beside his dying Cackles, and the whistling ended. Cackles closed her eyes for the last time. Herself and the heavenly music went off together out through the gap, out through the Hills-of-the-Past, the Valley of the Pig, the bog-land waste and on over Chieftain Hill, heading for the clouds and the heavenly sky.

Sing-me-a song took her dazed father down to the mighty waterfall where it continued to lash out into the dyke. Child though she was, she held him by the hand and stood him alongside her in the centre of the waterfall as it cascaded around them, soaking them to the skin. The sins of her father and herself (though the child knew not what they were, so innocent was she and so guileless was Johnnie-tackle-the-ass) were now being cleansed forever, and the children stood by and watched. A good crowd soon gathered and felt that the sins of everyone (however small) were being washed away as they peered down over the wall.

Sing-me-a-Song and her father went up the dyke on the other side by the spring-well. They came into Dowager's yard and crossed into her welcoming room. In their soaked skins, they stood there, not knowing what to say.

At last, Johnnie-tackle-the-ass spoke up. 'Cackles is dead,' said he.

'May the Lord have mercy on her soul,' sighed Dowager, and she put some sticks on the fire to bring them back the warmth.

By now, the neighbours had followed into the yard and were looking in over the half-door. Everyone's heart was as soft as a bog. Dowager poured out the last of the goose-soup and ladled it into the shivering Sing-me-a-song and her father. She hadn't a word to say, and for once in her life, her tongue was as thick as a cow's tail.

It wasn't as though Cackles was an old woman. Dowager could give her at least a 10-year start in the race towards old age. Nor had anyone ever seen the good woman giving a single day on the bed with any form of sickness.

Twisting the dishcloth in her hands, Dowager's heart raced out of her body, full of the joys of their lifelong friendship. It was Cackles with her kettles of boiling water and her hot towels that had helped deliver most of Dowager's children, apart from the one or two born in haste abroad in the fields or by the well-hole when she was caught out suddenly. It was Cackles that had rushed down the road with her candles and lamp and seemed to float through the air in her haste to get to the welcoming room at the time of each birth. It was Cackles' delicate and persuasive fingers that were needed as Dowager tossed and turned on the bed, and it was into Cackles' eyes that the little babies first peered. And when each child landed on the blanket, you should have seen the look of joy in Cackles and the happy tears rolling down her cheeks.

And now she was gone, leaving Johnny-tackle-the-ass behind her to walk up-and-down the creamery road for the short remainder of his life with his perplexed and disillusioned thoughts locked inside his head. No more would he tackle his ass and collect his load of ferns. Cackles, in her home in the Beyond, was merely waiting for the day (it would soon arrive) when the good man would come and join her in the happiest of all reunions.

SWIMMING IN
THE RAGING RIVER

1

It was getting towards the end of September. As soon as the hay was saved and the oats and barley thrashed, men had time on their hands. To celebrate, they would meet on a bright Sunday morning above at Sheep's Cross.

It was the same every year as far back as anyone could remember. With a little army of boys following in their wake, and each of them with a towel wrapped round his shoulders, they'd make their way into the hills and hurry to their favourite resort, the big sally hole, where they'd be sure to get a few good lungfuls of clean mountainy air (said Fiddler Joe to himself as he reached for his towel).

The sally hole lay on the hidden curves of Growl River, a river that made its way through Bog Boundless and on to the mighty Shannon River that was 12 miles away in Limerick. It was on the outskirts of the known world and hidden from the eyes of man and beast alike, not a single soul there except for one or two remote turf-gatherers like Ned-the-Herd and Joe Solitary. The unreal beauty of this tranquil spot (said the men) outshone even the bishop's palace over in Clare.

'It's a mile from the start of Obscurity,' said Dowager, 'and half-ways to Eternity.'

'Ah, it's you that have the great big rocks of words,' said My-Son-Jack, laughing across the firelight at his mother and her usual fanciful way of saying things.

Dowager gave him a shake of her head and stopped poking at the fire. 'The two eagles on top of Chieftain Hill,' said she, 'don't even know where this sally hole is, and it's an awful pity that they haven't got wind of it, or they'd come swooping down and snatch away some of our bold boys and their roguery and make a tidy meal out of them for always annoying old folk up in the hills.'

Today would be a day for holiday hearts and light laughter, a day for the men to try their hand at swimming and show off their fine strokes in the water. But there was always a practical purpose to such an outing: it was the one day in the year for them to wash their bodies from head to toe and make ample use of the carbolic soap, the one day when they felt they were being baptised all over again. Young Zeppity couldn't help shuddering when he recalled his recent far-from-light-hearted baptism by his big brothers below in the river.

For the rest of the children, it was going to be another day of intense excitement when they realised where they were going, and they threw themselves out from under the blankets with hearts as light as butterflies. It was earlier than usual to be hopping around the bedroom – so early that the cockerels hadn't yet stepped out to salute the day. Neither had the sunlight filtered its rays in over the windowsill geraniums to turn them from red to pink. Their new journey would do them a power of good, bringing them face to face with the roaring majesty of Growl River and see it snarling its way past the foot of Chieftain Hill. The men would point out the many scenic wonders on their way there and make sure the children felt the presence of those wilderness spirits who had roamed these banks since time immemorial.

After they'd hurried through their Blessing prayers and sprinkled each other with holy water, they each placed a few hard-boiled eggs in their pockets and got ready for the road. The women smiled proudly at their men, who turned on their heel and never looked back.

As soon as they reached Sheep's Cross, they met up with bands of other men, and soon the crowd was as noisy as the pig-and-cattle fair or the congestion at the creamery gates when the monthly money was being paid to the men for their cream. Sheep's Cross was a good spot to get together for this big outing; it was where their parents used to hold their crossroad dances when the farmers came back from the harvest-time mill, where the only music heard was Warbling Will's concertina and the squeeze-box of Hammer-the-Smith's father and the paper-and-comb polkas played from inside Shy Dennis's ditch by the shy Scissors Sisters (*'Don't ye be looking at us – we're too shy!')*.

2

At a goodly pace, the men were soon out past the forge, their heads held high and self-importantly as if they were a shower of Wran-boys going off to catch the little wren that betrayed Jesus when He was fretfully praying in the Garden of Gethsemane.

At the head of the procession was Lord-to-God and Simon-not-so-Simple as well as Split-the-Wind. These three had their own peculiar gifts, which compared favourably with men long vanished from our slopes. Lord-to-God was a short man, his face a mass of freckles. He was fat and bald-headed, and it was rumoured that his feet were webbed like a drake. The children couldn't wait to get a glimpse of this as soon as he took off his boots. Simon-not-so-simple was as thin as a yard brush, but it was said he had a pair of monumental legs with calf-muscles as swollen as mutton-chops. This too the children were anxious to see.

As for Split-the-wind, he had what some said was the greatest gift of all, having just recovered from an operation on his bowels. Some of the children had already witnessed his charming new gift. The rascal could emit the most captivating music from his bum, make squeaky mouse-like noises as well as long-drawn-out trumpet noises. All the time, he'd be looking around him as though wondering where on earth the sound was coming from. He'd pause for a second, keeping the children in a fit of frustration (*'Fart for us! Fart for us! Please fart for us!')* as to which of his musical notes he would make next. He was better than the Daffy-Duck Circus, and before he'd finished his quaint performance, he'd have them rolling round the grass in fits of laughter. His final performance was to turn himself into a thinking statue. The expectant children would be quieter than church mice. He'd put his hand to his ear as though listening for the sound of a distant train before letting out an enormous volley of thunder from the depths of his bum.

'Byze-oh-byze, that was a good one!' he'd say, and the children would tear down the fields in a heap of head-over-heels abandonment. At their first opportunity, they'd report the news of Split-the-Wind's extraordinary gift to their schoolmaster *(Dang-the-skin-of-it)*, and this be-whiskered gentleman would hide his face behind the blackboard and hold his aching sides in a scarcely-controlled bout of silent laughter.

Apart from the full washing and the scrubbing with the soap, this was the day when the children attempted to swim. In our world, only one or two grown-ups could swim even a stroke, for our men were a pack of timid lambs when it came to water, and they rarely let a drop of it near their bodies. This was true of the women too, who rarely, if ever, went into the shallows of the nearby river and only dabbed their wet fingertips to their cheeks when they were hurrying out the door to Mass. They'd rather be hiding underneath the horse-and-cart than putting their toe into anything as cold and frightening as a river.

Today, however, there was no time for the men to show such natural cowardliness of the river, and they threw out their chests.

'By the living Lord, we're not one bit afraid of ye, Growl River,' and they hid their fears from the boys and told them about the big splashes they were going to make in the sally hole, how they were going to quieten the very heart of this mighty river.

'Let the frightened women busy themselves with their cake-baking and knitting needles,' they said. 'Let the girls stay home and play on the ass-and-car with their coloured buttons and flowery chains.' The children felt they'd be learning a few good swimming-strokes before the day was over.

3

The bathers quickly reached the Hills-of-the-Past and went clambering on towards the Wild Moorland where nothing but black cattle and wild ponies grazed, the grass being too rough for the likes of their own spoilt cows. The warm sun was now splintering its rays down on them, and the sky was unbelievably blue with the gentlest of breezes and only a few ribbed clouds that were already bound for Galway.

The bathers soon found themselves hemmed in by twisted furze bushes and grasping hawthorn shrubs as the road curved itself on towards the great river itself before finally narrowing itself into a thin ribbon that became a disused laneway.

For a good stretch of the journey, the men had carried little ones like Cull and Little Dan on their shoulders till they got pins and needles in their arms and put them down to ramble on ahead with the bigger children. These little ones had never been so far away from home (not even Little Dan), and their eyes kept darting from left to right in wonder at the cascades of honeysuckle, foxgloves and blackberry bushes, the wild ponies and black cattle. They were now in a mystical place encircling their world.

The men were quickening their pace, anxious more than ever to get to the sally hole and put their toes in the water, and the little ones had to run to keep up with them, with no time for collecting blueberries or crab apples. At last, they came to the stepping-stones where the lane was just a yellow gully with a few worn-out briars and withered trees trying to choke their way.

My-Son-Jack again carried Little Dan on his back, and next to him, young Cull sat royally on Fiddler Joe's shoulders. They were as excited as calves to be seen perched so high and kept turning around to see the disappearing fields and the last of the cattle and ponies. The bigger boys ignored the briars and ran blindly down the final slope towards the river.

'Coom back, ye little fairy-men, or ye'll get yeerselves drowned,' yelled Red Scissors, racing after them. But they were full of exuberance and paid not the slightest heed to him and flung their arms out wide to greet the majestic roars of this mighty river.

And now some astonishing news reached the children. Sweeney had spent the last few days secretly hiding behind the bushes, burying his head in a bucket of water and trying to pick up with his teeth the three-penny-bit at the bottom of the bucket. And now, he boasted, he could accomplish this feat with ease. To witness the strut of the cocky fellow for you could never keep his spirits down – that's the way he was. The other children gasped when they heard this wonderful piece of news. What a great attraction he'd be! They couldn't wait to reach the sally hole where Sweeney would be the only boy able to dive beneath the water, and they felt like clapping him on the back. Even the men were bursting with anticipation to witness Sweeney's fearless skills when they reached the river.

The bigger boys were at the river's edge and looking down into the twinkling waters, daring each other to touch it with their toes. It was achingly cold with the hurt of snow in it. The purple heather was all around. Above it all towered Chieftain Hill, holding sway like a giant pyramid from old Egypt. The little ones marvelled afresh at the river's blustering hisses and bellowing roars as if it were saying, 'I'm more than a match for ye mere mortals – come towards me and swim in me if ye dare!'

The men now crossed the stepping-stones with the little ones almost glued to their backs, journeying almost reverently into an unforeseen dream-world. They felt sure they were in Wonderland when the bright sunlight reflected their bodies back up at them from the river's silvery wavelets. The bigger boys had already crossed onto the other bank, the river's roar unable to stifle their happy shouts as these merry half-men struggled their way up the bank like a flock of wild stags.

4

The only man that could swim more than a few strokes was Spare-Ribs, who was known to have the doggy-paddle off pat and was reputed to have swum the fabled Tigris River. Of course, our men were known for their tendency to exaggerate and tell huge lies if they got half a chance. Added to this tall tale, they said that Spare-Ribs had a few extra ribs to spare and that that was the reason why his mother had put such a peculiar name on him. None of the children had been given the chance to count his extra ribs, and they were looking forward to him stripping off his togs so that they could count his ribs and bring back another report to school – to go with Split-the-Wind's farting backside. The truth, however, was that Spare-Ribs hadn't one spare rib to his name and, if anything, was extremely thin and spare in that department of his body for he was always dying with the hunger and looking for an extra bite to eat, poor man.

And another thing – everyone knew that the best man at leaping from the top of High Rock into the 10-foot pool would be Matt-with-the-Machinery, a giant-of-a-man. If any man could terrify the life out of this fierce river, it would be Matt, and the younger children were looking forward to seeing him disappearing under the water with an almighty splash.

However, it was for a far less salubrious reason (as yet unknown to any of the children) that Matt would prove himself the greatest attraction on this memorable day and even Split-the-Wind and Spare-Ribs would have to take second place to him. Matt was a very shy and innocent man, but between his thighs, he had the most enormous piece of machinery, which, on every other day, was kept firmly concealed in his britches.

Today, however, it'd be the prime subject for discussion and envy, something an ass would be proud to call his own (said the wily Rambling Jack).

'Good-God-in-Heaven,' said he, 'Matt has the makings of a pure aristocrat.' When Sweeney (the devil that was in him) heard this outrageous news, he lewdly clamped a stick between his legs to demonstrate the size of Matt's machinery, and the other boys laughed nervously.

'Ah-ha!' said Red Scissors, 'The blessings of God on Spare-Ribs, our mighty swimmer, and on Matt with the great gift between his legs!'

The group had all crossed, the men's eyes forever fixed on the children in case one of them should fall into the current and get carried off towards Limerick and the ocean. There was half-a-mile to walk before they reached the sally hole, but it would be worth the trudge for its water came up to a man's chest and higher, and was the only pool deep enough to try a few handy swimming strokes, even if they were made with one leg firmly fixed to the ground.

At last, they were there, and the water was as bright as silver. The children's faces gleamed with excitement as the fairy breezes whispered in their ears. No sheep, no bird or wild beast had ever found this place before, and no twig or leaf had ever fallen into its clear waters. It was no wonder that our men had always chosen this magical spot. It was a piece of heaven itself.

The big men undressed and threw their shirts and britches to the four winds. Some had pink flesh as soft as meat and others had flesh as white as cream. All looked delicately-coloured against the lush background of the grass. The boys followed their example. Without a stitch on them, there was a mischievous look in the eyes of one or two growing boys, and they began to strut brazenly up and down the grass and flex their muscles. What a belt of the yard-brush mothers would have given a few of their older lads, could they have seen them, and not a trace of modesty about them.

It was different with the men. They gave the odd nervous cough and took shy, sheepish glances at the others' bodies and their own nakedness. Their memories went back to earlier years when they'd go and wash their bodies in the river back home, only to find that some of the more brazen women had taken stealthy steps down through the trees to spy on them. Since then, they had become the coy little fellows when it came to stripping off their togs, and a good few of them still felt that their soul was being exposed when they had no clothes to protect them.

The children sat on the grass and gazed at these new types of men with no shirts or britches on. They blinked and marvelled at the mass of hair on the men's chests, under their armpits and round their private bits and wondered would they themselves one day be as hairy as a bunch of apes like them. They could scarcely hold back their laughter at the sight of Matt as he stepped down to the edge of the river to test its coldness. Much to their disappointment, he had his hands clasped coyly round his precious piece of machinery, and they never got the chance to see it.

The other men followed Matt and tiptoed gingerly towards the edge of the pool, timidly dipping their toes into the water to test it. Then they went back a bit and took a mad rush from the bank and jumped into the pool with a tremendous roar, splashing one another to high heavens and pelting fountains of water into one another's eyes. The boys had never seen the men so abandoned and so excited – except at a hurling-match.

The bigger children stopped strutting around and stood shivering sheepishly on the bank. The men kept beckoning them to come and join them, but they were still too frightened to adventure past the river's edge. To avoid being labelled cowards, however, the older lads sought their own form of amusement and paraded up and down the grass, throwing out their chests and lifting their legs in comical and ungainly gestures.

And then Sweeney spread his legs and cried, 'Matt! Matt! Coom and look at this fine specimen!' The others pretended they were wild animals and cavorted through the heather. Their shouts and antics made Cull, Zeppity and Little Dan laugh themselves silly at all the fun.

With a nod from Lippy, Philly found his confidence and, rushing madly with his big brother towards the pool, tumbled in, pushing the heads of two startled men down under the surface as though they were trying to drown them.

5

Unlike the others, Zeppity was in no mood to take off his shirt and britches following the earlier baptism that Lippy and Philly had given him under Echo Bridge. He remained a little way off on his own.

Little Dan and Cull went down to the sandy shallows just below the pool, but the watchful eye of My-Son-Jack and By-Jiggery were constantly on them like hens with their chicks.

The three children were like cats caught out in the rain, their toes achingly cold and the stones as sharp as needles under their feet. The water crept up into their goose-pimply skin, making them shudder, but they soon got used to its smoothness and with tentative steps, stepped further and further in from the side of the river until the water reached their kneecaps. Finally, they ventured almost waist-deep, and the water began to feel warm. It was the most wonderful time they could ever remember.

What fine swimmers the older lads thought they were as they made their way along the shallower side of the pool, one leg glued firmly in the pebbles, the other leg floating aimlessly behind them like a young frog. Oh, the roguery of these little liars as they tried to impress the men with their so-called swimming as if nobody could see beneath the surface. Scoundrels like Lippy thought they'd fooled Spare-Ribs into believing they were a new breed of swimmers with their doggy-paddle as they continued to thrust their arms out in front and raise their chins like the great swimmer did. The other men shook their heads and smiled.

'Isn't nature a wonderful thing?' they mused, for they had used the very same piece of deceit when they were young, and now they sighed and applauded the lads' efforts to impress and praised them for the excellent style of their swimming strokes.

But, so intent were the boys on making their sly little hops on fixed leg, that they forgot to count the ribs of Spare-Ribs.

The day ticked along like a melody, with the twitching bodies of the little ones jumping up and down in the shallow stretches and Sweeney and the others running up the bank, then charging back into the water in an attempt to unsettle the men and knock them down all over again. There were enough shouts to frighten the river as the startled men fell in a pile beneath the surface, and the heather shook with the curses from the men ('*ye little feckers*'). They themselves were just like the boys and as playful as kittens. The two eagles in the cleft of Chieftain Hill would never get a minute's peace at this rate.

Then the men came up with a new game, and like a herd of galloping horses, full of spray and laughter, they made an almighty racket as they raced along the edge of the pool, upstream against the current. From the barefooted days of their childhood, they had feet as hard as leather and put no heed in the sharp stones.

The young ones copied them and plunged about in the shallower reaches. The men turned around and laughed at them and then went back to throwing themselves into their river races.

The next hour passed along most pleasantly, and the flushed faces of the bathers took away the dazzle from the glittering sun herself. So great was the excitement, that one or two boys sat at the edge of the river and slyly christened her with a stream of their poolie.

The men were tired from their races and came and joined them. They sat side-by-side and wallowed in the lapping shallows, their feet tearing at the little pebbles like the sow in her sty.

Sweeney came down to join them. Suddenly, he knelt down under the shallow water. He kept his eyes wide open and looked back up at them from beneath the surface, and they marvelled at the bravery of him. Was Sweeney still a mere boy? Was he turning himself into a fish? Was he now a fairy-man to be doing such a peculiar thing as this? Wishing to go one better and having everyone's attention, Sweeney took to doing handstands in the pool, and the children now realised that he had been completely bewitched by the spirits of the river. The bewildered Red Scissors was left scratching his head and was the first to speak.

'Did ye ever see the likes of Sweeney? Look at him and he upside-down and his head nowhere to be seen, and he wriggling his skinny legs in the air like a young pig that won't enter the cart on market day.' Even Spare-Ribs had to stop and stare in wonder at Sweeney.

After their refreshing rest from their river races and the time spent watching Sweeney's grand show, the men made their way to the centre of the sally hole where the water was up to their chests. The children looked on in awe as these hairy horses bobbed up and down like a load of floating corks.

The little ones would have loved to follow them, but My-Son-Jack and By-Jiggery shook their heads and told them keep away from that dangerous part of the pool in case they got drowned and taken off by the angels.

On the far bank there was the overhanging ledge (High Rock) and though it was a temptation for the bigger boys to climb it, not one of them (not even Sweeney) had the courage to go up and jump down into the 10-foot hole beneath it. But the men were fearless by now and climbed up onto the rock and held their nose with one hand and shyly cupped their other hand between their legs.

There was an expectant pause like the frustrating one that Split-the-Wind had made a few weeks back, and then with a sudden rush and a roar, the men leapt together out into space and (*Splash*!) landed in the middle of the pool.

What an unmerciful sight it was to see their heads coming back to the surface a second later! The children sighed with relief to see that their men were not dead. The renewed laughter of everyone filled the glade, and the men couldn't wait to climb back onto High Rock and start all over again. And now (what every child was waiting for) Matt himself scaled the rock's highest peak. He turned away his shy body and walked back a short distance from the rest of the men. Then, rocking back on his heel, he prepared to make his run. Suddenly, with the legs of a speeding greyhound, he raced across High Rock and, clasping his right knee up towards his chin, he sailed into the air and sliced through the glassy sheet of water with the splash of a mighty hippopotamus, almost drowning the rest of the swimmers with the towering waves his body made. The children wondered if there'd be a drop of water left in the river. What a noble baptism he had given them all!

Matt stayed under the water for what seemed an eternity, and the seconds passed by. The children grew frightened and thought the poor man had drowned himself and that they'd have to bury him. But then (*'Ah-ha! mee byze!'*) up he came with the roar of a bull, his black hair plastered to his head like satin and the water running out of his ears and nose. What with all the excitement of Matt's great leap, the children had missed getting a tiny peek at the famed machinery between his thighs.

The shy giant now chased the older boys across the pool and even waded down almost as far as the little one.

'Ye are not yet properly baptised like Jesus,' he roared with a wink at My-Son-Jack. Then he carried Lippy on his back and jogged up and down the river with him. My-Son-Jack got into the fun and did the same with Philly, the heather echoing the shrieks of these young lads as their laughter got mixed up with their tears whenever Matt threatened to throw them into the deepest part of the pool and submerge them for a new and hilarious christening. It was good sport, for this harmless man had the heart of a child and would never have subjected them to such a cruel atrocity.

Not to be outshone by Matt's merriment, Spare-Ribs challenged him and the rest of them to see which of them would remain under water the longest. All the men took up the great swimmer's challenge, and Sweeney now joined in the fun. Then they all went down under the water, and once more, the seconds ticked by.

The younger children wondered if the divers would ever come back to earth, or had Hell swallowed them forever. In the end, it was Spare-Ribs who stayed down longest and won the laurels of the day. By now, the outing had turned into a pure festival.

6

It was time for the men to produce the half-dozen bars of carbolic soap, and they began pelting the slippery bars across the sally hole, trying to hit one another on the jaw and knock each other down. Old-timers down the slopes must surely have heard the fierce curses (‘*feck, feck and feck again*’) pouring out of them when the soap slipped through their fingers, and they had to duck down under the water to catch it before it ran away on them. Once more, everyone was steeped in laughter.

The time had come for the earnest scrubbing of the children as requested by the women. In the evening when they got home, there’d be a full inspection and, if they weren’t as clean as new babies, they might find themselves the victims of a sound leathering with the yard-brush. For a while, all the laughter stopped as each child sadly prepared for the treatment.

The men marshalled them to the lower end of the pool where the water came gushing out of a shadowy rock, and they got down to the serious business of the washing, paying particular attention to the back of the children’s necks and inside their ears. They gave their hair a right good lathering, soaping it all over in case of head lice since these little nippers were experts at hopping from head to head back at school.

Getting fiercely scrubbed was taking a good bit of the fun out of the children’s day, and they quickly got tired of the men turning and twisting them about as though they were a few sops of hay. Even the little ones had a bit of pride in themselves and took the soap from the men and began washing themselves under the arms and around the top of their legs, tending especially to the bits of cow-dung that might be ingrained behind their knees.

Finally, they held their noses (for by now they were able to do this as good as the men) and ducked their heads down into the pool and washed off the soapy suds from their bodies.

When they came back up with their hair streaming and the water glistening on them, it was indeed as though they'd been baptised like their blessed Saviour. They shook themselves the way dogs do when getting out of a river, and they clapped each other on the back for being such brave little fellows. The men gave them a final look-over and nodded to one another in satisfaction: every child was as clean as a new priest.

7

There came a lull in the day, almost a delirium. The men, who had washed the boys so vigorously with their rough hands, now stood motionless and awkwardly beside them. One or two of the more rascally ones pointed to the sky, shielding their eyes as though they were trying to make out the outline of some imaginary eagle hurrying their way from Chieftain Hill. The bigger boys were still little innocents at heart, and they strained their own eyes and tried to get a glimpse of this new sighting.

Suddenly, the men grabbed them by their ankles. The unexpected unfairness of this sort of play-acting shattered the recent peace and calm (‘*Go ‘way ye pack of basthards!*’) with roars of blasphemy. They fired the water into the men's eyes, and the men fired it back at the boys, sweeping the spray at them like a flat stone skimming the pool.

Sweeney and the rest stumbled out of the river, glad to get away from the men's clutches and started running races through the rough ferns to dry themselves. Their feet were so fast they made the ferns whistle. The breezes scurried along the bank after them and tickled their bellies.

Some of the boys drifted further along the bank to reach the shadier side of the river and sat on the boulders like wagtails, dangling their feet in the river. Others played higher and higher and jumped over sticks stretched across the bushes. More ran up into the heather and played hide-and-go-seek amid the peeping shadows. Then they rolled all over the grass and dried the last of the water off of their bodies. They lay there sprawled beneath the reddening sun that was turning their skin a shadowy pink, their hair trailing behind them in the grass. It was one of the few listless moments in their young lives, their one chance to breathe into their lungs this profound silence. Closing their eyes, they fell into a doze, lulled into a mood of enchantment by the river fairies of this ancient place. And all the while the river and its distant sound (increasingly lively since Matt's mighty splash) travelled majestically onwards towards the Shannon River.

Such an endless moment of enrichment couldn't last forever, and mad abandonment and caprice again came out to play and took a hold of their spirits. The mood of Lippy and Philly turned to downright lewdness, and they grabbed each other from behind and tried to squeeze the life out of each other's private particles, and all along the bank, you'd hear their delirious shouts ('*sweet suffering saints, aren't ye the dirty whoors?*'). But soon they were worn out and lay down again and laughed till the tears of joy rolled down their jaws.

Zeppity still had his shirt and britches on and with Little Dan and Cull had wandered down along the bank where the river wound its way round a few small tree roots, and there were no sharp rocks to be seen. It was a shallow and seemingly harmless stretch of water and made a smooth sandy bank where it went into a curve.

Their sharp eyes scanned the riverbed for coloured stones to add to their collection of drawing stones back home. They bent down in the wet sand, and with the palm of their hands, squashed out sandy ditches like they did with the mud and horse-dung on the creamery road. In the end, they'd made a ditch almost 20 feet long. Then they aimlessly tiptoed into the twinkling water. By now, they were having a great time of it, their toes clenching into the yellow sand and dashing to pieces the tiny crystal wavelets.

Lippy added to the fun and made a spider-thin flaggard-boat from the nearby rushes and showed Zeppity how to sail it into the little wavelets and watch it ride off on its journey over the pebbles. They made more boats for each of them, then sailed them out into the water to slip away into the current and disappear towards the stepping-stones.

They were as happy as larks and watched the trout, slippery-quick and smooth, hanging on the current before gobbling up the gnats and midges and hurrying away, frightened by the children's presence.

By now, Zeppity had forgotten his earlier fears and was getting braver by the minute. He rolled up his britches above his knees and paddled further in ahead of the other three.

Suddenly (would they ever forget it?), his feet slipped out from under him into a huge hole underneath his legs. *WHOOSH!* In a second, the poor child had disappeared from view – clean gone!

Oh, poor Zeppity! – he, who had come out for a day's recreation and fun like everybody else had stepped too far out into the middle of the river. The sand had been too soft and had given way beneath his feet. Down he sank, the water whirling around him, dragging at his body to claim his life if it could. His little friends could see his wide staring eyes and his legs floundering, could see him up to his neck in the river. His face seemed to bulge in sheer terror, and then his head was buried beneath the snarling river, and all that could be seen were his two little arms thrashing wildly at the air, and then he had disappeared altogether, and they could only see the splattering air-bubbles.

'Oh, Zeppity! Poor Zeppity! Will we ever see you again? Gone to an early grave before your time was up!' *The wilderness fairies* heard the screams of the children and called to the heavens for help, and God smiled down and stretched out His hands towards Zeppity. Their screams had alarmed the men in the deep pool, giving them not a second to think or blink. Running faster than the wind, My-Son-Jack sped through the air, and his powerful arms stretched out past the terrified children as he threw himself into the middle of the river to get to Zeppity and rescue him from death. But

By-Jiggery had already reached the drowning child before he could get there. For Zeppity was his son.

Would their little friend live or die? The bathers were out of their minds with worry as they watched this mighty confrontation between Man and Growl River. With the strength of wild horses, the two men broke the fierce spirit of the river demon and scraped up the drowning child in their arms – and a cartload of sand along with him! It was impossible to describe the chattering-teethed Zeppity and he in the very jaws of death. The two men carried him out and up onto the bank and shook him the way you would a wet rag and shushed the other little boys away as he lay there on the grass, outstretched like a corpse. The britches that the once-shy Zeppity had refused to take off were dragged from him along with his shirt.

By-Jiggery rinsed the sand out of them and left them on a bush to dry. Little Dan and Cull sat huddled under a bush. Leppity's lungs (they thought) must be saturated with a gallon of water and sand and maybe a few fishes too! They tried to laugh a little nervously to one another, but it was no use. They were sadder than a dead rabbit, and they believed that Zeppity was dead and gone from them and that he'd be buried before the week was out and be covered up with clay below in Abbey Acres.

Miracles do happen, and the saints and angels are often close at hand, for in a few minutes, Zeppity got back a little of his old strength. He was crying and was ashamed at not being able to control the river like the rest of the children or able to avoid getting himself half-drowned. Without any clothes, he sat there at the edge of the river and shivered. He felt mournful, lost and alone in his own small world. On realising how near to death he had been, he was utterly afraid and silently pissed into the river and at last felt better.

The near-tragedy of Zeppity had taken the joy out of the day. The bathers had no more heart for swimming and bathing. They murmured among themselves and said what a terrible thing it was to have seen poor Zeppity almost drowned and to see him looking so wretched and sad in the middle of them. They made up their minds to put the heart back into him, and once more, they clambered up the slippery rocks at the far side of the pool. Together, they jumped down into the sally hole and sent splashes to the heavens in imitation of Matt.

The next minute, Lippy's eyes were bulging in his head, and he nudged Zeppity and pointed up at High Rock.

'Will ye look at Matt!' And then the tear-stained Zeppity saw Matt looking down at them. The giant lifted up his mighty arms, and his chest puffed out like a pig's bladder as he got ready for his final big splash of the day. Like Lippy, Zeppity's own eyes went spinning like saucers as he finally beheld the great size of Matt's famous machinery and, to the joy of everyone, he found himself laughing out loud. He couldn't wait to get home and tell his mother of the enormity of Matt's great big machinery.

8

The day of the swimming had come to an end. The children (including Zeppity) sat on the bank and watched the men racing each other through the ferns like a crowd of schoolchildren, watched the older boys (oh, how they'd like to be men themselves!) challenging the big men to the races and the wrestling bouts. The good-natured men *('We're not too old to trounce ye at the races or the wrestling bouts')* were full of the fun of it.

Like Lazarus, Zeppity had been restored to life, and everything was sunshiny once more. The men were exhausted from all the day's sport, and they flopped down on the grass and lit their pipes. Their eyes twinkled inside the smoke, and the honey-sweet smell of the tobacco filled the children's mouths and noses as the men spat down into the river. Their talk was as delicious as a ripe apple, and for once in their lives, *the river fairies and moorland fairies* were outdone, and the men and boys had become the new hobgoblins.

At length ('Well, byze, 'tis sad to be leaving the river'), they all put on their clothes and with the swish of their wellingtons returned to the stepping-stones.

Once more, the men carried the little ones on their shoulders. It was goodbye to the Wilderness and Chieftain Hill, soon to be hidden in clouds, goodbye to the pearly waters of Growl River and the sally hole – lonely now with the echoes of their laughter and shouts now gone from it.

It had been a day in a lifetime, and the men, weary as they now were, felt better than getting themselves drunk below in Curl 'n' Stripes' drinking-shop as they tramped out onto the bog road near Tracey's Sandpit.

Everyone was ravenous with the hunger, and the children went hunting for crab-apples, blackberries (never mind the maggots!) and wild strawberries. The bathers were dyed with the redness of evening, and the sun in her final moments was preparing herself for twilight. The evening chill would soon come on, and the day would fade away from them.

'It's been a picture-book of a day,' said My-Son-Jack to himself as he looked down at his little brother. There was a peaceful intimacy between them all as they strolled home. A little sadness, however, had crept into them too, especially the children for they knew they were no longer in Fairyland and had become their own selves once more.

Except for the mournful cry of the curlew, there was silence. There was stillness. Nobody spoke (just their reveries), and the day was frozen timelessly in their minds like an old brown photograph. The little ones couldn't wait to get home and tell their mothers the tale of the day – how Zeppity had nearly got himself drowned and had swallowed a dozen fishes and how they had seen the two eagles flying all day above Chieftain Hill and their wings as big as houses (the little liars!).

Oh, how their mothers ('Ah-ha, mee fine night-walkers!') would tussle their hair and turn their own faces away towards the fire to prevent being seen laughing when they heard about Matt's famous machinery, and they'd smile to themselves ('*that'll do, child*!'), recalling a memory or two of their past girlhood.

From that day onwards, the summertime would fade from them all. They knew that, like the past itself, they would never get this day back again. But they knew they'd be going to Growl River again the following year and the year after that and would thrash this mighty river with their laughter and tears. Yes, indeed they would!

THE END

www.ingramcontent.com/pod-product-compliance
Lightning Source LLC
LaVergne TN
LVHW091035080826
845145LV00002B/510

* 9 7 8 1 8 3 9 7 5 6 6 4 1 *